A NOVEL BASED ON THE LIFE OF

ERNEST GALLO

HARVESTING
THE AMERICAN DREAM

Karen Richardson

Harvesting the American Dream is a work of fiction. Some incidents, dialogue, and characters are products of the author's imagination and are not to be construed as real. Where real-life historical figures appear, the situations, incidents, and dialogue concerning those persons are based on or inspired by actual events. In all other respects, any resemblance to actual persons, living or dead, events, or locales is entirely coincidental.

The Mentoris Project
P.O. Box 1019
Temple City, CA 91780

Cover photo: Everett Collection Historical / Alamy Stock Photo
Cover design by Suzanne Turpin

More information at www.mentorisproject.org

ISBN: 978-1-947431-01-0

Library of Congress Control Number: 2017954684

All net proceeds from the sale of this book will be donated to Barbera Foundation, Inc. whose mission is to support educational initiatives that foster an appreciation of history and culture to encourage and inspire young people to create a stronger future.

The Mentoris Project is a series of novels and biographies about the lives of great Italians and Italian-Americans: men and women who have changed history through their contributions as scientists, inventors, explorers, thinkers, and creators. The Barbera Foundation sponsors this series in the hope that, like a mentor, each book will inspire the reader to discover how she or he can make a positive contribution to society.

Contents

Foreword

First and foremost, Mentor was a person. We tend to think of the word *mentor* as a noun (a mentor) or a verb (to mentor), but there is a very human dimension embedded in the term. Mentor appears in Homer's *Odyssey* as the old friend entrusted to care for Odysseus's household and his son Telemachus during the Trojan War. When years pass and Telemachus sets out to search for his missing father, the goddess Athena assumes the form of Mentor to accompany him. The human being welcomes a human form for counsel. From its very origins, becoming a mentor is a transcendent act; it carries with it something of the holy.

The Barbera Foundation's Mentoris Project sets out on an Athena-like mission: We hope the books that form this series will be an inspiration to all those who are seekers, to those of the twenty-first century who are on their own odysseys, trying to find enduring principles that will guide them to a spiritual home. The stories that comprise the series are all deeply human. These books dramatize the lives of great Italians and Italian-Americans whose stories bridge the ancient and the modern, taking many forms, just as Athena did, but always holding up a light for those living today.

Whether in novel form or traditional biography, these books plumb the individual characters of our heroes' journeys. The power of storytelling has always been to envelop the reader in a vivid and continuous dream, and to forge a link with the subject. Our goal is for that link to guide the reader home with a new inspiration.

What is a mentor? A guide, a moral compass, an inspiration. A friend who points you toward true north. We hope that the Mentoris Project will become that friend, and it will help us all transcend our daily lives with something that can only be called holy.

—Robert J. Barbera, President, Barbera Foundation
—Ken LaZebnik, Editor, The Mentoris Project

Prologue

"D*on't worry about me. I just want you boys to get along and take care of each other."*

The words ricocheted against the walls of twenty-four-year-old Ernest Gallo's skull. Just as he seemed to grasp their import, they would scuttle away from any hope of understanding. They were among his mother's last, uttered just the day before to his brother, Julio.

As Ernest drove south through California's Central Valley to Fresno, he tried to brace himself for the misery that awaited him. To think that Julio had driven this road twenty-four hours ago in the same Model T flatbed to bring their younger brother, Joe, back to Modesto for the summer. How could it be that their lives had changed so tragically with one rotation of the earth, while for others it was just another Wednesday?

Ernest berated himself. He had been living so far in the future that he had failed the present. He had missed all the warning signs. While his head had been in cerulean skies, the barometer had been dropping around him, too low to ever recover. For the last few weeks, any free time he had after tending his father's vineyards had been spent driving the dusty roads of the San Joaquin

Valley. Were Father to question his motives, Ernest would have said he was checking in with their growers, estimating harvest times to anticipate their shipping needs in the fall. But in truth, Ernest had been interviewing old-time vintners and trying to learn as much as he could about how to make wine. And while he had slept, dreaming of barrels brimming with rich red nectar, a tempest had swept in.

After last year's disastrous grape crop, this year's was coming in strong. In fact, Ernest had been thinning the Alicante Bouschet vines when Julio's wife had come hurrying out to the vineyard. As soon as he had seen her expression he had known something was terribly wrong.

"Ernest, there's a reporter from the *Bee* on the phone. You need to come in."

Ernest hadn't been able to answer—let alone comprehend—the questions from the newspaper reporter that had spilled from the phone. He stared at the dirty field boots he hadn't thought to take off before coming into the kitchen. He was transfixed by the cracks that spiderwebbed across the worn leather. The shiny black receiver in his grip was like an anchor pulling him under. One by one he looked into the eyes of his family standing mute around him: his wife, Amelia; his brother, Julio, and his wife, Aileen; and thirteen-year-old Joe. None of them could save him. It would be up to *him* to save *them*.

The next couple of hours went by in a blur. He must have cleaned up before he left the farm. Though there was some dirt under his fingernails, his hands were cleaner than they should have been after a day in the vineyard. The vibrations from the steering wheel rattled his body as he pushed the truck toward its top speed of 45 mph. Though he was certainly in no hurry to get to Fresno, Ernest couldn't seem to keep the weight of his foot off the pedal. He prayed for guidance, strength, and wisdom.

Ernest recognized the orchards and pastures that lined the route. He must be near Merced. Halfway there. He looked down at his watch. When he returned his attention back to the road, he jumped in surprise. Though the sky had been perfect and blue all day, a black cloud had suddenly filled his windshield. He instinctively slammed on the brakes and veered to the road's shoulder. By the time the locked wheels skidded to a stop, the cloud was gone. He hung his head, squeezed his eyes shut, and opened them to a bloodbath. The truck's windshield was a splatter of clear, golden yellow, and red stains. The black cloud had been a swarm of flies, the most populous inhabitants of the Central Valley. Ernest sighed, reached for an old flour sack he kept on the floor, and stepped on the running board to clean up the mess.

Chapter One

JUICE

After making sure his wife was settled, Battista Bianco placed his hands under his grandson's armpits and propelled him into the air onto the wagon's flat bench. He then climbed up next to his wife and handed the five-year-old the worn reins. "Ernest, I need you to drive today," he said. "You have magic way with this stubborn mare. She no listen to old men like me."

Battista pulled his pipe out of his pocket, stuck it in the side of his mouth, and began his practiced routine. Ernest was eager to hear one of his grandfather's stories, but knew he'd have to wait for his *nonno* to finish his ritual. As Nonno tapped his pipe against the side of his boot, he reached back into his pocket and pulled out his leather pouch. He carefully sprinkled a pinch of tobacco into the bowl of the pipe and pressed it down with his thick thumb. He did this two more times before gingerly holding a lit match over the bowl. When his cheeks hollowed, the flame lowered to the bowl. A few more puffs and a curtain of satisfaction fell over the old Italian's sunbaked face.

Some Sundays they would go to Mass early so they could bring the wine to Father Michael. Battista would usually tell his grandson stories during the dusty ride. Ernest had heard most of them before, but he didn't mind. He had his favorites.

"Nonno, tell me the story about the pirates and the sea monster."

"Ah, are you sure? It's not too scary?"

"No," Ernest boasted. "You know I'm big now. I'm not scared."

Though he spoke English, Ernest understood his grandparents' native Piedmontese dialect and knew the story his nonno was about to tell by heart.

"Well, Nino, you know I wanted to make wine like my father and *my* nonno. Your mamma and her sisters were little girls and Uncle Walter was the same age you are now. My cousins had come to California and wrote home about how much it was like Asti. I told your *nonna,* 'Ginnie, I'm going to go to buy a vineyard in California. They're cheap there and I'll never be able to afford the land here. I will send you money so you can join me. The children can stay with our parents. When I have the money, they can come join us—'"

"Nonno, get to the part about the pirates and the sea monsters. *Per favoreeee,*" Ernest begged. Sometimes it took Nonno so long to get to the good part.

Nonno took a long draw on his pipe and noticed Ernest had dropped the reins. He picked them up and handed them back to the boy. "Ernest, you must hold tight."

"I know, Nonno. I'm sorry."

"So where was I? Yes. My mamma cried. So many young people from our village had gone to America. Not many came back. Only the ones who were too sick. They never even got a peek at Lady Liberty before they were sent right back where they came from. But I was Battista Bianco! I was strong and healthy.

I took the train to Genoa to get the boat. It was the biggest machine I had ever seen. The SS *Werra.* Bigger than my whole village. There were so many people. Young men like me. Mothers. Children. Someone even tried to bring a chicken on the ship. Can you imagine? A chicken crossing the Atlantic Ocean? Bah.

"We had been on the sea for three days when a young hand came down below deck. He couldn't have been more than—"

"Thirteen. Right, Nonno? He was thirteen," Ernest interjected.

"Ernest! You must respect your elders. It's not polite to interrupt," Nonna gently reminded.

"Your nonna's right, Nino. As I was saying…he couldn't have been more than thirteen. I was asleep when my new friend, Antonio, poked me awake. 'Battista, wake up. They're looking for you.' I stood up and carefully stepped over all the people in my way. I didn't want to step on anybody! So many sleeping bodies.

"'Are you Battista Bianco?' the boy asked me.

"I said, '*Sì.*'

"'*Signore,* Captain Pohle needs to see you immediately,' he said. I couldn't imagine why the captain would want to speak with me, but I followed the young lad up the stairs. The captain was a big man and he looked at me and said, 'Signore Bianco? I understand you have brought treasure onto my ship. Now we have pirates onboard and they want to speak to you.'

"'*Mio Dio.* Pirates?' I said. 'And they want *my* treasure? Let me see these scoundrels.' The captain led me into his private chamber where there were two savage-looking knaves waiting for me. One had a patch over his eye and the other had only one leg. And oh, how they smelled!"

Nonno squeezed his nose with his fingers and Ernest and his grandmother both giggled.

"So I tell these pirates to follow me. I will go get my treasure," Nonno continued. "We walk across the deck where all the fancy people are and I lead the pirates to the rail. You see, Ernest, I had a plan. That afternoon the water was still. Like glass. And the sun—it was a golden orange. And you could see its reflection on the water. I said to the pirates, 'Why do you want my treasure when there are greater riches right here in the sea?'

"The fellow with the patch looked to where I pointed and his one eye squinted with greed. The sun played a trick on him and he thought there was gold under the water. He jumped off the ship and his stupid friend followed him. And my treasure was safe."

"Your cuttings, right, Nonno?"

"Smart boy. You remember. Yes. The wine we are bringing to Father Michael came from the vines that grew from those Asti cuttings. Our family in Italy drinks the same wine." And then he added with a wink, "But mine is better."

"Now, the part about the sea monster," Ernest urged.

"Another time, Nino. There's the church. I'll join you and Nonna inside after I see Father Michael."

Nonna took her grandson's hand and led him to the wrought-iron stand of votive candles inside the small narthex. She reached into her purse and gave him a penny for the collection box. She then struck a wooden match, which Ernest solemnly and carefully accepted. He stepped on tippy toes and gingerly lit the highest candle he could reach and hurriedly puffed the match out before the flame could reach his fingers. He watched his grandmother give the sign of the cross and copied her motions. After Nonna said hello to a few of her friends, they made their way to their usual pew and waited for Mass to begin.

"Shh, Nino. Be still," Virginia Bianco whispered in her grandson's ear. The boy had skinned his knees the week before. He had been teaching cousin Stella the steps to "Giro Giro Tondo" when his feet got tangled and he fell on the rocky soil. Through the scabs Ernest could feel every groove of the pine plank under his knees. He shifted his weight from side to side, taking a bit of the pressure off one knee at a time, but any relief he felt was short-lived.

Ernest tugged on the skirts of his grandmother's ankle-length dress. "But Nonna…"

"No, Ernest. *Silenzio*."

He wrinkled his nose and twisted his mouth. He caught a small smile on his grandmother's face as she turned away from him. Even when she was stern, Ernest felt the warmth of her love. He wondered if sometimes she was just pretending to be cross.

Nonno joined them and the priest began to talk. Ernest shifted his gaze to the streaks of blue and gold reflected on the floor. He traced the source to the sunlight streaming through the window to his right. From the glass, the Madonna gazed down at the babe in her arms. Ernest was captivated by the honey-colored circles that arched over the tops of their heads. He wondered if they were attached and if Mary had to take off her baby's before she put him to bed. In the picture at Nonna and Nonno's, they had a soft glow, but these looked heavy and awkward. Ernest continued to examine the window until his thoughts were interrupted by the tinkling of a small bell.

This was his favorite part. Father Michael was about to turn Nonno's wine into Jesus's blood. He didn't understand why anyone would want to drink someone's blood, even God's, but he knew it was a miracle. Ernest could feel a thumping inside his ears every Sunday at this part of the Mass. He forgot all about the pain in his knees, and he straightened his spine and pulled his shoulders down as he looked up at the gold chalice raised over the priest's head. Ernest snuck a peek at his grandfather. If it weren't for him, there would be no wine and no miracle.

Ernest didn't really understand why he had been sent down to Hanford, California, in 1910 to live with his nonna and nonno. He was one year old at the time and his newborn brother, Julio, had stayed in Oakland, a few hours away, with their mother and father. Nonna said it was because his mother worked too hard cleaning and cooking three meals a day for all the *pensioners* at his father's boardinghouse. Susie couldn't possibly manage all that *and* care for a new baby with a toddler underfoot. But when his parents came to visit, his father would say, "Don't ask so many questions."

Almost eighty miles south of the state's exact center, the Biancos' farm was known to all in the quiet agricultural community. The veil of dust that fomented along the driveway signaling a visitor's arrival hardly had time to settle before its next disturbance. Sundays were the busiest, when family and friends came over right after Mass. Nonna served her famous ravioli and each family would bring something to share: bread, sausages, cheese, and fruit. Of course, Nonno provided the wine. Most people brought gallon-size earthen jugs and gave Nonno five cents to fill them up straight from one of the barrels in his basement. People were always coming to buy wine. Some were shepherds from foreign lands. Ernest didn't understand their funny words and it seemed that Nonno didn't, either, but their empty jugs and the nickels in their outstretched hands said everything that needed to be said.

When the sun rose to cooler days, an entirely new crowd emerged from the dust cloud that hung over the driveway. Some faces were familiar, but each year there would be new ones. They had come to help Nonno with the harvest and crush. Battista's vineyards stretched across Hanford. He grew different kinds of grapes and each vineyard ripened in its own time. Family, friends, and hired hands filled wooden lug boxes with sun-sweetened handpicked clusters. The crates were carried to wagons and unloaded at the shed behind the white shingled farmhouse.

Father Michael came to bless the first crush of the season. Ernest, cousin Stella, and the other barefoot children were placed into a big tub of rich purple fruit where they jumped and danced, infused by the day's holiday-like atmosphere. Without fail, there would be one child who stepped on a stem and cried for his mother to lift him out of the goo. But Ernest loved the squishy feeling between his toes, the sticky sweet smell in the air, and the excitement that came with each year's jubilee.

As the children did their part, the bulk of the grapes were crushed next to the shed in a machine manned by two men. One poured the fruit into the hopper while the other turned a bank vault–style wheel to spin two metal shafts that squeezed the clusters of grapes. A bucket underneath collected the thick mash of juice, pulp, skins, and stems that spilled from the machine. The mixture was then poured into sixty-gallon barrels inside the shed to ferment for a week or so.

One September afternoon in 1914, Ernest was bored. The fervor of the harvest had subsided, and Nonno, Uncle Walter, Aunt Lydia, and Stella had all gone into town on errands. Nonna had fallen asleep in her chair while knitting, and Ernest couldn't think of anything to do. He heard muffled voices in the backyard and went outside to investigate. Two of Nonno's helpers were in the backyard shed pressing the wine—the big fat man and the one with the scar on his arm. Ernest watched attentively. They dipped a bucket into one of the big fermenting tanks and emptied the smelly mixture into the press. The device looked like a tiny wooden barrel, except maybe the man who made it hadn't done such a good job. There were gaps between the planks and liquid was coming out the sides. But the men didn't seem worried.

The big fat man covered the press with a round wooden lid. The other man attached a long metal handle and started winching it back and forth. More and more juice spilled out of the sides and from a groove in front where the milky purple nectar poured into another bucket. When the bucket was full, one of the men would pour it into a barrel or one of Nonno's big baskets that had a glass jug inside.

"Can I have a turn?" Ernest asked the man with the scar.

"I don't know. This is hard work…let me see your muscles."

Ernest pushed up his shirtsleeve and flexed his bicep with all his might. His face turned red as he held his breath.

The big man laughed, "Why, Gianni, I think he's stronger than you."

Gianni stacked a couple of lug boxes on top of each other to give the little boy a higher perch. It was harder to pull the handle than Ernest had expected. While he pushed all his weight against the metal bar, the two men held a tin cup under the press and drank some of the fresh juice. The wooden lid sunk into the growing cake of dross with each pull or push, and soon Gianni had to put some wooden blocks between the lid and the mechanism to keep the pressure on the mash of grapes.

"Boy oh boy, I need a break," the five-year-old exhaled after a few minutes. Ernest jumped off his perch and the men resumed their work. His brown hair was stuck to his forehead and he was mighty thirsty. He picked up the tin cup and gulped down the sweet juice as he had seen the men do. The men laughed.

Pushing the press wasn't as much fun as it had looked, but Ernest stayed and rolled empty barrels and casks to the men as they continued their work. But that was difficult too. Ernest took another drink of juice. The men laughed even louder.

Enjoying the attention, Ernest put a farm basket on his head and put on a show. He placed his hands on his hips as he danced, spun, and jumped in circles. He felt a warmth rush through his body and an energizing tingle course through his limbs.

"I'm a little old woman," he screeched. "I'm a donkey," he brayed. "Watch me kick my legs." He gave the performance of his life.

Suddenly the walls of the shed felt like they were closing in on him. He had to get outside. There, he ran faster than he had ever run in his life. He sprang up from one foot and hung in the air forever before his other foot hit the ground. He felt like he was flying.

When Ernest woke up, he slammed his eyes closed as fast as he could. It was dark and he couldn't tell where he was. But all the shadowed shapes around him were spinning faster than anything could possibly move. He cautiously opened one eye and saw that the sky outside the window was darker than the pressed grapes. He raised his other eyelid and grandmother's bed started to twirl. He squeezed his eyes closed again and began to cry.

"Hush, Nino, everything will be good," came Nonna's soothing voice.

"Nonna, I'm dying," Ernest squeaked.

"No, Nino. You will be okay. Silly boy, you had too much wine."

"No, Nonna. I didn't drink any wine. I'm dying." Ernest stifled a sob.

"Ernest, when the grapes are in Nonno's shed, they turn into wine. But don't worry. Keep your eyes closed and go back to sleep." Grandmother Bianco looked into her grandson's scared brown eyes and placed a damp cloth on his brow. She sang softly.

Fa la ninna, fa la nanna
Nella braccia della Mamma
Fa la ninna bel bambin,
Fa la nanna bambin bel,
Fa la ninna, fal la nanna
Nella braccia della Mamma

"But Nonna, why can't you come too?"

"What would I do in the big city? And who would cook for Nonno? And what about the chickens? You know I'm the one who feeds them every day," Grandmother soothed.

"Why, they can come too! It would make Mamma so happy to have you with us," Ernest rebuffed.

Virginia Bianco was breaking into a million pieces on the inside, but she remained steady for her grandson. Her daughter and no-good son-in-law were on their way to collect him. Battista's lungs were in poor health again and it was time to try a different climate. In any case, it was certainly time for Ernest to live with his mamma and papà. Julio was five already and the brothers were practically strangers. Maybe Giuseppe had changed like Assunta had assured them. Oh, how could her daughter have made such a poor choice? And then for her younger sister, Celia, to go ahead and marry Giuseppe's brother Michaelo? Such foolish girls!

Ernest knew he belonged with his mamma and papà, and he was excited to live in the city and go to school to become smart. But he couldn't remember a time when Nonna and Nonno hadn't taken care of him. He wondered if Mamma knew how to make ravioli and if Papà knew any good stories. He wondered what it would be like to have a little brother. He had spent time with Julio during holidays, but only for a few days at a time. He seemed okay and they did have fun playing together. But one thing he knew for sure: He needed to make it clear right away that Julio knew who was in charge. Julio was the baby. Ernest was big. His throat ached and he tried to wipe away the warm tears he felt on his cheek before Nonna could see them. Big boys didn't cry.

Nonna knelt down to her grandson's height and pulled him against her bosom. "Nino, remember what I always say: *Avanti e corragio. Il Signore chudera la porta ma apre un altro.* Let's go ahead with courage. When God closes one door, He opens another."

Chapter Two

HARD KNOCKS

"I don't wanna tell him. You tell him," Ernest said emphatically.

"Uh-uh. I told him last time. It's your turn," Julio argued.

Ernest thought for a minute before speaking again. "Um, okay, but here's the deal. I'll tell him. But you have to feed the cows for two weeks."

"No way. *Two weeks?* That's not fair. One week," Julio countered.

"Okay, one week." Ernest sighed dramatically for Julio's benefit. He wanted Julio to feel like he had conceded while his plan all along had been to agree to one week. He stifled a small smile, not wanting to hurt Julio's pride or seem like a bully. Plus, one week was more than fair considering what he was about to do.

Ernest twisted around to look back at the crooked line the plow had etched along the surface of the hardpan. The furrow certainly wasn't deep enough for the potatoes his father planned to grow. He pushed down on the lever to lift the plowshare and jumped down to the dirt. It had been a long summer. His arms ached and his legs were weak from standing all day. He hadn't been able to sit down as his feet didn't reach the floor of the plow. He was only able to control the four-mule team when he stood.

He walked around the lathered, huffing animals to his brother. Each boy spit in his right palm before sealing the deal with a handshake. Julio held the lead mule's halter while his brother headed for the barn. Ernest turned back once and was struck by the expanse of the brown field. It stretched as far as he could see, no matter which direction he looked. It seemed he and Julio had little to show for their last three weeks of labor.

Father had bought the farm in Antioch, California, six months before, in the spring of 1917. Ernest remembered the dark mood leading up to the move. One night after Father had closed his Oakland saloon for the evening, Ernest and Julio had been awakened by his shouts breaking through their bedroom floorboards like the harsh light of an oncoming train. "The Drys are going to ruin this country! You watch!" Ernest was accustomed to his father's temper, but this outburst was lasting longer than most. He heard Mamma quietly trying to soften Father's mood. It would be still for a few moments and Ernest would hold his breath, praying it was over. But then the shouting would begin again. The ugly insults his father hurled at his mother slapped at the boy's ears. Chairs scraped against the floor below and he heard Mamma cry out. Ernest tucked the pillow around his head and held it in place with the crook of his right arm. He reached his left arm over to Julio's twin bed and found his brother's waiting hand, and in it, the comfort and assurance he needed to fall back to sleep.

The next morning, Ernest noticed everything took Mamma twice as long as usual—pouring their milk, buttering their bread, putting the lunches together for school. She moved like one of those hypnotized people at the carny. "Boys," she said, "your father is selling the *pensione*. The government won't let anyone sell wine or alcohol anymore. He found a nice farm not far from here. One hundred and twenty acres. You'll still be able to see your cousins. We can grow all our own food and you will have a lot of exploring to do. Imagine the games of hide-and-seek you can have. And I won't have to cook and clean for all these strangers anymore. It will just be the four of us. Won't that be nice?"

But so far, Antioch had been anything but "nice." Now, another beam on the plow had snapped in two. That was the third one in as many weeks and Father had been apoplectic about the first. As Ernest trudged to the barn to inform his father, he rehearsed a speech he knew he would never deliver. *"Papà, no one else is plowing their fields right now. The ground is too hard and the draught horses we used last time only made the soil worse. I'm only eight and Julio's only seven. We're doing our best. Please don't be mad at us."* Ernest willed these disrespectful and dangerous thoughts out of his head. A swift whipping would come if Father ever read his mind or smelled a whiff of criticism. Best he just tell Father quickly. Get it over with and endure the hollering and whatever punishment came with it.

"Father?"

"What is it now?" Father was perched on a bale of straw, pencil in hand, carefully examining the W. F. Pitts seed catalog. Father didn't speak English, let alone read it. Ernest knew *he* could read most of the words, but didn't dare offer to help. He knew better than to insult his father. If Father wanted his help, he would ask for it. The immigrant's eyes remained fixed on the small, tight words while his young son stood by his side reaching deep within for courage and, at the same time, steeling himself for the worst.

"Another beam broke," Ernest stated. The fewer words, he'd learned, the better.

"*È la vita.* That's life," his father answered flatly. "Wipe down the mules and feed all the animals before your mother has dinner ready. And make sure the sheep have water. Tomorrow you will start cutting the Thompsons in the vineyard and Julio will weed between the rows. I need them to be ready to graft the Zinfandels and Alicantes in the spring."

"Yes, Father." Ernest's chest heaved in relief. That was the rub with Father. You never knew what you were going to get.

Born Giuseppe Gallo in 1882, Ernest's father now went by the Americanized version of his name: Joe. He had arrived in Oakland just in time for the big earthquake of 1906. Within a year Joe had saved enough money to buy a horse and small wagon. He spent three days of each week making trips to local winemakers. He left before the sun rose and returned to the city at nightfall with eight barrels of homemade wine. He sold the wine along the sides of the city's cobblestoned streets, mostly to immigrants from Northern Italy like himself. The hearty red wine made by their fellow countrymen tasted like home. When the last drop had fallen into the last buyer's jug, he returned to the wineries to refill his barrels. This was how he met his wife, Susie, for he used to buy wine from her father, Battista Bianco.

Joe had saved his money and, with his younger brother Mike's help, bought an Oakland boardinghouse with a first-floor saloon that catered to the Bay Area's influx of Northern Italians. Though Susie had worked tirelessly to keep the boardinghouse clean and the *pensioners* well fed, most of their income had come from the five-gallon kegs of wine that stood on the downstairs bar. However, in Joe's opinion, this new country had some *pazze,* or crazy, ideas about wine and liquor. Somehow politicians thought they could reduce alcoholism through government-induced temperance. With the passage of the Eighteenth Amendment, prohibiting the sale of alcohol, and the onset of Prohibition, Joe needed to find a new way to support his family. While his brother Mike was laying the foundation for an illicit future, Joe was determined to obey the law of the land no matter how ridiculous he thought it to be.

Joe had always enjoyed his forays to the local wineries. The agrarian lifestyle seemed honest and reminded him of home. The farmers he knew were simple people, maybe even simpleminded. If they could farm successfully, surely he could too. How hard could it possibly be? If he could find some affordable land near Oakland, he could come to town and sell produce just like he had sold wine years before.

The Antioch property had satisfied the top three requirements on Joe's wish list: the price was right, it was close to Oakland, and the land was already productive—vineyards of Thompson seedless grapes covered a third of the land. Thompsons grew well in the region and were a dependable, all-purpose variety. They were the standard table grape, but could be made into both raisins and wine.

For although the *sale* of wine was forbidden under the Constitution's new amendment, its *manufacture* wasn't. At least, not exactly. Wineries could still make medicinal and sacramental wine, but more importantly, the head of each household in the country could make two hundred gallons a year for his family's personal use. Thousands of Northern Italian immigrants had moved into the Bay Area and now they would be making their own wine. It would be breeze for Joe to sell any grapes he grew.

The new amendment, however, had opened up an even bigger market for grapes—a national one. Families throughout the country cleared space in their basements for "Papà's new hobby" and Papà needed grapes. Most of the country's wine drinkers were French, Italian, and German immigrants who lived in the Midwest and on the east coast. For decades locomotives had towed tank cars filled with California wine to the east. But now they delivered refrigerated cars with a much more fragile cargo: grapes. The journey was unforgiving, and growers, shippers, and home winemakers quickly came to prefer Alicante Bouschet grapes over Thompsons.

The thick skins of the Alicantes kept them from breaking during transit and decreased the subsequent mold. Alicantes also made the type of rich, deep red wine preferred by immigrants. The grape was so sturdy it could be pressed multiple times. With some added water and sugar, a ton of Alicantes could produce 700 gallons of wine, significantly more than the 150 gallons most other varieties yielded. Joe saw the opportunity and decided to graft Alicante cuttings onto his Thompsons' rootstocks.

But, as his eldest son, Ernest, soon concluded, Joe Gallo knew nothing about farming. And he didn't have the aptitude, the instinct, or the patience for it. He was like King Midas, but instead of turning everything into gold, everything he touched either withered and died or remained dormant in the ground. The vegetables that persevered in spite of all the indignities they suffered were half the size and half as sweet or flavorful as they should be. Susie barely had enough tomatoes and garlic to feed and can for her own family. Selling anything in Oakland or beyond was out of the question.

Ernest and Julio never did play hide-and-seek on the family's new farm. Their chores knew no end, no matter the day of the week or the season. But the brothers were in it together and rarely complained. What good would it do? There were always animals to feed and vineyards to tend. Complaining wouldn't change that. Nor would it mollify Father's endless expectations and demands.

Unlike most of Ernest's classmates—many of them farmers' sons too—Ernest was grateful when school resumed in the fall. While some of the kids had their summer vacations, Ernest had been working hard on the farm. But now he had recess. Twice a day, even! He could sit most of the day and was the best in his class at math. He even appreciated when Miss Peterson corrected some of his Italian ways and helped him become more American. Even though he was born in California, he sometimes felt more Italian than American.

One spring day during his last year of elementary school, the teacher dismissed them early. Ernest had forgotten it was a half day. He met Julio outside his classroom as per their unspoken routine. As they were about to leave the building, they passed a group of Julio's friends. One of them was carrying a basketball.

"Hey, Julio, why don't you and your brother come with us?" one of them invited.

"Thanks, I wish I could, but I need to get home," Julio shrugged.

The Gallo brothers turned right at the end of the path and dutifully headed for their never-satisfied fields. They were about halfway home when Ernest suddenly stopped.

"Julio! What's wrong with us? We need to live, brother!" He pivoted in front of Julio and put both hands on his shoulders. He turned his younger brother 180 degrees, and with his arms outstretched, gently nudged his brother back toward school.

"Ernest, what are you doing?"

"Not what *I'm* doing. What *we're* doing. *I* didn't know it was a half day. *You* didn't know it was a half day. And more importantly, *Father* doesn't know it's a half day. Let's have some fun for once."

"Um...I don't know. We've got so much to do. If Father found out, he'd kill us," Julio argued. "There's no wind today. He'll probably want us to sulfur the vines some more."

"He'll never find out. We'll make sure to get home at the usual time and we'll still get all our chores done." Ernest looked into his brother's bloodshot eyes and imagined his must be just as red. He had told concerned teachers that he was suffering from seasonal hay fever, not wanting to admit that he had been in the field from three until seven in the morning sprinkling sulfur on the grapevines to prevent mildew. The yellow powder made his eyes itch and sting like nobody's business.

"But—"

"Come on, Julio, you know I'm right...and your eyes need a break. Mine do too," Ernest appealed.

His logic was hard to refute.

"All right," Julio agreed. "Last one there's a rotten egg!"

He took off running and Ernest gamely followed, though he knew he had no chance of catching up. Julio was arguably the more athletic of the two.

When they got to the playground, none of Julio's friends were there. Some older boys were playing basketball. The middle school must have been released early too. Undeterred, Julio approached the boys to see if they could join their game.

"Hey, aren't you Julio? You go to school with my sister," one of the boys said.

"Don't you mean *Hooo-lio*?" asked the one with the slicked-back blond hair. "*Hooo-lio,* are you a dago or a beaner?"

"It's Julio. Like July. And I don't know what a 'dago' or 'beaner' is, so I don't know if I'm either," the fifth-grader innocently responded.

A rage fell over Ernest and suppressed all his senses like a thick woolen blanket when he registered the slur to his brother. This rowdy had just insulted his brother, his family, his people. Seeing nothing but the entitled face below the slicked-back blond hair, Ernest suddenly felt his feet propel him forward before Julio had even finished his last sentence. Without any deliberation or awareness, Ernest sprung up and quickly jabbed the bully in the nose. Though Ernest was shorter by a full head, he enjoyed the element of surprise. He grabbed Julio by the collar.

"Quick! Run!"

The brothers gathered their books without missing a stride and rounded the corner of the Queen Anne schoolhouse… straight into Joe Gallo.

"Just what I thought! How dare you! How dare you take advantage of me," Father growled between clenched teeth. He grabbed each boy by the ear and dragged them to his waiting truck.

Julio started to cry, but Ernest remained stoic. It was all his fault. How could Father have known? Ernest looked up at the red-faced Italian and saw a little dab of shaving cream in the hollow of his ear. He must have been at the barbershop that was right across the street from the drugstore. A lot of the school kids had probably gone there to buy candy to celebrate their early liberation. Father must have put it together that school had been dismissed early. He'd probably gone to look for his sons after returning home and discovering their insubordination.

"Father, it's all my fault," Ernest admitted. "Julio wanted to go straight home, but I made him stay."

"Exactly, Ernest. It *is* all your fault. You are the big brother and I expect more from you. What kind of example are you? And what of your baby brother, Joseph? Is this the kind of behavior you will teach him too?"

Joe stooped down so he could look Ernest straight in the eye and seethed, "I'm ashamed you bear my name. You're not worthy." With that, he stood up and spit on the ground. The thick wad landed on Ernest's left shoe. "Remember those long pants I promised you for your graduation? No? Neither do I."

Ernest took a quick look around to make sure none of his classmates were nearby but, thankfully, they were alone. Graduating in his old, worn knickers would be humiliation enough. He took a long look at the belt around Father's waist. Maybe by staring it down he would become its master, weakening its power so it would hurt less later on. Then, as if Mother Nature were in on Father's mood, the sky darkened and cold, fat raindrops began to fall.

By the time they got home it was pouring. Blinded by the tumult of his guilt and shame and his father's unfairness, Ernest hadn't noticed the mound of old rubber tires that filled the truck bed. He started walking toward the shabby house. Finding a comfortable home for his family clearly hadn't been one of Father's priorities when leaving Oakland.

"Whoa, boy! Where do you think you're going? Get your rear end back here and help me with these tires! You too, Julio!" Father bellowed, even though his sons were just a few feet away.

"Yes, Father," they replied in unison.

The job took a good couple of hours. One by one, they rolled each tire over to the vineyard. Neither boy asked why; they both just followed Father's instructions. By the time they were finished, there were tires scattered down each row and the three

Gallos were soaked to their marrow. The wind had picked up and the temperature was dropping. Ernest shivered. He couldn't imagine ever feeling warm and dry again.

Though dinner was late that night, Mamma's polenta was extra good. Ernest caught her putting a few more drops of wine than usual in his water and the two exchanged a quick smile. Even if the rest of him was still cold, he was grateful for the warmth in his stomach. He was also hopeful that Father had forgotten about the whipping. Moving the tires had been difficult, but maybe there was a silver lining. He nudged Julio and asked to be excused so they could wash the dishes. The cookware and plates had never been cleaned faster than they were that night. As soon as the last spoon was dried and placed in its wobbly drawer, Ernest rushed to his bedroom to do his homework. If Father couldn't see him, maybe he'd forget about the beating.

Ernest fell asleep to the sound of the rain against the roof. It seemed that each spring his bedroom ceiling would sprout a new leak, and no matter where he placed his mattress the fissure was sure to be right overhead. As dog-tired as he was, deep sleep wasn't in the cards that night. His unconscious mind lay in wait for that first drop. When he started to nod off, he dreamt of rough seas with waves taller than the house, in which he and Julio were frantically trying to row the dinghy that held them toward an unseen but certain shore.

"*Ernest! Julio! Get up! Immediatamente!*" Father's voice boomed through the house.

Of course, Ernest thought, Father had remembered his undelivered thrashing. He rubbed his eyes and wondered what time it was. The rain had stopped but the sky was still dark.

His father stood in the doorway. "Get dressed now! Meet me in the vineyard."

Ernest pulled the thick sweater Nonna had knit him over his overalls. Two years later and the sleeves were still two inches too long—his long-awaited growth spurt yet but a promise. He met Julio at the back door. They laced up their boots, grabbed a couple of lamps, and ran to the vineyard.

Father handed Ernest a can of gasoline and urged, "Pour this over the tires. We have to protect the vines from the frost." The words left his mouth in a crystalized puff. Suddenly Ernest noticed how cold it was.

Joe trailed his eldest son, dropping a lit match on each wet tire. As the rubber began to burn, it snuffed out the flames. The vineyard was soon blanketed in a thick black smoke. Ernest choked and couldn't see where he was going. He tripped over the untouched tires behind him, pulled the hem of his sweater over his nose, and hurried to finish the task.

No one within twenty-five miles saw the sun rise the next day. The light that managed to leach through the shroud over Joe Gallo's vineyard revealed rows of charred vines that would never bear fruit again. Ernest's stomach churned. Yesterday the Zinfandels and Alicantes they had grafted onto the Thompson rootstocks had been full of young buds and the promise of an abundant crop. He inwardly berated his father. Joe's pride was lethal. Ever since moving to Antioch, Father had planted the wrong crop in the wrong place at the wrong time. Ernest couldn't understand why his father never asked more experienced farmers for advice or paid attention to their habits. It wasn't a sign of weakness; it was the smart thing to do. If he knew that at twelve, why couldn't his thirty-nine-year-old father see that?

"That's it! I quit this stupid farm. This stupid way of life!" Joe wailed to his speechless family before striding back to the house.

Joe's most efficient accomplishment of those four years in Antioch was the speed with which he sold the farm. They headed south just two weeks after the conflagration, Ernest and Julio hanging on to the taut jute that secured their three mattresses to the truck. Any possessions that didn't fit in the truck's bed or couldn't be strapped to the roof or bumpers had to be left behind. Ernest wriggled to find a spot where he wouldn't be poked by a protruding pot handle or tool. Baby Joe sat between Father and Mamma in the front seat.

As the farmhouse disappeared from sight, Ernest tipped his cap. "Good riddance!" he shouted. "I hope I never see you again!" He flopped on his back and looked up at the blue sky. He remembered Nonna's words: *Let's go ahead with courage. When God closes one door, He opens another.*

Chapter Three

THE PROPHECY

Uncle Mike had just bought a house in Oakland, but his recent prosperity had made it possible for him to hold on to his cattle ranch in the nearby town of Livermore too. He had suggested that his brother Joe and his family move in. That way he could stay in Oakland and Joe could manage the ranch and take a share of the profits until he figured out his next move. Mike also offered to take the boys for a week so Joe and Susie could get settled. Ernest and Julio divided one week every summer between Mamma's sister, Aunt Tillie, in San Francisco and Uncle Mike and Aunt Celia, who were always moving around the Bay Area. But given their family's circumstances in 1921, their vacation came earlier than usual.

Ernest couldn't believe his luck. He loved Oakland and San Francisco. Uncle Mike had always given the boys plenty of money to spend and they could do whatever they wanted as long as they were home in time for dinner. Between the trolley cars and ferries, there wasn't anywhere Ernest couldn't go or anything he couldn't do. And it meant a week without chores to boot.

When Father pulled up to the Livermore house, Ernest's jaw fell open.

"Uncle Mike, Uncle Mike, is that your new car?" Julio shouted.

"Sure is, squirt," Mike grinned. "Come take a look." In his double-breasted pinstriped suit, felt Borsalino hat, and diamond pinkie ring, Father's brother looked a little ridiculous in the rustic setting, but perfectly right next to the shiny Packard Runabout.

Ernest and Julio jumped down from the truck bed to admire the machine. The paint was the color of an aged red wine and looked that much richer next to the spoked whitewall tires.

"Here, lemme show you the engine. She's a V-12," Mike boasted as he popped the hood open.

"It's beautiful, Mike, but there's no room for the boys. I thought you were taking them to Oakland," Susie said.

Ernest's spirits plummeted as he realized his mother was right. Uncle Mike's car sure was sweet, but it only had one seat. It couldn't fit two adults and two boys.

"Ah, Susie. Ever the worrier. Not a problem. Celia will sit in front with me. And watch this." Mike walked to the rounded back side of the car and a lid popped up, revealing a hidden seat in the trunk. "The boys can sit here."

"Whoa, Uncle Mike!" Ernest exclaimed.

"Nice, brother. Enjoy her. She's a beaut," Joe said. He was smiling, but Ernest detected a slight strain in his voice.

"It's called a rumble seat," Mike explained.

"I know what it's called," Joe mumbled under his breath, though Ernest was the only one close enough to hear him.

"Uncle Mike, tell us about San Quentin!" Julio burst out.

Twelve-year-old Ernest quickly scolded his eleven-year-old brother for mentioning the prison. "Shh, Julio. We don't talk about that."

"Don't worry, Julio. I'll tell you all about it later. All righty, boys, let's go. Joe, wait till you hear her motor. *Celia! Let's go! Time's a-wasting!*" Mike hollered toward the house.

The drive to Oakland was exhilarating. And loud. Ernest had never moved so fast in his life. Well, except for the Bob Sled Dipper at Chutes at the Beach. He wondered if the amusement park at Ocean Beach had any new rides and then realized he would soon see for himself.

The boys spent the first half of the week with Aunt Tillie in the part of San Francisco called North Beach, home to an enclave of Northern Italian immigrants. Aunt Tillie lived on the third floor of a building Nonna and Nonno owned near Columbus Avenue. It was an easy walk to the Palace Theater, which was playing the new Buster Keaton picture. Aunt Tillie had given each boy fifteen cents, so even after buying a bag of dried shrimp for the show, they had enough leftover change to buy some *canestrelli* from Victoria's. Ernest let the lemon cookies dissolve in his mouth and savored the alternating sweet and tart flavors. Though he had never been to Italy, Ernest imagined Columbus Avenue was about as close as you could get. All the Ligurian voices around him sounded like everyone in his family and the aromas spilling from the restaurants, delis, and bakeries smelled like Mamma's kitchen.

On the boys' last day in San Francisco, Ernest broke off on his own. It was something he did every year. The Powell-Mason cable car took him most of the way. Even though automobiles were taking over the streets, there were still plenty of horses and wagons. As one drove by him on Mission Street, Ernest hopped on the back without the driver noticing. He held on tightly and jumped off right in front of the courthouse.

The Beaux Arts masterpiece of a building had survived the great earthquake of 1906 and bore the solemnity of a house of God. Ernest's steps echoed off the entryway's mosaic floor and the veined marble walls. Accustomed as he was to feeling small, this was an entirely different sense of insignificance. The building was a testament to the gifts bestowed on man by the Creator. Only He could have formed the exquisite marble and given man the ingenuity and resourcefulness to ship it from Italy, and the imagination and skill to build this monument to justice.

Men sped down the hallway as if pulled by strings on a toddler's toy. Ernest was sure the smooth leather briefcases they gripped cost more than his father's truck. All the men and women were wearing their best suits and hats, their shoes polished to a scuffless shine. There was an urgency and gravity to their whispers and voices. Ernest took the stairway to the third floor and waited for permission to enter the courtroom. He found a seat in the back. The wooden benches reminded him of the pews in Hanford and reinforced his sense of being in a hallowed space. The judge easily could have been wearing Father Michael's robes.

But Ernest left earlier than he had planned. He usually liked to spend hours in the courthouse listening to the lawyers' arguments and rhetoric. But the judge was hearing a divorce case. No one in his family had ever been divorced and he understood it to be a sin. Hearing these strangers' marital problems made him feel like a Peeping Tom. As Mamma always said, "What happens in the family stays in the family."

Ernest left the courthouse feeling somber, but confident that a night at Chutes at the Beach would cheer him up. Cotton candy, a salty breeze, and the glow of a million electric lights had turned many a dull mood.

~

"Tell me about your week, Ernest," Mamma asked.

"*Sì, avvocato,* tell us about your week," Father added derisively.

Ernest blushed. He hated when Father called him "the lawyer." He regretted ever telling him about his visits to the courthouse.

"Please excuse me, Aunt Celia," Ernest mumbled as he pushed his chair away and left the dining room. He paced around the parlor, hands clasped behind his back. He wasn't ready for the week to end. And he wasn't ready for Father. Ernest had been so relieved to leave the farm behind, he hadn't thought of what Livermore would bring. Given the size of Uncle Mike's farm, there couldn't possibly be as many chores to do as there had been in Antioch. Though living, breathing beings, cows surely didn't need as much attention as grapes. They seemed pretty self-sufficient as long as they had access to food and water. But he knew Father would find a way to keep him and Julio busy. He walked back and forth in the small room as if each footfall could release his worries. He sensed a shift in the tone of the conversation coming from the dining room and listened in.

"It'll be the easiest money you've ever made. These last two years have been the most lucrative of my life," Uncle Mike purred. "If the Drys only knew! Anyway, it's all set up. I'll handle all the business. You just gotta keep her running and bring the juice into the city. And, Susie, don't you worry. I got this thing wired. I've got a lotta friends. And in all the right places. It's perfectly safe."

Ernest wasn't certain what they were talking about, but he had a pretty good idea. The anger that he had been pacing away was coming back. What was Father getting them into now? Though his uncle's swagger and largesse were alluring, Ernest didn't completely trust him. Uncle Mike's approach to life was similar to how he drove his car: fast, loose, quick to overtake anyone in his way, and always looking for a shortcut. As much fun as it was to ride shotgun, each trip ended with relief and wonder that you had survived. If Father was taking advice from Uncle Mike, it couldn't be good.

Ernest pivoted at the window to see Aunt Tillie standing in the doorway.

"Nino? I didn't forget my promise. I brought my cards. How about we see what they have to say?"

"Yeah, that'd be swell," Ernest replied, grateful for any distraction.

You could always count on Aunt Tillie to be abreast of the latest fad. She was the first woman in the family to drive and the first to start smoking. Last summer she was all excited about her Chinese tile game. This year it was her cards. Ernest sat on the sofa and Aunt Tillie pulled a chair up to the low table in front of her nephew. He was skeptical about anyone's ability to foretell the future, but what harm could it do?

Aunt Tillie pulled a candle and a box of matches out of her handbag and placed them on the table. With theatrical flourish, she struck a wooden match against the box's red phosphorus strip and lit the candle. She placed the cards face down on the table. They were bigger than any playing cards Ernest had ever seen and he watched as she spread them out into a big mess. She moved them around with her palms, not picking any up, just shuffling them over and under.

"Ernest," she said softly, "pick a card. Which one are you drawn to?"

The boy's brown eyes moved over the pile until he settled on one. After he pointed to it, Aunt Tillie picked it up and turned it over.

"The Ten of Pentacles! The lord of wealth!"

"What does that mean?" Ernest asked, certain it had to be good news.

"One second. You need to turn over some more cards."

Ernest tried to make sense of the unusual-looking images Aunt Tillie studied. Her lips moved silently while she unraveled the mystery that lay between them.

"The cards say you're going to be a very successful businessman."

"Really? What else?"

"Just a second, I'm still looking…seems to be the oil business…or the wine business."

Chapter Four

THE LADY WITH A THOUSAND FACES

"Ernest! We have to go! Go over everything one more time with your brother," Father instructed before hurrying out of the barn.

"Julio, you know how to do this. It's not that hard. You just have to keep an eye on this part here to make sure nothing leaks out." Ernest pointed to a soldered seam on the copper contraption. "If any vapor comes out, you and everything in here will shoot up to the moon faster than you can say 'phonus balonus.'"

"That's exactly what's making me nervous. You're not helping any."

"It'll be fine. I rubbed some paste on it this morning just to be safe," Ernest assured. Though he was grateful for any chance to be away from the still where Uncle Mike made his illegal alcohol, the trade-off wasn't that much better. Both boys dreaded Father's "errands."

As Ernest expected, their chores in Livermore were different from those at the old farm. But there was just as much work to be done. Part of the deal Father had made with Uncle Mike was that he would keep his illegal still in the barn in operation—or, put another way, Ernest and Julio would keep his illegal still in operation. Yet, Ernest had to admit, life had improved. His mother seemed happier. He had never known what a beautiful voice she had. And he realized he had never heard her sing until they moved to Livermore. He couldn't believe how many arias she knew.

Father seemed happier too. Although he often chastised Uncle Mike for his flashy cars, silk shirts, and diamond fob, he himself had bought a new car. A Hudson. It stood out in a farming community where all the other fathers drove trucks and horse-drawn wagons. In any case, Father was more relaxed than Ernest had ever seen him, despite the incredible risk he was taking with the law. His uncle and father acted as if an invisible perimeter had been drawn around San Francisco, and the sleepy cow town of Livermore forty-five miles to the east was out of the prohibition agents' sight and minds. "They just want the headlines and big speakeasy raids," Father would reassure his family. But his eldest son knew all about prohibition agents Tom Threepersons…and masters of disguise Izzy and Moe…and the Lady Hooch Hunter, also known as the Lady with a Thousand Faces. Their names alone instilled a fear Ernest couldn't shake.

"Watch the flames to make sure they don't get too high or too low," he continued explaining to Julio. "And pay attention to the bottle or jug you're filling. Have the next bottle ready to go. I promise you Father will know if even one drop gets spilled. It takes about an hour to fill one jug. And keep the barn door open so fresh air can get in. There's plenty of pomace and sugar next to the pot still so you can refill it when you need to."

"Thanks, Ernest. Be careful…Oh, and watch out for the Lady with a Thousand Faces. I hear she's everywhere," Julio teased, trying to get his brother back for scaring him about blowing up the barn.

"Noble experiment, my *posteriore,*" Joe Gallo laughed. "California is wetter than ever! Let's go make some money, son!"

Ernest wished he could have shared some of his father's enthusiasm, but he couldn't shake the feeling that something was about to go horribly wrong. He didn't know anyone who supported the Eighteenth Amendment, but the law was the law. After all, look at what had happened to Uncle Mike. *Prison*. Ernest tried to reassure himself. They had never been stopped or questioned in their two years in Livermore. And at fourteen, he was still a kid. They probably wouldn't send him to jail. But no matter how he tried to settle his mind, the worry continued to chip away at any composure he managed to muster.

The anxious preteen tried to make the best of the drive. The countryside was beautiful. The winter rains had turned the grass and brush into a sea of green. Ernest's gaze followed the shadows of the clouds scudding over the rolling hills and the cows grazing among the spreading oaks. The almond, peach, and apple orchards were in different stages of bloom and their pink and white blossoms filled their branches or lay in a carpet between their trunks. In places it looked like the Creator had randomly swung a broad brush dipped in buckets of pastels over the landscape. The almond groves were Ernest's favorite. They looked like they were covered with snow. With his elbow resting on the open window frame, he closed his eyes and inhaled the sweet fragrance.

Their first stop was The Highway Inn. Father parked the car behind the restaurant. Ernest opened the car's rear passenger door and reached in for the wicker laundry basket. Should anyone ask, he was delivering linens his mother had washed and ironed. Hoping to disguise the basket's true weight, he carried it higher than what would have been comfortable. The bottles of grappa must have weighed at least sixty pounds and he prayed Julio had packed the basket carefully so it wouldn't clink when he carried it to the hotel's rear entrance. His heart didn't stop pounding until he returned to the car and they were back on the road.

Soon after, Father pulled behind a roadside barn so Ernest could repack the basket. A friend of Uncle Mike's had replaced the Hudson's rear seat with a hollow compartment. Ernest had filled it with pressed linens and bottles of their homemade brandy that morning. He refilled the basket and they motored to the Santa Rita Inn. They repeated this drill three more times until the compartment was empty. Ernest's heart got a little lighter each time. Maybe luck was on their side.

Their last stop was a white clapboard house on the edge of town nicknamed Old Mexico. Ernest had never been to the house before, but Father had told him the password and how many times to knock. He wished just once Father would do something other than drive the car.

"Father, can you please do this one?" he asked.

"So I end up in the slammer? You know I can't. You get caught, you get a slap on the wrist. Me? Well, that's a whole different ball of wax," Father shrugged.

Empty-handed, Ernest climbed the steps to the back door, knocked twice, waited a second, and knocked three more times. When he heard someone on the other side, he whispered, "Goats galore." The door cracked open and a middle-aged woman peeked out.

He stopped breathing. It was the Lady with a Thousand Faces. A mistress of disguises, the Lady Hooch Hunter was one of the most famous "prohis," or Prohibition agents. Though no one could say what she really looked like, Ernest *knew* it was her. He stumbled backwards down the last step and bolted for the car.

"Honey, where's the fire?" she called after him. "I know I ain't the prettiest, but I never seen no one scared off like that before."

Ernest scrambled into the front seat. "Hurry, Father! We've gotta get out of here! It was her. The Lady with a Thousand Faces!"

The fourteen-year-old had never been so scared. Hadn't he known this day would come? How could Father have done this to him? And why the heck weren't they moving? Father hadn't made a sound. He hadn't even started the engine. Ernest looked over to see his whole body was trembling. His face was red, and what Ernest and Julio called his "angry vein" in the middle of his forehead looked like it might burst. And then came the most thunderous belly laugh Ernest had ever heard anyone release.

"Hahahaha...You should've seen your face! I bet...hahaha...I bet you wet your pants," Father roared. "That's Mrs. Molly!" He turned toward the woman. "Molly!" he yelled out. "Come meet my son Ernest."

"Joe, he's just a child," the full-figured woman scolded. She looked at Ernest. "Come with me, honey. You look like you seen a ghost."

Joe nodded at his son and Ernest reluctantly followed Mrs. Molly into her small kitchen. She opened a bottle of Coca-Cola and placed a straw inside. Ernest was shaken and too embarrassed to look her in the eye.

"Here you go. The sugar should do you some good. Bring some color back to your cheeks."

"Thanks, ma'am."

"You just drink up. Then you can carry those empties to your father." She pointed to a stack of crates next to the stove. "And when he fills them up again, you have *him* bring them back to me."

Father was in fine spirits as they drove back to the farm, but Ernest remained quiet and brooding. Though he still felt like a fool, he was relieved he had made it through another day of "errands." He tried to enjoy the view as he had earlier in the day, but the pinks weren't as pink, the greens as green, and the wonders of the valley as wondrous. He craved the sense of awe he had felt that morning, but it was lost. It was as if the Lady with a Thousand Faces had clawed her way up his back and was clinging on for dear life.

Uncle Mike's pastures covered two rolling hills. The Guernseys were grazing and Ernest envied their worry-free existence. The house and barn atop the second hill were a picturesque advertisement for good country living. But as they got closer, Ernest felt the spirit of the Lady amusing herself with the fine hairs on the back of his neck…and then he felt her nails—

"Father," he choked, "are those trucks?"

"*Per amor di Dio! Non è possibile!*" Joe cried out.

They were trucks indeed. Two of them—parked in the hilltop driveway. Ernest made out the shape of a covered truck and the sheriff's wagon.

"It's a raid!" Father shouted as he pushed his foot into the gas pedal and sped past the turn to the house.

"But what about Mamma? And Julio? We have to go help them! And Joe Junior!" Ernest yelled. "What are you doing? Turn around!"

"*Non fare lo stupido!* Don't be stupid! You saw what they did to Uncle Mike. Be quiet and let me think."

Ernest felt sick. Father was driving too fast on the snaking road. The boy could feel the soda pop percolating in his stomach and was afraid it would come spewing out. Suddenly, Father hit the brakes and the car skidded to a stop behind a government-funded billboard admonishing "Money Spent for Booze Cannot Buy Shoes." But Joe Gallo couldn't read English and the irony was lost on his bewildered son.

"We wait here. One hour and they'll be gone."

"And Mamma? They probably already arrested her!" Ernest worried.

"We wait here. One hour," Father hissed through clenched teeth. "Now shut your trap."

Ernest didn't have a watch and didn't dare ask his father how long they had been sitting at the side of the road. The valley had a warm pink cast, but the car was completely engulfed by the billboard's shadow. Ernest wished he had brought a coat. He couldn't remember ever saying so many "Our Fathers" or "Hail Marys" in a row and hoped He was listening.

At last Father started the engine, pulled out the choke, and put the car in gear.

From the main road Ernest could see that the trucks were gone. He felt his body unfold with relief, but as they pulled up the driveway, something didn't feel right. Then he smelled it—the astringent odor of alcohol mixed with the sweet, fruity aroma of grape pomace. Grappa. A light amber trickle snaked down the dirt driveway, filling small ruts and circumventing obstacles as it carved a path to the bordering ditch. Father was still setting the parking brake when the armed men surrounded the car. Ernest recognized Sheriff Van Patten but not the others.

Ernest felt like he was back at the Palace on Columbus Avenue watching a gangster movie unspool. The event played in front of him in a series of vignettes and still images. And just like in the theater, there was no sound. Ernest's eyes darted across the scene. Gun barrels were pointed at him and Father. Handguns. Rifles. Double-barreled shotguns. He looked past them to the splintered barn door. The casks on their sides—dead soldiers, still bleeding out. Joe Junior in Mamma's arms. Her drawn face. Swollen eyes. Julio standing bravely by her side. The copper still, dragged outside the barn, buckled in half like the cookies they sold in Chinatown, the setting sun glinting off the indentations the axes had inflicted. The empty bottles lined up like carnival knockdown dolls.

The reel ended and Ernest was standing next to Julio. Father was facing the sheriff's wagon while one of the suited men slapped a pair of handcuffs on his thin wrists. For the first time in his life Ernest noticed how slight Father was. The man who had towered over him his whole life now looked small and vulnerable. Weak. Pathetic, even. Something shifted inside Ernest and he wondered how he could ever respect his father again. He wished he could feel sorry for him. Even a little bit. Pity might feel better than the bitterness and disappointment that filled his soul.

Father turned and faced his family. His mouth was moving up and down, up and down. Ernest tilted his head and stared at Father's moustache, fascinated by how it jumped in time with his mouth. He wondered when he'd see him again.

"Ow! What'd you do that for?" Ernest snapped when Julio's elbow jabbed him in the ribs.

"Answer Father!" Julio hissed.

Only then did he hear Father's voice.

"Ernest! Take care of your mother and brothers!" he growled.

"C'mon, you greasy dago. Get in the car," the sheriff snarled, pushing Father into the back seat and slamming the door.

Chapter Five

THE COCK CROWS

Joe Gallo was released the next day and the charges against him for violating the Volstead Act—the legislation Congress had passed to enforce the Eighteenth Amendment—were dismissed later that year. Uncle Mike really did have friends in all the right places. Mamma insisted they never refer to the shameful event again, which suited Ernest just fine. He worried that anyone who found out might question his own character. If a man is judged by the company he keeps, how harsh a sentence can his own family impose?

With the Feds' knowledge of the brandy still, there was nothing left for Joe in Livermore. With money borrowed from Uncle Mike, he bought a farm in Escalon, just fifty miles to the east. Joe and his wife and children lived there for a short time, until 1924, before settling thirteen miles away in Modesto, the heart of the San Joaquin Valley.

Nestled between the coastal mountains and the Sierra Nevada range, the valley surrounding Modesto provided fertile soil and a Mediterranean climate with hot, dry summers. A complex irrigation system of canals, tunnels, flumes, dams, and reservoirs delivered life-giving water. Tomatoes, almonds, cotton, asparagus, and a cornucopia of other fruits and vegetables flourished in the "nation's salad bowl." Though the climate was too hot for finer grape varieties, it was perfect for the reliable Thompson seedless.

In his latest foray into farming, Joe had bought arable land. He seemed to have learned from past mistakes. His vineyards were thriving and his timing couldn't have been better. Before Prohibition, a ton of grapes had sold for five to seven dollars, but in the past few years, growers had fetched up to $150 a ton. Financial security had made for a calmer home for the Gallos—and a brand-new house—but still required unremitting work. By age sixteen, Ernest had spent more hours in the field than many twice his age. And though his chores hadn't gotten any easier, it was what he knew. And if he had to do it, he was going to do it better than anyone else. Otherwise, what was the point?

Most California grape growers sold their grapes to a shipper for a fixed price, but in 1925, Joe decided to try a different—and he hoped, more profitable—approach. He would go to Chicago himself and work in tandem with a consignment broker to negotiate the best price for his grapes on the railroad sales tracks. Ernest and Julio would be in charge of harvesting the grapes, packaging them, and loading them onto boxcars—all while starting their freshman and junior years of high school.

Each harvest came with predictable stresses and worries. It was imperative to pick the grapes when the sugar content was highest, but before they became overripe. One extra day on the vine could have critical ramifications. Growers also had to keep a keen eye on weather patterns as a heavy rain right before harvest could bruise or even rupture the plump berries and destroy an entire year's worth of work.

The leaves on the bushy vines had grown to the size of Ernest's hand. On some, the three lobes had grown in a way that created a surprised spooky face. Clusters of Alicante Bouschets hung like heavy Christmas ornaments meant for much stronger limbs. The plump grapes were so tightly packed, it would be hard to pull just one from a cluster without damaging the neighboring berries. The fruit appeared either black or blue, depending on the angle of sunlight, and dangled invitingly for hungry critters. In fact, a deer had broken through the fence that surrounded the lush vineyard, and Joe and his boys were making repairs when Julio did the unthinkable.

It had been an exceptionally bad time for the high school track coach to ask him to run in the next day's meet. Though he trained with the team during school hours, he rarely competed due to his arduous responsibilities at home. But a key runner had the stomach flu and the coach begged Julio to come to the team's rescue.

"Father, I know it's not a good time, but Coach Marquam really needs me to run in the race tomorrow," Julio said. "Tommy's out sick and he's our best relay runner. If I don't go, they might have to forfeit the race, which will put us out of state championships."

"This is a joke, right?" Joe barked. "Now? Right when we're about to pick the crop, you want to go chase a stick? Please."

"Just this once, Father. I'll be home by seven. I'll just miss a few hours of work. I wouldn't ask, but I don't want to let the fellas down."

"What about your family? It's okay to let us down? Let *me* down?" Joe's voice was getting louder.

Ernest could feel his temper escalate in tandem with Father's. He had always worked hard to control his anger. To put a cork on his rage and keep everything inside. He had seen the damage Father's words and fists had inflicted and had vowed he would never do that to others. But as he heard the foul invectives spew from Father's mouth and felt Julio deflating by his side, the cork that stoppered his own anger popped, followed by a spray of pent-up resentments.

"Stop it!" Ernest yelled. "Just shut up right now."

Father froze. "What did you say? What did you say to *me*?"

"I'm sick of your disgusting language! Your lack of appreciation. And the way you treat us. We're out here every day. We never complain. You give us nothing in return!" Ernest shouted.

Ernest noted how tightly Joe squeezed the claw hammer in his right hand. His left fist was balled, knobby knuckles protruding from dry, fissured skin. But the fence was between them and his fear of Father had tempered over the years as his own confidence had grown.

"Julio is one of the best athletes at school, but you wouldn't know that, would you? You know what? *No one* knows that because he never gets a chance to play. Basketball, baseball, track… nope, not for Julio Gallo. He can't play. He has to sulfur the grapes, feed the pigs, irrigate the fields, while his father watches from the water tower. Just to make sure he doesn't dare slack off.

"And me, Father? Would it kill you to admit that I just might know something you don't? I tried to tell you there would be a glut of Alicantes, and Zinfandels would be a better long-term investment. I tried to tell you it would be better not to prune too early in the spring. But you don't listen. And guess what? I was right. But you're too thick and pig-headed to think that Julio and I might be anything more than a pair of mules to do your bidding."

Ernest wiped the spittle that had sprayed the side of his face and paused to take a breath. But his eyes never left Father's clenched right hand and he watched in disbelief as his old man raised his right hand and threw the hammer like he was flicking a dart and the bull's-eye was his son's face. The tool flew straight at Ernest, but he somehow ducked just in time.

"How dare you!" Ernest snarled as he lunged toward the fence that separated father and son.

"Ernest, don't," Julio said as he pulled his brother back. "Both of you. Just stop."

"You need us," Ernest spat at his father. "You want to spend the next two months in Chicago waiting for grapes that never arrive? See these sixty acres? We can just let them rot on the vine. And what are you going to do about it? Julio is running in that track meet tomorrow. You're going to Chicago. And everything will go on as before, even if Julio misses three whole hours of work."

"You!" Joe shouted, pointing at his eldest son. "You never talk to me like that again! You ungrateful runt. And *you*!" he said, pointing at Julio. "You go chase your stupid stick tomorrow. I'm done with both of you." He stormed away with one last rejoinder. "Now fix that fence."

The next day, Julio came home with two blue ribbons.

And the day after that, Father left for Chicago.

The mood in the Gallo house had lifted even before the last whistle had blown announcing the departure of Father's train from the station.

While waiting the last few days for the grapes to reach an ideal sugar level, Ernest and Julio spent their afternoons in the barn building wooden lug boxes that would be used during harvest to collect the grapes and then ship them to Chicago. After

Ernest built each box, Julio stenciled GALLO in red paint on the side. Six-year-old Joe Junior was working his way through a can of crooked nails, hammering them straight.

"Time to take a break," Mamma sang out as she entered the barn bearing a tray with glasses of milk and biscotti. "Such strong, hard workers, my boys." She glanced over at the stacks of lug boxes. "You've done a lot today. Don't you think you have enough?"

"Not sure. It's hard to tell, but I think we're close," Ernest surmised. He sat down on a knee-high, three-legged stool and took a long gulp of milk. He stretched out his fingers, cramped from holding the hammer. The scent of fresh pine permeated the barn. To Ernest, the scent of the lumber and paint combined with that of the fresh hay smelled like opportunity and promise. He took out the notebook he always kept in his back pocket and began to count the finished lug boxes, making tally marks as he went along. He bit into a crunchy cookie and stared at the boxes.

"Something's missing," he said.

"What's that?" Julio asked.

"The lug boxes. They're not labeled," Ernest replied.

"Jeez, Ernest, what do you think I've been doing?" Julio said as he held up his paint-stained hands.

"No, I mean…we don't have enough time—or money—to have labels printed, but we need something more than 'Gallo,' don't you think? Something that separates our grapes from everyone else's."

"I could paint something on them…over the name," Julio suggested.

"A fire truck," suggested Joe Junior.

"A bunch of grapes," offered Mamma.

"Um, I don't know…let me think," Ernest said. "What would fit with 'Gallo'?" His eyes lit up. "I've got it! A rooster! *Gallo* is Italian for 'rooster' and we've already got the red paint. What do you think?"

They all agreed it was a fitting image. A rooster represented rural life, courage, and perseverance. It announced the dawn of each new day. As they raised their glasses of milk in a toast, their own rooster crowed from outside the barn. They all laughed in astonishment at the timing.

The Alicantes had been the first to ripen. Luckily, it was a Saturday, so school wouldn't interfere. The temporary workers arrived as the sun was cresting the horizon. Bathed in golden light, the vineyard was a model of efficiency—Henry Ford would have approved. Each worker was given a hooked harvest knife and an empty lug box. The pickers lined the rows of the vineyard and their filled boxes were passed to the person to their left. The boxes accumulated at the end of each row and were then loaded into the back of the truck. Ernest and Julio thoroughly inspected every box and discarded any withered or moldy grapes and made sure that each box weighed twenty-five pounds—no more, no less.

As the day progressed, coats and sweaters were peeled off, sleeves rolled up. Mamma served lunch at eleven. Spaghetti, fresh bread, and wine. Everyone sat on bales of hay around a makeshift table that Ernest and Julio had assembled from an old barn door. The strangers were unified in their shared goal and experience: the camaraderie and satisfaction that came from honest outdoor work reaping the land's gifts.

Long after the pickers had gone home to their families and beds, Ernest and Julio were still at it. As soon as the clusters were plucked from the vine, their shelf life shortened with each sweep of the second hand. Chicago buyers were discriminating and only paid top price for the freshest grapes. Hundreds of other growers had harvested today and they would all be competing against each other in the eastern markets. Luckily it was a short drive to the closest railroad spur, where the railcar they had reserved was waiting. It was dark. It took three hours and three round trips back home to load up the truck and fill the railcar. Two hundred boxes. It would take the grapes five days to reach Chicago, where Father was waiting.

Exhausted but exhilarated from their sense of accomplishment, the Gallo boys drove home under a nearly full moon.

"Ernest, what about that last row of grapes?" Julio asked.

"Wanna pick them when we get home?"

"Sure. Why not? What's another two hours without sleep?" Julio joked.

"We're out of lug boxes," Ernest remembered.

"Then we'll make more. Tell you what, I'll pick the berries and you make the boxes," Julio suggested.

"It's a deal. I bet I can make the boxes faster than you can fill them," Ernest boasted.

"Oh, I'm sure I can pick faster than you can nail them together," Julio challenged.

"You're on," Ernest grinned, his grime- and sweat-streaked face illuminated in the blue moonlight.

It took six more weeks to harvest the rest of the vineyards. The boys kept atop their schoolwork in spite of the enormous responsibilities they shouldered. Ernest, already a member of the school's Agriculture Club, managed to stay on the honor roll, and to his delight, was elected to the school's Hi-Y Club, where a young man's good character was the most important criteria for membership.

Father returned in the middle of November. His pockets were full yet he was dispirited. He had hated everything about Chicago: the crowds, the noise, the food, and, most vehemently, the haggling.

"*Mio Dio*. It was the worst. Nothing but thieves. Their word means nothing. They look at your grapes with their noses in the air. They tell you your grapes are no good. Too expensive. And they peck at you for a better deal. Like *avvoltoi,* vultures. You give them what they want. You shake on it. And then they come back later and ask for a better price. *Sì*. I made good money, but never will I deal with those hustlers again. Never."

Ernest knew his father well enough to guess what had really happened. Joe Gallo was as thin-skinned and easily bruised as a Sangiovese berry. Of course the buyers in Chicago were trying to get the most for every dollar. That was business. You couldn't fault them and you couldn't just walk away. You had to stay and play the game. Fouls were unavoidable. The trick was to get what you wanted while making the other guy feel like he had won.

Though only sixteen, Ernest was confident he could hold his own in Chicago. There was too much money at stake to just give up. It didn't make any sense to walk away. Unlike his father, he was patient and even-tempered. He would never let a buyer get under his skin to the point where he lost a sale.

It took discretion and cunning, but over the next year Ernest convinced Father to let him try his hand in the Windy City.

Chapter Six

THE RAIL YARDS

The sun beat against the large panes of glass. Every so often an overheated passenger would open a window for relief, only to slam it shut immediately—the smoke and soot from the engine proving too high a price for cooler air. The five-day trip to Chicago was especially uncomfortable in the straight, wooden, third-class seat. At least Ernest's seatmate had disembarked in Salt Lake City, allowing him to curl up at night with Father's heavy wool coat for a blanket. As unpleasant as the accommodations were, nothing could quash the sense of independence and adventure he felt. He couldn't believe Father had said yes and that his teachers had granted him a six-week leave of absence.

Upon his arrival in Chicago, Ernest walked to the address Father had given him. The city reminded him of San Francisco, though he soon came to the conclusion that until now he hadn't truly known what it meant to be cold. It was just September, but the tips of his ears burned and more than once he had to hold on to a streetlamp for fear of being swept aloft like Dorothy Gale in *The Wizard of Oz*. The wind slashed through Father's warmest coat and at times literally took Ernest's breath away. But nothing could chill the fire he felt inside—to be alone at seventeen in this storied metropolis to perform a man's job.

The hotel was a mile from Lake Michigan and, even inside, wind whistled through the drafty hallways. His room was spare, serviceable, and, for the next month and a half, blissfully all his. Ernest unpacked his few belongings and splashed some cold water on his face. Looking at his reflection in the mirror, he decided he ought to start shaving soon. Although his first car of grapes wasn't due for two days, he thought it wise to go to the tracks and get his bearings.

He hopped off the streetcar at Twenty-First Street. At first glance, the Santa Fe Railroad yard looked like a monochromatic photograph. A thick, bleak gloom hung overhead in one unbroken mass, the cloud cover mixing with the exhaust rising from the tracks. The surrounding buildings were coated in black soot. The sellers and buyers were clad in gray and black tweed or shades of brown. The horses came in the same colors as their owners. The steam engines, cars, and waiting wagons and trucks were all black. Even the people's expressions were gray.

Ernest walked through the gates and found a place to stand where he wouldn't be in anyone's way. As he watched the surrounding chaos, the colors began to seep through—not in what he saw, but through what he heard and smelled.

He flinched at the locomotives' shrill brakes and throaty whistles. The strident sounds always seemed to take him unawares. He tried to separate the hum of voices—jobbers promoting their products, vendors selling their wares, excited buyers petitioning for a better price. Many of the accents and languages were strange, though his ears keyed in on the familiar—Italian and English. The cacophony was completed by idling motors, barking dogs, and horses' jangling harnesses and clopping hooves. Ernest found the tumult exhilarating.

He inhaled the mix of odors carried by the brisk air. All stations shared the familiar scent of expended coal and steam. But here there was a comingling of lake water, burning tar, horse manure, and smoke from cigarettes, pipes, and cigars. Curls of gray rose from scattered barrels surrounded by folk trying to warm their stiff hands over makeshift fires. Ernest's stomach rumbled when the wind shifted and delivered the aroma of steaming hot dogs. At three cents each, he decided he could afford two and walked over to the cart to get in line.

"Haven't seen you here before," came a voice from behind.

Ernest turned to look up at a friendly face. The fine lines around the man's eyes foretold kindness and good humor.

"It's my first time," Ernest shared. "I'm here to sell my father's grapes."

"Are you now? Tell me, son, how old are you?"

"Almost twenty-five," Ernest fibbed.

"Is that so?" the man played along. "Well, I'm Calvin Coolidge. Pleased to make your acquaintance." He stretched out his hand for Ernest to shake.

"I'm no stooge, sir," Ernest replied, pulling his hand back and stepping forward in line.

"Of course not. I was just funning. I'm Charles Barbera. Been at these tracks my whole life. Shake?"

Ernest turned around and shook the stranger's hand. "Ernest. Ernest Gallo, sir."

"Tell me about your business, Ernest. Maybe I can help you find your feet. This can be a pretty troublesome place, these tracks."

Ernest checked his gut. His father had warned him about all the crooks on the yards. He had thought Father's descriptions of the tracks had been exaggerated, but now that he was here, he was getting a sense of the enormity and seriousness of the operation. He saw right away that these Chicagoans weren't people you wanted to mess with.

Fear was whispering in his ear. He blushed at his own naiveté. He was in *way* over his head and only now did he realize it.

Ernest paid for his hot dogs and stood nearby while the stranger bought his. He recognized he would need help. His gut told him Barbera was a decent man. Plus, there were hundreds of people around. He reasoned if the stranger tried any funny business he could surely outrun him while shouting for help.

"Sure, Mr. Barbera. That'd be swell. Thank you, sir."

Barbera led Ernest to the tracks and explained that this time of year two hundred cars of grapes came through every day, all from different growers. They were sold by the carload. Some would sell here in Chicago, others would be forwarded east to New York and other cities, depending on demand and where the sellers expected to get the highest price. The shippers met their grapes on the tracks. Most had long-standing relationships with "jobbers" who negotiated a price for one railcar at a time. As Ernest likely knew, one railcar held 1,100 twenty-five-pound boxes of grapes. The jobbers then sold the grapes by the box to individual buyers—presumably there to buy enough grapes to make their legal limit of two hundred gallons of wine per year.

"Here's what you have going against you," Barbera advised. "Nobody here knows you. Some of these guys have known each other for twenty, thirty years, when they used to ship barrels and tank cars of wine. Now it's grapes, but the faces are the same. They do business with the same guys every year.

"But here's what you have going for you. These shippers and jobbers? They don't know grapes. It's just a product. Business. Something to sell. In a month, it'll be Christmas trees. Then broccoli and carrots. But you grew these grapes, right? You've raised them from babies. Use that. Turn your disadvantage into an advantage."

"Thanks, Mr. Barbera."

"A couple of other things. As soon as you sell your cars, get in a cab and go straight to the bank. Get that dough outta your pocket and someplace safe. See those guys over there? There's toughs all over here waiting to pick you clean. Syndicate men. They'll try to extort 'protection' money from you. Now you seen 'em. Don't even look at 'em again."

Yikes, Ernest thought. Barbera was confirming everything Father had said. He needed to come up with a strategy for every possible scenario. No way, no how was he going to let some scofflaw take everything he and Julio had sweat and bled for.

"One more thing. Sears, Roebuck just opened a store on Homan Avenue. Do yourself a favor and get yourself a proper hat...and a razor."

Ernest unconsciously touched the flat corduroy cap on his head. Barbera was right. He probably looked like he had just fallen off the turnip truck. At five foot four, sunbaked, and seventeen, no one here would take him seriously. The odds were already against him. He had to leave Chicago knowing he had done everything within his power to succeed.

"Thank you, sir. I truly appreciate all your help."

"My pleasure, kid. See you around." Ernest's guardian angel tipped his hat, cupped his hand around his mouth to light a cigarette, and strolled away.

~

Ernest soon found his place among the shippers and jobbers. The older men admired the boy's audacity and tenacity. His grapes were good; his prices, just. Father sent one to two cars every few days. Ernest got his highest prices the first day, when the grapes were freshest. If he had to, he'd lower the price the second day. He wanted to make sure the cars were sold before the next shipment arrived. He also had to keep track of what varieties the other sellers were offering, their quality, and how much they were charging. Prices were as fluid as the wine the grapes would bear.

"You! Dago! You owe me money. Those boxes you sold me two days ago were packed light. You owe me ten cents a box."

Ernest bristled at the slur, instantly recognizing the high-pitched voice and poor English before he turned around. The unpleasant, greasy man had bought a carload of Zinfandels two days earlier. Ernest braced himself for whatever anger and vitriol the man might spew.

Though their boxes weren't filled at a packing house like those of their more established and better financed competitors, Ernest knew Father and Julio had added or removed grapes from each box to ensure every one weighed exactly twenty-five pounds. He quickly did the math. At ten cents a box, the man was asking for a refund of more than a hundred dollars. Grape prices had dropped in the last two days and Ernest surmised that the man hadn't been able to sell the carload for more than he had paid. This was the kind of thing that had driven Father nuts. Father would have told the man to take a hike and would never have done business with him again.

But Ernest wasn't going to lose a customer. Even if the customer was wrong.

"Well, I know for a fact that those boxes weren't light, but I'll tell you what. How 'bout I give you a break on the next carload. Fair enough?"

"You kidding? Why would I do any more business with a cheat?" the man complained.

"Listen, I have a carload over there at a dollar thirty a box."

"That's more than I paid for the last car," the man shrieked. "That was a dollar twenty. You think I'm a fool? What is it with you guineas? You're all the same."

"Hey, mister! There's no need for the name-calling," Ernest snapped, then resolved to keep his temper in check. "These grapes are better. A dozen buyers are interested in this load. Plus, the market is stronger today."

"I don't know. Maybe I look at other grapes. I buy from someone else," the man countered.

"My grapes here will make a fine, hearty wine." Ernest paused a few seconds before adding, "Listen, for you, I'll take a dime off. How's that?"

The man was visibly calmer. Ernest remained quiet while the man considered his options. He waited a bit more before adding, "Hey, I'm new here and I want you to buy grapes from me next year. How about I take another nickel off?"

The greasy man was too deep in his own greed to detect the false reluctance in Ernest's voice.

"Okay. That's good," the man said, pleased as punch for haggling Ernest down from a dollar thirty a box to a dollar fifteen. What he didn't know was that the savvy teenager had started his day planning to sell that carload for a dollar fifteen.

Ernest led the buyer behind the railcar to finish their business. The man unlaced his boot and peeled off a fetid wool sock. He removed a wad of bills that had stuck to the bottom of his foot and counted out his payment. He handed the damp bills to Ernest, who gingerly and quickly recounted the bills while holding his breath. He looked around quickly to make sure no one had seen the transaction.

As Ernest did at the end of every sale, he heeded Charles Barbera's advice to get out of dodge as soon as he had money in his pocket. He had also instituted one extra precaution. On his third day in Chicago, he had asked a policeman where he could get a gun for protection. The next day, the copper had sold him a Smith & Wesson for ten dollars. For the rest of his stay in Chicago, Ernest carried the revolver in a pocket he had sewn on the inside of his coat. He prayed he would never have to use it, but found comfort in its heft.

He nonchalantly bypassed the sharks that circled the gates, hopped in a cab, and headed straight for the Continental Bank. He deposited the cash, mailed a check to Father, and returned to the tracks.

Though the accommodations were equally uncomfortable on the train trip back home, Ernest hardly noticed. The seat didn't feel as hard, nor the air as stale. He floated on a cushion of confidence and achievement. It had been a life-changing six weeks. He literally felt like he had left Modesto a boy and was returning a man. How many men could pinpoint the moment in their lives when they crossed that line, he wondered.

"This seat taken?" asked a familiar-looking older man. "Giuseppe Franzia. I recognize you from the yards."

"Please, sit down," Ernest replied before standing and removing his new felt hat in a sign of respect.

Franzia took off his coat and pushed a large wicker basket under his seat. "Where you headed?"

"Modesto. I'm Ernest Gallo."

"I'm getting off at Modesto too," Franzia said. "Looks like we're going to get to know each other, *sì*?"

"Yes, sir." Ernest resumed his careful examination of his notebook.

"A lot of numbers there, if you don't mind me saying. How did you do?"

"Well, I sold seventeen carloads, so that's about two hundred and twenty tons."

"Not bad. This your first year?"

"Yes, sir."

"Mine too. Got tired of paying the shipper. Might as well just sell them ourselves. Why pay the middleman, *sì*? Since those idiots in Washington won't let me make wine anymore, I gotta do what I can. Thirsty?"

Franzia dragged the wicker basket out from under the seat and poured two glasses of wine. "*Salute*," he toasted.

Through the course of the journey, Ernest's companion pulled a variety of fragrant foods from his seemingly limitless basket: sausages, cheeses, whole bulbs of garlic, and the biggest red onions Ernest had ever seen. By the time they reached Omaha, Nebraska, Ernest noticed that despite the hordes he had seen boarding the train, their car was conspicuously empty.

Ernest had consulted his notebook during the rest of the journey. Even though he had earned several thousand dollars more than Father had made last year, he needed to figure out how he could increase it next time. He knew he should feel satisfied. Seventeen thousand dollars was a lot of money in 1926. It would take most men thirteen years to make that much. But he knew he could do better. He pored over the data he had collected, looking for a pattern or trend and factoring in the days of the week, the different grape varieties, and how much he earned per car compared to his competitors. He spent the rest of the trip designing a strategy for the next year.

"Hey. Wake up. We're here." Franzia shook the boy's shoulder.

Ernest took a deep breath and stretched his cramped limbs.

"Come see me sometime. You're an interesting young man," Franzia mumbled as he made his way down the aisle, valise held in one hand, wicker basket in the other, and disappeared.

Julio was waiting at the station with the truck, eager to hear all about Chicago. It was a short drive home and everyone was anxious to see Ernest. Julio knew he'd have to wait until it was just the two of them to get the *real* story. But they'd be back in the fields together tomorrow. He wouldn't have to be too patient.

As they turned into the long driveway, Ernest saw Mamma waiting, framed by two of the white pillars that lined the front porch. Only then did he realize how much he had missed her. Mamma swept down from the porch, her apron brushing from side to side in time with the calico dress she had sewn last spring. She embraced her boy. Just when Ernest began to wonder if she'd ever let go, she took two steps back.

"Look at you. Who is this man? What have you done with my Nino?" she teased. "You're too skinny. Have you eaten anything since you left?"

"I'm good, Mamma. Look, I got you something." Ernest popped the latches on his suitcase and reached under his folded clothes. He pulled out a small package of tissue paper. "Here, Mamma. Well…open it!"

Mamma carefully unfolded the tissue. She put her hand over her open mouth when she saw the engraved cameo brooch.

"Oh, Ernest. It's beautiful. But you shouldn't have."

"I had to get it, Mamma. She looks like you. But not as beautiful."

"I thought I heard a car," Father said, trailing the family's pet greyhounds, King and Queenie, and barefoot seven-year-old Joe Junior. "Welcome home, son. It's good to have you back."

"Hey, Joey. I have something for you." Ernest handed his little brother a small box. "Be careful. Don't drop it."

Joe Junior lifted the package's cardboard flap and pulled out a glass orb the size of a baseball. Ernest took advantage of the moment to finally give the two spinning dogs the attention they so emphatically demanded.

"What is it? What is it, Ernest?" Joe Junior puzzled.

Ernest knelt down to his brother's height. "See the little doggie inside? Now shake the ball and see what happens," Ernest replied.

"Whoa! Is that snow?"

"Sure is,"

"Is it real? Did you see real snow, Ernest? Did you?" Joe Junior asked.

"I did! Brrrrr. It was cold!" He turned to his father and smiled. "Father, come here." Ernest handed him a silver cigarette case with an ornate "G" engraved on the front. "I wasn't sure if I should get 'J' for Joseph or 'G' for Giuseppe. Then I realized it could be 'G' for Gallo and I couldn't go wrong," Ernest laughed.

Joe wiped his oil-stained palms on his trousers before accepting the shiny object. He turned it over in his hands, admiring the lines and swirls delicately etched in the silver before opening and closing the case. "Thanks, son. It's—"

"Don't get it dirty," Susie admonished as she looked over at her husband's blackened fingers. "Your father was just working on the engine," she explained.

As Joe placed the case in his front pocket, he lowered his chin and made a point of locking his eyes with Susie's. No words were spoken, but volumes were said.

Ernest instinctively assessed the ripple of tension and knew how quickly it could turn into a storm. Not only had Mamma interrupted Father—a landmine in and of itself—but she had also criticized him. A lethal combination. Maybe with some levity and sleight of hand Ernest could keep the mood lighthearted.

"And I didn't forget you, Julio." Ernest took off his fedora and placed it on his brother's head. "There. Perfect fit," he grinned, looking at Julio, but fully aware of Father's every breath and movement, no matter how slight.

"Ernest, did you make a lot of money?" Joe Junior innocently asked. "Are you rich now?"

Great. Here we go, Ernest thought. He heard the hairs in Father's nose whistle as he filled his lungs. Father's shoulders rose and his elbows moved away from his torso in an unmistakable and ominous signal. And there it was. The angry vein. Things were about to get ugly. Ernest was acutely aware of the muscles in his own body tightening. He sensed Mamma and Julio stiffen too. They had all been here too many times before. Experience had taught Ernest that he had two options: stand up to Father, defend himself, protect the family, and endure an ugliness that could last for hours—or be passive and let Father vent until his tank had nothing left. He'd have to choose his tack carefully while preserving his own dignity and without causing any harm to the rest of the family.

"Is *Ernest* rich?" The insult in Father's voice was palpable. "Did you just ask if Ernest was *rich*?!"

Joe Junior cringed, realizing he had clearly said something wrong, but confused as to how he had erred. He was certain he had heard Mamma telling Aunt Tillie that his big brother had made a lot of money in Chicago. Hadn't Mamma sounded happy, like it was a good thing?

Ernest seized the opportunity. "No, Joseph. I'm not rich," he said forcefully. "I just got lucky. Father grows the best grapes and everyone in Chicago knows—"

"That's damn right and don't you forget it. You got lucky," Father sneered. "You come home strutting like a peacock looking like a real dandy in that ridiculous hat. Just who do you think you are?" As he spat out his last sentence, he reached over and snatched the fedora off Julio's head. He twisted the hat in his grease-stained hands before throwing it on the ground and grinding the felt into the dirt like a spent cigarette under the sole of his boot.

A tremor ripped through Ernest's nervous system. On the train back from Chicago he had blithely imagined his homecoming like a Norman Rockwell cover from *The Saturday Evening Post*: an intimate moment captured between a doting father and his clever almost-grown son with a caption underneath reading, "Proud father." He knew it was a ridiculous fantasy and had tried to suppress the idea, knowing how far it would be from the hurtful reality that likely awaited him.

Ernest had known Father would feel humiliated by his son's success and would only see it through the prism of his own failures. He had expected Father to be bitter and ungrateful. He had tried to put himself in Father's shoes. Of course he had no idea what it was like to be a father, but when he searched his darkest, basest, and most inflated self, he couldn't imagine not being able to give his son—or anyone, for that matter—a deserved kind word or pat on the back. Father's abhorrent behavior hadn't come as a surprise. But it still stung. In fact, it stung more than the fear, loneliness, and frozen nights of the past month and a half.

"Giuseppe!" Mamma rang out. "*Basta!* Our boy just got home. Stop your nonsense. Our family is together and that's what matters right now." Mamma's eyes were ablaze and everyone was stunned into silence. Even Father.

Ernest drank it in. Mamma standing toe to toe with Father. He watched as she briefly took one hand off her hip to tame an errant hair that had slipped from her bun. Her hand returned to her hip and Ernest's heart swam with emotion. Love. Respect. Admiration. Gratitude. Sadness. He wondered what she had first seen in Father, and even more, why she had stayed with him. After all, though still scandalous, divorce was becoming more common, and Aunt Celia had left Uncle Mike. He had heard Mamma weep when she thought no one could hear. He had fought the urge to comfort her and offer an understanding ear. For he was her son, not her confidant. There was only so much he could do, and over the last few months he had done his best. And that's what he would always do.

Chapter Seven

A DAY WITHOUT SUN

Though his most basic needs had always been met, in some years more easily than others, Ernest hungered for financial security and independence from his family. Father had never given his sons a regular allowance or salary—with no free time, where and how would they spend money anyway? But now he was in college and had no savings or anything to show for his years of hard work.

He was the reason Father's business had grown. Only because of *his* three years of success in Chicago had Father been able to buy more vineyards, bringing his total holdings to 230 acres by 1929. Though they were able to hire extra hands, Ernest worked harder than ever, all while juggling a full load of courses at Modesto Junior College. The growth of Father's business had broadened his responsibilities at home just when school had become more demanding.

Ernest also carried some of Julio's unspoken resentment. In addition to growing more grapes, Father had started to buy them from other growers. With more product to sell each year, he needed more buyers and the Chicago market was already saturated. So while Ernest continued to disembark in Chicago,

Julio remained on the eastbound trains until they reached the New Jersey auction yards. While his older brother thrived on the excitement of the sell, Julio hated everything about it. He came home drained and cheerless. Julio was a country boy. A farmer at heart. But Father either couldn't see that or, more likely, didn't care.

What profits Father hadn't spent on land, he had invested in a single stock: Transamerica, Bank of America's holding company. Ernest didn't know one successful Italian who didn't own the stock. The bank's founder, A. P. Giannini, was a hero in Northern California's Italian community. With Giannini's help, North Beach's "Little Italy" had recovered from the great earthquake of 1906 faster than any other neighborhood in San Francisco. The personable and engaging Giannini had launched many an Italian-owned business as the founder of Bank of Italy—later renamed Bank of America, to the disappointment of many account holders. Owning Transamerica stock was a source of pride for the maligned immigrants still trying to find their place and earn respect in their new country. Look what another Italian had accomplished! Besides that, they needed to support their own kind in a land that had labeled them as primitive, violent, and untrustworthy.

With Joe's blessing, his eldest son managed his investments. Ernest called their stockbroker almost every day—sometimes even two or three times—for Transamerica's closing price. Each time he churned with conflict as he placed the receiver in the cradle. The surge of excitement any good news brought would quickly crumble as a little voice in his head would whisper, "But none of it's yours."

~

"I'm twenty years old and I need to think of my future. I want to have my own family someday," Ernest began awkwardly.

The family was walking back home from Easter Mass at Saint Stanislaus. Ernest and Father led the way and had spent most of the half-hour walk in silence, the son trying to summon the nerve and the right approach to open the taboo subject. They were almost home and the opportunity would soon be lost, so the conversation had started a little more stiffly than he had hoped.

"What are you getting at?" Father asked.

"You promised me you would give me my own land, remember? I don't need much. Just enough to get started," Ernest said.

"*Give* it to you? Or *sell* it to you?"

"Either way. If you want to give it to me, that'd be swell," Ernest smiled. "But if it's on loan, that's fine too. I promise I'll pay you back."

"You know, my father never gave me nothing. None of us. He was relieved when me and my brothers left. Fewer mouths to feed." He looked off into the distance, never making eye contact. "I'll think about it."

"That's what you said last time," Ernest said in exasperation. "Look, if there's no future for me here, I need to know. That's all." He tried not to show his frustration and disappointment. It had been three months since their last conversation and nothing had changed.

"I said I'll think about it. That's the end of that," Father snapped.

Ernest seethed inside. He didn't want to start a fight. Not on Easter. Not in front of Mamma. He was completely at Father's mercy. He had nothing to bargain with. Why would Father ever want to change anything when he and Julio continued to work fourteen-hour days, seven days a week, for free? Father had them over a barrel. Ernest felt restless and knew he couldn't—or wouldn't—go on like this much longer. Something had to change.

Ernest spent the fall of 1929 back in Chicago. It was his fourth straight selling season. Julio was miserable somewhere in New Jersey. Joe worked with his sons to make sure they got the highest prices possible. Ernest had to keep track of Julio's supply, keep his finger on the pulse in Chicago, and monitor the unavoidable deterioration of their grapes to determine if he'd get the best price by keeping the cars in Chicago or forwarding them to Julio. He needed to sell everything before the next shipment arrived from Modesto.

It was a complicated dance and Ernest was having a hard time tuning in to the market's rhythm. He couldn't find a pattern in his numbers. Prices were fluctuating and sales were down. Rumors abounded that the stock market was in trouble. The recent seesaw had been unnerving. Wall Street seemed to have stabilized but everyone was still nervous. The Gallos' San Francisco broker had come to expect the daily three o'clock calls from Ernest and continued to reassure the anxious young man that everything would be okay. "The worst thing anyone can do right now is panic," he would say. But Ernest struggled to keep his concern at a reasonable tenor. After all, the family's entire savings were invested in Transamerica stock. He had pleaded with Father to diversify his investments, to no avail.

"It's me," Julio's voice crackled over the earpiece one evening. "I gotta talk to you about what's going on here. Have you seen the papers?"

"Yeah. It's bad. No one's buying," Ernest replied from one of the hotel lobby's phone booths.

"Same here. I still got those seven carloads you sent. Mold was setting in when I got 'em and now they're only getting worse. I can't just sit here and watch them rot, so I'm going to forward everything to Kearny and try to unload them there in the auction," Julio explained.

"All right. Do what you can. I trust you. I sent Father a wire and told him not to pick any more grapes or send anything else until we figure out what's going on. I'll talk to you tomorrow."

Ernest had just opened the door to leave the booth when the phone rang. He picked it up tentatively, and after identifying himself, the operator patched through a call for him.

"Ernest? Is this Ernest? Ernest Gallo?"

"It is. Mamma? Hi. Is everything all right?"

"You need to come home," Mamma said urgently.

"It's okay, Mamma. We need to sell the rest of grapes. Prices have dropped, but we're getting what we can. Better than nothing."

"It's your father. Uncle Mike is putting crazy ideas in his head and he won't listen to me. Please come home."

"I told Father not to send anything else. Julio and I are almost done. We'll be back in less than—"

"He's making wine. I'm afraid he's going to get in trouble again."

"I'll be back as soon as I can, Mamma. Don't worry. It will be okay," Ernest soothed.

After a few more reassurances, he hung up and fumed. Why did Father have to make everything worse? He didn't think things through. One should never act out of fear. So this year wouldn't be their best. That was the nature of agriculture. One had to welcome the good years, but prepare for the bad. What they didn't need was Father in jail. Ernest resigned himself to slashing his prices the next day until his last car was empty. He had to get home.

But Ernest didn't sell a solitary grape the next day. While he lay awake in bed worrying about his family in Modesto, it seemed an indifferent but powerful force had come along and nudged the earth off its axis. When he awoke at his usual 5:00 a.m., his room appeared unchanged. Dingy. Spare. As cold as ever. He dressed quickly, placed the revolver in his inside coat pocket, grabbed his umbrella, and hurried down the four flights of stairs to the lobby. The revolving door discharged him onto a sidewalk not yet wetted by an approaching storm.

Though the day had started like any other, it was one Ernest would never forget. He thought about it often—too often—trying to recall the moment when he must have known. The moment before he saw the headlines, before Joan at the donut shop had blurted the news in a nonsensical flurry of blubbering. Surely he must have sensed something. How could the whole world just collapse around you without you instinctively knowing? Ernest would come to think of it as a "Where were you when…?" day. *Where were you when your family lost all their savings? Where were you when you found out the stock market crashed? Where were you when your father started to go nuts?*

Coffee and half-eaten donut in hand, Ernest rushed back to the hotel to call the stockbroker. All three phone booths were occupied, so he waited impatiently for his turn as a line formed behind him. The switchboard operators were overwhelmed with calls, but he was eventually patched through, only to learn that Father's Transamerica stock had plummeted along with everything else.

The astute twenty-year-old understood the personal impact immediately. Father had no cash or savings. In fact, against Ernest's advice, Joe had used the Transamerica stock as collateral for the mortgage he had just taken out on the 160 raw acres across the street from their house. Things were going to get difficult. But Ernest didn't immediately grasp the greater picture—the ramifications for the country and its citizens. No one did.

Ernest's "Where were you when?" day would go down in history as "Black Thursday," the beginning of the Great Depression: October 24, 1929. The ten-year economic and social blight that followed devoured the country like a beast, claiming jobs, homes, lives, and hope. In its wake it left hunger and despair. Unemployment peaked at fifteen million. Banks were replaced by soup kitchens; chorus lines by breadlines.

Ernest met Julio at the new Union Station, where they caught the first train heading west. All the cars were full, but a kind soul changed seats so the brothers could sit together. Julio took the window seat, and Ernest, the aisle, where he was buffeted by a blast of cold air every time a new passenger boarded the train. He paid no mind to the chill as he appreciated the opportunity to quiz each newcomer for the latest news. He was antsy and desperate to know what the papers were saying.

Ten-year-old Joe Junior carefully pulled up to the Modesto station, half-standing, and craning his neck to make sure the front wheel didn't hit the curb. It was the first time he had been allowed to take the truck into town and he was giddy with the sudden responsibility and trust. Maybe Ernest and Julio would stop treating him like a dumb kid. Though his big brothers initially were surprised to see him, they didn't seem all that impressed. In fact, Ernest quietly picked up the stack of magazines that Joe had sat on to see over the steering wheel, moved them to the floor, and signaled for Joe to slide over to the middle as he indifferently assumed the driver's seat and continued his conversation with Julio. The older brothers talked over Joe as if he wasn't even there.

Ernest was grateful to be off the train. Out of abeyance and back on terra firma, where he could get out of his own head and actually do something. Hopefully, Father had come to his senses and would listen to some of the ideas he had been mulling over on the interminable journey back home. Ernest parked the truck in the gravel driveway and stumbled briefly when he stepped out of the cab. His balance was off-kilter, having spent the last five days acclimating to the train's rhythmic cadence.

Cool by California standards, the air felt almost balmy after the Windy City. Curls of smoke smudged the flawless blue sky that stretched over Modesto. Farmers had awoken to a still and windless day—perfect for burning brush, vine trimmings, and household refuse. It smelled like fall. Then another smell tickled Ernest's nose: the sweet odor of overripe grapes with a hint of mold—almost pleasant, but not quite—days away, or maybe just hours, from becoming foul. Ernest heard a commotion behind the house. It sounded like the crusher. He stretched out his arms, interlaced his fingers, cracked his knuckles, and went to investigate. It had been almost a week since Mamma's frantic call. Surely Father had come to his senses since then.

But there was Father. There was the crusher. And there were the truckloads of grapes that would never leave California. The ones for which Joe Gallo had promised his growers too much money.

Julio stopped at Ernest's side and whispered, "What the—"

"What in the world are you doing?" Ernest boomed as both hands clasped his head in disbelief.

It wasn't clear if Joe hadn't heard his son or had just chosen to ignore him. Regardless, the question went unanswered and the resolute Italian remained intent on his task: turning the crusher's wheel, hand over hand over hand. From fifty yards away Ernest couldn't see a barrel or bucket under the crusher to collect the juice and tried to make sense of it as he hurried forward.

As he got closer, Ernest could see that the crusher was atop one of five manholes in a newly excavated part of the yard. The nearest one was still open and Ernest looked down into a stew of dark juice, crushed skin and stems afloat on top.

"I said, 'What in the world are you doing?!'" he yelled again as he walked over to his father.

Stooped at the crusher, Father looked like he hadn't shaved, eaten, or slept in days. His head seemed too heavy for his neck. His chin rested on his chest as his eyes blankly considered the red stain spreading over the barely set concrete at the bottom of the six-foot hole. He sensed another soul's presence, took his hands off the crank, and slowly straightened his spine. He squinted in the sun and held his hand at his brow to block the glare.

"Leave me alone. Can't you see I'm busy?" Joe snapped when he saw his son.

"Stop. Let's just talk. Tell me what you're doing," Ernest said, desperately trying to sound calm and mask his fear and confusion, while swatting away a cluster of flies.

Joe stood, shuffled a few yards to his right, picked up a nearby lug box of moldy grapes, and dumped them into the hopper. "Gotta save the berries, gotta save the berries," he huffed.

Knowing he had to do something, but unsure what, Ernest looked over to Julio, searching his brother's face for reassurance, a suggestion, a nod of encouragement—any kind of handhold. Julio was about to say something when Mamma came bustling out the back door.

"See?" she shouted. "He's *pazzo,* crazy! Thank God you boys are home."

Ernest twisted himself between Father and the crusher and placed his hands on the bewildered man's shoulders. "Look at me," he ordered.

Father shrugged off his son. "Gotta save the berries, gotta save the berries."

"Stop!" Ernest yelled as he grabbed his father by the front of his shirt. "Stop right now! Julio and I will finish. Get some rest. It's okay. I've got this." Ernest put his right arm around his father and signaled to Julio to take his other side. Together they led Joe inside the house.

"Mamma, can you please get Father a drink of water?" Julio asked. "Here, Father, sit down." Ernest pulled out a chair and they eased Joe into it, his body stiff and uncooperative, his joints seemingly frozen from hours manning the crusher.

The family gathered uncomfortably on the back porch. Father rocked back and forth, continuing his rant, "Gotta save the berries, gotta save the berries."

Mamma explained how Joe had snapped like a violin string that had been tightened too much when he had heard about the collapse of his prized Transamerica stock. "I can't let the berries rot on the vines!" he had screeched. "That's like throwing money away. I gotta save the berries!" He had chased all the pickers off his land and tried to pluck the vines clean himself. He went three days with no sleep, harvesting by moonlight and lamplight. Then last week, with Uncle Mike's help, he had excavated a giant hole in the backyard and built an underground tank. She couldn't imagine that the concrete had even cured before he'd started crushing the berries, many of which had already started to rot.

Despite the grim situation, Ernest couldn't help but be impressed at how fast Father had built the underground tank. He guessed it could hold at least twenty-five thousand gallons. It was actually not such a bad idea. Using their remaining grapes to make wine was the only way to save their now-worthless crop. Turning lemons into lemonade, so to speak. He almost laughed aloud at the analogy. Too bad it was illegal.

"He needs sleep. Give him some wine. I'll talk to him in the morning," Ernest instructed. "Julio, can you stay with Mamma and help her with Father? I need to think."

Ernest went outside and sat in one of the two rocking chairs on the front porch. On another evening he might have appreciated the crickets' burgeoning symphony or called Mamma out to see the fiery hunter's moon swelling over the horizon. But despite his two months of city frenzy, Ernest was too preoccupied to enjoy the wonders and comforts of home.

He tried to keep his mind focused on one problem at a time and not get lost in all the unknowns and things that were out of his control. Though Father was still the head of the household, he was the oldest son and he needed to step in. Father could bounce back from this...this...whatever this was...or he could be permanently incapacitated. He had always had his moods and tempers, but his behavior today was bizarre and unnerving.

Ernest had never seen anything like it. He had heard of people having nervous breakdowns, but no one ever talked about what they looked like or what the signs were. Could that be what this was? And if so, how long would it last? And what was to be done? He could call Dr. Maxwell, but that would be too embarrassing. Best to keep it in the family. With so many unanswered questions, he decided it prudent to wait and see how Father was in the morning and go from there.

One thing he knew for certain was that there was no way he would let Father get into bootlegging again. The Livermore raid had terrified all of them, especially Mamma. He wouldn't let Father hurt her like that again. He'd call the prohis and turn him in himself if he had to.

It occurred to Ernest that the expanse drenched in moonlight in front of him was now an even bigger problem: the undeveloped 160 acres Father had leveraged with his Transamerica stock. He decided to call the broker in the morning to see if there was any news. Maybe the panic sweeping through the nation and the house behind him would have all been for naught. For all anyone knew, the stock market and banks could bounce right back.

"Ernest, you should come inside," Mamma soothed through the screen door. "Father's asleep now and you should get some sleep too. You've had such a long day. I'm sure Father will be better now that his boys are home. *Ti amo, Nino mio.*"

Thankfully, Father's rendezvous with madness hadn't lasted. Upon the boys' return he didn't have the will to fight all the forces telling him to stand down. He resigned himself to giving his sons more control over decision-making and the farm's day-to-day operations. The underground tanks were abandoned and Ernest and Julio resumed their seasonal chores in the vineyards. But as Joe Gallo scratched his way up from rock bottom, his choler and rancor returned. And it was worse than before, for a new sentiment had spilled into his emotional cocktail: despondency.

Joe's new persona stretched Ernest to the limits of his patience, understanding, and sympathy. He had learned to navigate Father's moods like an experienced seaman, steering his ship between reefs and jutting rocks on a black night—knowing when to push the engine to its limits, when to pull back, and when to let the current carry him through. But now Father was in a boat of his own, in the middle of a still, windless expanse. He had sailed into the doldrums and there seemed to be no way to get him out.

There would be days when Father wouldn't get out of bed and days where he would make it as far as the living room armchair, only to sit there staring blankly ahead, rocking his head ever so slightly up and down or from side to side in weak reply to the family's questions. There were some decisions Ernest had to make without consulting his father. And time after time, as he was executing them, Father would suddenly find his way and berate his son for being an idiot. The state of the economy combined with the pressure and responsibility of managing the farm and taking care of the family weighed heavily on the young man.

Like farming of any kind, there was little security in growing grapes, even in the best of times. Poor weather, disease, and pests were as much a threat as the chain of supply and demand was unpredictable. The grape business ran on an annual cycle that kept growers in debt for most of the year. Borrowing season began in January, when farmers would traditionally start collecting the funds they needed for their operating expenses—equipment purchases and rentals, supplies, labor, and shipping. Debts were paid off the following December after the crop had been sold. Hopefully there would be profits. Then the cycle would begin again. The Depression had made it almost impossible to borrow money, so growers were cutting overhead wherever they could. The banks were in a tough spot, for their only chance of getting a return on their investment was if growers had fruit to sell.

Though the southern plains had been ravaged by the Dust Bowl, Mother Nature had been kinder to the Central Valley, delivering enough sunshine and water to produce respectable yields. Despite or maybe even because of the economy, folks were still making wine and there was still a demand for grapes. Ernest and Julio continued to tend the vines, harvest the crops, and make their annual sales trips to Chicago and New Jersey.

As if to mock their financial straits, Ernest was confronted by their fallow burden every time he stepped out onto the front porch: those 160 brambly, weedy acres Father had mortgaged just before the crash. The bank hadn't been able to do much about the Gallos' debt. Buyers weren't exactly beating down the door for Central Valley farmland, but the family desperately needed the land to deliver. It would take a newly planted field three long years to start producing grapes. But first the land needed to be leveled and groomed.

Four straight days of rain had turned the field into a basin of mud. Trying to stay dry, Ernest and Julio stood on the porch mapping out their strategy for tackling the land, and agreed they would start on the southwestern corner and work their way out from there after the first of the year. They would have to knock down trees, pull out the stumps and roots, level the land, and fill in the gullies for irrigation and drainage.

Over the staccato of the downpour on the Spanish-tiled roof, they heard a clatter of heavy equipment coming down Maze Road. The young men turned in unison to the east to see Father behind the wheel of a Caterpillar tractor, a bouncing and rattling LeTourneau scraper in tow. He stopped in front of the house and Ernest and Julio pulled their jackets over their heads and ran out into the pouring rain to greet him.

"Twenty dollars a day they charge me. But they no say how long a day is," Father shouted over the engine. "You boys start now."

"What? In this weather?" Julio asked.

"Yes, in this weather. Otherwise it would be twenty-five," Joe scoffed. "Now, start! *Vai!*"

The brothers were puzzled by Father's words, "they no say how long a day is," but Joe soon made it clear. To get the most for his money, he instructed Ernest and Julio to work the fields in twelve-hour shifts. To Ernest's relief, Julio volunteered to work nights. It was an unseasonably wet and cold winter and the wretched weather turned what should have been a manageable job into pure misery. The slog through the mud felt endless. And there was no relief, for even when Ernest lay in bed at night, he could hear the rumble of the Cat as Julio drove the beast back and forth, back and forth.

It was had been late to place grape cuttings, so they grew melons and beans. Yet the land held a grudge that would last for years. In their tireless battle with the elements, numb hands and chilled bones notwithstanding, the Gallos had almost irreparably damaged the soil by scraping it while it was soaking wet. Their first vines succumbed to red spider mites and the next were felled by disease and poor crop set. It would take the land almost a decade to recover from the brutality it had suffered.

By the summer of 1930 Ernest couldn't bear to be around Father's mood swings, ingratitude, dictatorial tirades, and sullenness any longer. If Father entered a room he was in, Ernest would find a reason to leave. He took his meals after the family had finished eating. The grueling work on the new land had kept him from finishing the semester at Modesto Junior College and it didn't seem like he'd ever be able to graduate. His life and future were in his father's hands—unsteady and cruel hands, at that. Hands he didn't trust. He was expected to work like a man, but was still treated like a boy.

Ernest rapped softly on Julio's bedroom door. "Can I come in? I need to talk to you."

Julio rubbed his eyes and sat up. "What time is it?"

"I know. Sorry. I just had to tell you now," Ernest explained.

"Tell me what?"

"I can't stay here anymore. I can't be around Father. I just can't live like this anymore. It's killing me."

"But what else can you do? Where would you go? It's not like there are any jobs out there. I know it's hard, but here you've got family, food, a roof over—"

"I know. I've got a plan. Maybe you'll join me. I'm going to El Centro."

"Where's that?" Julio asked.

"The Imperial Valley. Just north of Mexico. It's time for the melon and onion harvest. There should be plenty of work. I figure I'll talk to the owners and tell them how much I know about shipping and selling. If they send me to Chicago, I'll get them a better price than anyone. I know all the guys there. It's the same lot who buy our grapes."

"Wow. I didn't see this coming," Julio admitted, sitting up straighter and fluffing the pillow behind his back.

"I just decided tonight. I wanted to tell you before anyone else. I hope you'll come with me. Think about it," Ernest urged.

"When are you going?"

"Two days."

"What? Two days? Father's going to have a cow!"

"What else is new?" Ernest said sarcastically.

Though he didn't know a soul in the Imperial Valley, Ernest had no doubt he would land on his feet. But the excitement he felt about his venture wasn't absolute. It was certainly acceptable for a twenty-one-year-old man to leave home, but shadows of guilt and worry kept his buoyancy in check. He worried how his absence would affect Mamma and tried to rationalize that she would be better off. He could see how much his antipathy toward Father wounded her and there would surely be less arguing and tension in the house with him gone. He would send her money and make sure she and Joe Junior were taken care of. If Julio joined him, Father would have to manage the vineyards on his own. But maybe then he would be too busy to fall into any more funks. The longer Ernest thought about it, the more convinced he became that he had to go.

He joined the family for dinner the next night and shared his news.

"Why do you do this to me? To your family?!" Father blustered.

"Father, you were younger than me when you left Italy," Ernest reminded him. "You had dreams. I have dreams."

"And so do I," Julio added. "I'm going with Ernest."

"What?! You too? Dreams?! This is about *dreams*? You're both stupid. Crazy. How am I supposed to manage the vineyards on my own?"

"You'll find a way. Joe's old enough to help. All he does around here is shoot rabbits. At his age Julio and I—"

"That's not fair. I help," Joe Junior protested.

Ernest detected a quiver to his right and turned to see tears in his mother's eyes.

"It's okay, Mamma. It's the right thing to do. You'll see," Ernest assured. He reached his arm over her shoulder and pulled her close.

"Right for who?" Father shouted. "Right for *you,* you mean! But isn't that just like you to think only of yourself? No care for anyone else. Go to Mexico. Go and fail. I say you'll be back in one month with your tails between your legs!" He slammed his fist on the table and stormed out of the room.

With one suitcase between them, the brothers boarded a Greyhound bus the next morning and headed south.

Chapter Eight

WINE AND ROSES

Joe Gallo's parting words to his sons proved somewhat prophetic. But it wouldn't be them who held their tails between their legs.

At the turn of the century, developers had built a series of irrigation canals to divert the Colorado River to the Imperial Valley's sub-sea-level desert near the Salton Sea in Southern California. The rows of corn, beans, and melons that the native Quechan Indians had struggled to propagate on the barren land now stretched to every horizon and fed families 2,500 miles away. But the industry was still young and was hit hard by the Depression.

Farmers were going out of business and couldn't pay the seasonal pickers gathered at their gates looking for a day's work. Crops rotted in fields as hungry day laborers were turned away. Ernest apologized to Julio that El Centro wasn't the land of milk and honey he had promised, but they both remained optimistic and set out every morning looking for work. Ernest could handle the uncertain lifestyle, but felt guilty for dragging his younger brother along. But he would see it through—if not for himself and Julio, then just to prove Father wrong.

When they did manage to find work, it was demanding: hours cramped in one position, sidling along a row of beans under a white-hot sun much hotter than the one in Modesto. Their fingers were cut and swollen, stiff from their repetitive chore. All for fifty cents a day—just enough to cover their shared hotel room. But neither complained; the work was no harder than that in Modesto. And more importantly, no one was lurking nearby ready to hurl insults as they toiled. No straw boss could injure them like their own father. The freedom and independence the brothers felt was like a life-sustaining spirit filling their hearts and lungs. Though Ernest never stopped worrying about Mamma and Joe Junior, he never called them in case Father answered the phone. Instead he talked to Aunt Tillie in San Francisco once a week and she acted as an intermediary.

"Please, Nino. You and Julio must go home. Your mother needs you," Aunt Tillie urged.

"I told you last week—and the week before—I just can't. I miss Mamma, but you know Father. I can't bear to be around him. It's no good for anyone. I'll start sending Mamma money soon," Ernest explained.

"It's not about the money," his aunt scolded. "It's your family. They all need you. Susie says your Father wants you home too. He realizes his mistakes and has promised to treat you better. Please, Ernest. Your mother calls me every week and cries, begging me to convince you to come home. Her heart is broken. I'm worried about her. Joe says he'll give you your own land. Julio too. Susie says he means it. He's changed. He really has."

The little boy who still lived deep in Ernest's soul desperately wanted to believe it was true. His father missed him, loved him, needed him. He had finally recognized that Ernest was a good son. Honest. Loyal. Smart. Ernest's heart swelled with hope. But grown-up Ernest knew better and spoke up. Father was desperate. He couldn't handle the vineyards without his indentured servants. He would say anything to get his sons home. He couldn't be believed or trusted.

Ernest and Julio considered their options. Neither felt they owed Father anything, but both were concerned about Mamma and Joe Junior. They hadn't been able to send a single dollar home since they had left. If Father botched up the vineyards, the family could lose everything. If he wasn't going to take care of their mother and little brother, they would have to. It took two days to hitchhike back home, giving them time to develop a plan and a list of ultimatums.

The young men were back in Modesto in time to prepare for the 1930 harvest. Father had humbly welcomed them home, but Ernest knew his reserve wouldn't last. At some point he'd break his oath and Ernest would be forced to find some way to protect Mamma and Joe Junior and move on. He rededicated his bones and muscle to the vineyards, but his mind and heart were elsewhere, planning his next move.

No one with any sense thought Herbert Hoover would be reelected and many believed the country's next president would put an end to Prohibition. The national ban on the sale of alcohol had been too difficult to enforce. In the past decade, drinking had increased, organized crime had flourished, and the government had lost an estimated $11 billion in taxes. Repealing the amendment would create jobs and revenue. When Ernest added everything up, he was convinced it was almost the perfect time to enter the wine business.

The more he thought about it, the more his excitement grew. Wine was in his blood. His grandfather and great-grandfather were winemakers and he would continue the family tradition. His earliest memory was of waking up from a nap in a blanket-lined lug box in the Bianco vineyard, Nonna awash in sunshine as she plucked the clusters that dangled over his head. The image filled him with warmth. Those had been happy days. He remembered everyone laughing after Zia Tillie had read his fortune and said he would be successful in the wine business, but now he was starting to think it was meant to be.

He would need to convince Father that switching their business from grapes to wine would be an easy transition and a smart investment. Father would surely be cynical, so he had to come up with a budget and an impenetrable business plan. He decided to start by visiting wineries and other growers and learning as much as he could from those with experience.

Ernest walked up the steps again, louder this time, landing each foot with purpose. When he got to the porch, he coughed.

"Ah. *Buon pomeriggio,*" the middle-aged farmer said, raising his chin from his chest. "You caught me dozing off."

"Hello, Signor Franzia! Ernest Gallo, sir."

"*Sì. Mi ricordo.* Ready for Chicago?"

"Yes, sir. Though it looks like our yield will be lower than I'd like."

"Mine too. Here, have a seat," Giuseppe Franzia said, pointing to a chair next to his. "Amelia!" he shouted toward the front door.

"Thank you, sir," Ernest replied.

"Amelia!" Franzia yelled again.

"Yes, Papà," came a voice from behind the screen door.

"Get Mr. Gallo here and me something to drink," Franzia ordered gruffly.

Ernest stretched his neck toward the front door, curious to see to whom Franzia was speaking, but it was impossible to see through the door's fine mesh. Shortly, a teenaged girl carried out a tray with a couple of jars of wine and a plate of crusty bread, a slab of cheese, and an apple.

"Ernest, this is my daughter Ann."

"I thought your name was Amelia," Ernest said, confused. He stood, removed his hat, and nodded his head.

"No, Amelia's my big sister," she giggled. "She's somewhat bashful."

Franzia pulled a small knife from his front pocket and peeled the apple in one long spiral. He offered Ernest half as they began to talk business. They discussed the latest trends in fertilization and irrigation. Though Ernest was well read on the subjects and had his own opinions, he peppered Franzia with questions about his techniques. He was always hungry to learn as much from everyone he met and mentally stockpiled the information. You never knew when one idea could collide with another, seemingly unrelated, and spark a creative windfall.

During the discussion, Ernest's eyes were drawn by a flutter in the window behind Franzia. He thought he was imagining it, but the third time it happened, his eyes locked with a pair of blue eyes peeking out from behind the voile curtain. His heart skipped and he lost his place in the conversation.

"Well?" Franzia asked.

"Huh?" Ernest replied, briefly forgetting his manners.

"I said, what do you…"

But Ernest had tuned out again. He did his best to reengage in the conversation, but was having difficulty concentrating and maintaining eye contact. Wondering if "she" was still there, he couldn't keep his eyes from shifting back to the window. He finally had the awareness and good sense to excuse himself before Franzia thought him a complete buffoon.

The mysterious blue eyes had stirred up something deep inside Ernest. He tried to make sense of the strange feeling, but only grew more confused. Though he had never had much time to socialize, he had gone to school with plenty of girls. But none had made him feel like this. *Amelia.* That was her name. *Amelia Franzia.* The words flowed off his tongue as he whispered them aloud on the drive back to Modesto. His thumping heart kept him awake most of the night. Could there be such a thing as love at first sight? He didn't know the answer, but he knew he had to meet her. As soon as possible.

Ernest drove back to Ripon to see Franzia the next day. To justify his visit, he brought a pamphlet about innovations in rootstock grafting that one of his professors had written. To Ernest's dismay, Ann answered the door and there was no sign of her blue-eyed sister.

"You again," she stated matter-of-factly when she saw Ernest. She pointed to the fields east of the house. "Papà's in the vineyard," she explained.

Ernest did what was expected of him and went looking for Franzia. His disappointment at not seeing Amelia had been immediately offset by relief. For what if he had said something stupid? He had never really talked to a girl in that way. He could talk to anyone about business. That didn't scare him. But girls? Jeez. He'd never had the time or the chance. And what if she was too tall? It was highly possible, considering he was only five foot four. Or what if he met her and the feeling went away? After all, he'd only glimpsed her through the glare of the sun reflecting off the window.

Enough what-ifs, he decided. No sense in worrying about things he couldn't control. He'd just have to try his best.

Franzia was deep in a row of old vines. Ernest entered the leafy canopy, pausing to observe the trellis system the grower employed. Father grew his vines along two wires—a low wire that trained the two gnarly cordons to reach from the vine's trunk like the letter "T" and an upper wire where they would tie the tender shoots. But Ernest noticed Franzia's system used three extra sets of parallel horizontal wires. He was contemplating the merits of the technique when Franzia shouted at him.

"Mr. Gallo. What brings you back so soon?"

"*Buongiorno, signor!*" Ernest yelled back as he hurried down the shaded aisle. "I was thinking about our conversation and thought you might find this pamphlet here interesting."

"*Grazie*. I'm afraid I don't have time to jabber today, though. Too much to do."

"I understand. I just wanted to give you this. I'll be on my way." Ernest took a few steps back through the row before he summoned his courage. He turned back to Franzia. "Sir?"

"What is it?"

"Er…I was wondering if I could have your permission to ask your daughter out." The words came out faster than Ernest had intended and the relief he felt was immediate. There. He had done it. Taken the first step.

"My daughter?"

"Amelia, sir."

"But you've never even met her. *Have you?*" Franzia scowled.

"No, sir, but—"

"Well. This does come as a surprise. You're a nice enough young man. Good head on your shoulders. Hardworking. Too many questions maybe, but full of ideas."

"Yes, sir?" Ernest said, encouraged. This was going better than he had expected.

"But—"

"But?" Ernest worried.

"I don't know your parents that well, but I've heard some things about your uncle. A real lady's man, they say…prison…" Franzia said.

"But sir, if I may—"

"Nope. There's nothing to be said. I need to get to know you better. Because I like you, you can come here. Meet Amelia. Spend time with the family. But never alone. And no leaving my farm," Franzia warned.

"Yes, sir. I understand. Thank you."

The conversation would replay itself in Ernest's head for days. He was thrilled Franzia had given him permission to court Amelia. It wasn't exactly how he had hoped to spend time with her, always chaperoned, but he would take what he could get. The bit about Uncle Mike burned deep. Ernest had suspected he was a philanderer, but hadn't known for sure. And though his uncle's run-ins with the law had been in the Oakland and San Francisco newspapers, Ernest had no idea that word had traveled as far as the sleepy Central Valley. He felt ashamed and somehow accused. As if he were the bootlegger and cheat. He'd just have to prove to Franzia that he was a good guy—moral and honest—and good enough for his daughter.

For the third day in a row, Ernest set off on the twenty-minute drive to the Franzia farm. He had cleaned up and combed Brylcreem through his dark brown hair. He stopped the truck a few hundred yards from his house to pick some red roses that punctuated the end of every other vineyard row. Ernest had planted them a few summers ago for mostly utilitarian reasons.

The thorny bushes were susceptible to the same diseases as grapes, but reacted sooner. So if he ever noted a white powder coating the rose leaves, he knew it was time to sulfur the grapes to prevent mildew. He snapped the thorns off the stems, pleased with himself for thinking of picking them.

To his delight, Amelia answered the door. His first impression was that she was more beautiful than he had imagined. His second, that she was tiny. Definitely under five feet. Ernest awkwardly thrust the flowers toward Amelia, who accepted them even more awkwardly.

"I'll go get Papà," she mumbled, looking down at the roses and avoiding Ernest's eyes.

"No!" Ernest snapped, instantly shocked and embarrassed at how strident he sounded. "I mean…um…you don't have to. I came to see you."

Amelia's cheeks turned pink and she mumbled something about putting the flowers in water and coming right back. But she didn't come right back. Ernest rocked back and forth on his feet wondering if he had misunderstood. She was gone so long he thought about leaving. As he worked to rebuild his confidence, he heard a buzzing sound by his ear. A yellow jacket. He leapt to the side, swung his arms around, and flapped his wrists trying to shoo the pest away. He swiveled his head in a circle, thankful to see there were no witnesses to his unmanly performance.

She finally returned, carrying a tray of fresh lemonade, apologizing that it had taken so long to make. She placed the tray on a low table and the two sat down in a pair of forward-facing chairs. Ernest tirelessly quizzed Amelia about her school years, hobbies, and family, but her answers were short and perfunctory. He couldn't get a conversation going. It was bordering on uncomfortable, but he didn't want to leave. Thinking it might help if they were looking at each other, Ernest shifted his chair along the deck to face her.

The move caused Amelia to recoil slightly and she picked up her lemonade to cover her involuntary flinch. Her drink spilled and she quickly picked up a napkin to hide the evidence. Ernest could see he had made her even more uncomfortable and stood to leave.

"I should probably be going. I have a lot of work to do..." he started to explain, but was distracted by a buzz overhead. He looked up and then down to see the yellow jacket alight on the rim of the lemonade pitcher. Ernest reached down to the table and flicked his hand. The wasp dodged the swat only to land on Amelia's bare arm. Ernest's hand reached out with no conscious orders from his brain.

And before the sound reached his ears Ernest had already regretted his move. Amelia released a startled yelp as Ernest's hand made contact with her skin. Her blue eyes filled with tears. His face turned crimson as he realized he must have hit the wasp harder than he intended. He had only meant to slap it away. He berated himself. When he had dreamed of touching her creamy skin for the first time, this wasn't at all what he had imagined. A quick "I'm really sorry!" and he was past the old walnut tree that graced the front yard, in his truck, and on his way back to Modesto.

Though he had wanted to return the next day and give a proper apology, he had to go to San Francisco with Father to pick up some used lumber. They spent the night with Aunt Celia and stopped in Stockton on the way home. Four days passed before he was able to see Amelia again.

She answered the door drying her hands in a faded towel. She didn't seem surprised to see Ernest and her reserve had softened. Sensing his discomfort, she invited him inside. She led him back to the kitchen where Ann sat at the table, fingers splayed, her palms flat on a small towel. Ernest stayed in the doorway holding his hat in front of him with both hands.

"Join us," Ann beckoned. "Amelia just finished giving me a manicure. Now it's your turn."

"Ha," Ernest coughed out. "No, thank you."

"Oh, come on. Don't be shy," she ribbed. "You'll like it. Promise."

Ernest caught a small smile on Amelia's face, and when their eyes met, she shrugged.

"Well, sure. Why not?" he laughed, quickly calculating it would give him a reason to stay longer. Amelia seemed more relaxed, and her younger sister had already broken the ice. "What do I need to do?"

"Just sit down and we'll take care of the rest. Roll up your sleeves," Ann instructed.

Ernest self-consciously bared his broad, hairy forearms and placed the fingers of his right hand in the delicate, pink crinoline bowl of warm, sudsy water as directed by Ann. His thick fingers displaced half the water. No sooner had Amelia prepared a bowl for his other hand and sat down next to him than Ann swiftly excused herself.

An awkward silence filled the void Ann left, but thankfully it was short-lived. Ernest shared stories from his escapades in Chicago while his fingers soaked. He thrilled when he made Amelia laugh, tickled that he had brought her joy. His breath stopped when she told him to lift his hands so she could dry them. Her fingers slipped through the towel and brushed against his. A tingle tripped through him and his heart hammered in his chest. While she was focused on his hands, he looked up and drank in every detail of her wavy hair and the curve of her neck. He had just noticed the scratch on her arm when she turned his hands over, palms facing up. He looked down at the ugly yellow calluses at the base of each finger and realized that those might have been the source of her injury the other day. Maybe he hadn't slapped her hard after all.

He was about to explain when a young man burst through the back door. Ernest recognized him immediately as John Franzia, Amelia's brother. The young men knew each other from selling grapes in Chicago.

"Oh…uh…sorry. I didn't mean to interrupt," John stammered. "I was just coming in to make a sandwich."

Ernest stood instinctively, both out of polite habit and sheer embarrassment. He must have looked like a real fop—the dainty pink bowls in front of him, John's sister dabbing at his beefy mitts. He laughed nervously and Amelia joined in. John quickly excused himself while the couple's chuckles filled the air behind him.

Over time and with his wife's urgings, Giuseppe Franzia had accepted that his little girl had become a young woman with a heart and mind of her own. Though he hadn't quite warmed to the idea of her dating, he had at least begun to thaw. She could certainly have done worse than the modest, likable, and hardworking Ernest Gallo. On top of that, he was Italian and Catholic, shared their values, and made his Amelia happier and more confident than he had ever seen her. So when Ernest asked for his blessing and his daughter's hand in marriage, Franzia obliged.

Ernest thoroughly enjoyed his time with the Franzias. Although they had been hit as hard by the Depression as anyone else, their home remained relaxed and lively. He had spent very little time with any family other than his own and took in every custom, habit, and inside joke. He spent as much time as he could there. Father complained he wasn't doing enough work, but his bellyaching fell on deaf ears. Ernest was in love.

Back in Modesto, Ernest would hold on to the vision of Amelia's face and the warmth of her breath to sustain him through their time apart. But life at home had gone from bad to worse. They couldn't afford fuel for the tractor and had returned to using mules. For someone who was always looking to the future and trying to increase efficiency and profits, Ernest felt like he was running in place, or worse, slipping back in time. He had to work harder just to keep his chin above water, never mind moving forward. When he told Father he was going into town to buy grain, he was met by hollow eyes and grim words.

"We have no money to feed the animals," Father had said flatly.

And that was why, the night before his wedding, Ernest found himself on Maze Road grazing the mules on the side of the road at midnight. He cursed his life. The animals' ribs looked even more sunken in the moonlight. They couldn't go on like this. Opportunists had recently found loopholes in the Volstead Act. They were selling grape concentrate and unfermented juice for more than they would get for whole grapes. Some were even selling wine "bricks" with a company called Fruit Industries, going as far as marketing Vine-Glo, a dehydrated grape concentrate compressed into the shape of a brick. The product came with very specific instructions: "After dissolving the brick in a gallon of water, do not place the liquid in a jug away in the cupboard for twenty days, because then it would turn into wine." Ernest vowed to have another talk with Father about ways to improve their situation, but first he was going to marry the love of his life.

Deep in thought, Ernest almost missed the gray tarpaulin carefully draped over the brush in the roadside ditch, but the mules had abruptly stopped their foraging and raised their heads in unison. Ernest looked in their direction and heard the sound that had interrupted their feeding. A whimper. Slight and forlorn. His senses heightened, his eyes adjusted to the monochromatic ditch untouched by the moon's light. He made out the profile of a young woman, sitting on the ground, arms wrapped tightly around her knees.

"Are you alright?" he asked.

The woman startled at the sound of his voice and rose to her feet.

"I'm sorry. I didn't mean to frighten you. In fact, you frightened me. Didn't even see you here," Ernest spoke softly.

"I'm sorry, mister. My family's sleeping and I didn't want to wake them," she explained.

The dim light couldn't hide the woman's frail condition or her frayed dress and bare feet. Ernest then saw the old jalopy parked behind the makeshift tent. There was a mattress strapped on the roof and pots and pans had been hung to dry from the rear bumper. Migrants. As far as he was concerned, they had been dealt a bum hand. He couldn't understand people's derision and judgment of them. Hadn't everyone in America come from somewhere else? For the same reason? To leave an inhospitable life in the hope of building something better? Hadn't that been why Father and Nonno had come here and why he and Julio had moved to El Centro?

These people weren't looking for a handout. They wanted to work. He had hired plenty of migrants over the years, whether from Oklahoma or Mexico or as far away as the Philippines. He found they worked harder than almost anyone he knew. He understood their suffering. The toil the work took on their bodies, the sun took on their skin. Each time he saw their overburdened automobiles, held together with spit and string, a profound bell tolled deep in his soul. Invariably there would be a few scruffy children sunk into the mattresses layered on the truck's bed, their faces filled with hope and adventure. Not so long ago that had been Julio and him. *There but for the grace of God go I,* he would think. *And did I,* he would add. He was grateful when he had work to offer the desperate parents of these kids and always paid as much as he could, even if it was more than the going rate.

He chastised himself for his resentment over having to graze the mules. How dare he feel sorry for himself or complain that they couldn't buy fuel or grain when so many Americans wondered where their next meal would come from. Their pantry was full of food Mamma had lovingly canned. He ate sun-ripened peaches on the coldest winter days. Joe Junior hunted rabbits and gathered the chickens' eggs every morning. And should it ever get to the point where they didn't have cash to buy milk, they would always have something to trade.

"Did you pick this week?" Ernest asked the woman.

"Yes, sir. The wages were fair, but we're still hungry."

"I know." Ernest turned back and pointed to his house. "I live there. Did you work for me?"

"Yes, mister," she nodded.

"Come by at sunrise. I can give you some eggs," Ernest said kindly. "I hear the Depression's almost over. Things will get better. We've gotta have faith."

"God bless you, mister. Thank you for your kindness."

~

Ernest and Amelia were married on August 31, 1931, in a small Catholic church near the Franzia ranch. Giuseppe and Teresa Franzia hosted the reception in their home's cavernous basement. The brick walls provided the five hundred guests with welcome relief from the suffocating late-summer heat. Ernest, Julio, and Joe Junior wore identical dark three-piece suits and matching white ties, making it even more difficult for Amelia's distant relatives to tell the older two apart. When asked, each brother gave the same response: "You can always tell me because I'm the better-looking one."

The platters of antipasti, shrimp, oysters, mussels, grilled fish, and vegetables, and bowls of gnocchi, risotto, and ravioli that circled the golden roasted *porchetta* were replenished throughout the feast. When one keg of wine was drained, one of Amelia's five brothers was quick to put another in commission.

Best man Julio gave a warm toast and teased Ernest for not kissing his bride on the altar. "I didn't know! This is my first wedding!" Ernest shouted back to the room's amusement, giving his petite bride yet another smooch to atone for his grievous mistake.

The day after the wedding, Amelia accompanied Ernest on his annual sales trek to the Midwest. It was to be a working honeymoon. Like the rest of the economy, the grape market was in shambles and Ernest barely came out ahead. But the following year was even worse. Father had promised his growers too much money and Ernest had left Chicago with seventy cars of unsold grapes. On top of that, he owed the railroad $70,000 for shipping and demurrage. He was sickened at the loss. For all the bitter 4:00 a.m. mornings, backbreaking days, and sleepless nights to result in over nine hundred tons of slop and certain bankruptcy was soul-crushing. Joe made raisins from the grapes that hadn't made it to the train, but then couldn't find any buyers.

Though he and Amelia had their own two-bedroom rental in Modesto, Ernest still saw Father almost every day. After all, he still worked for him. Every time they met, Ernest examined the defeated man, searching for early signs of another meltdown. Father's mood fluctuated between hopelessness, acceptance, and anger. It took its toll on the rest of the family. October 1929 was the standard they used to assess his state and he hadn't yet reached those depths. Ernest had become the head of the family pro tem. It was an unenviable position. And as always, Father still had the final word.

"Father, I just heard Hoover's speech. He wants to repeal Volstead. So, even if Roosevelt loses, whoever's president is on our side," Ernest crowed as he entered the family home.

Joe looked up from his chair in front of the empty fireplace. He was having one of his hopeless days. The white strands that had been slowly peppering his hair had taken over in the last couple of years. His face was drawn. He looked frail and far older than his forty-nine years.

"What do you mean?" he asked.

"It's time to move ahead on a winery. Hoover wants to turn alcohol over to the states. So if we apply for a permit now, we can be one of the first, which will give us a significant advantage. The states won't legalize it all at once, so we can sell to one at a time and then exp—"

"What in the world are you babbling about?"

Ernest took a deep breath and made an effort to slow down. He told his father all about the research he had been doing. He rattled off the numbers stored in his head: the initial capital needed; how many gallons each acre of land would produce; the predicted price per gallon once the amendment was overturned; projected gross profits; and, with a flourish at the end, the generous net profits the Gallos would enjoy.

Joe leaned forward in his chair. Maybe his son had actually found a way out of the abyss. "Go on. Tell me more."

"Joseph can help Julio and me with the vineyards," Ernest gushed. "I've got some leads on refurbished equipment. If we get it now, we'll beat the rush and I'll get a good deal. I'll handle everything."

Father's eyes brightened. His son's enthusiasm was contagious. He rubbed his palm along his stubbly cheek as he considered Ernest's proposal.

"You know what? I think you may be right. I'll go to Bank of America and see what I can work out. Can you write out your numbers so I can bring them with me? We've got the grapes, yes? Why not make wine?"

Ernest couldn't believe how quickly Father had agreed. It had been a thrill to resuscitate his father's broken spirit and fill him with hope. Father had approved. Father was proud. He couldn't wait to get home and share the news with his bride. This was his chance to secure his own future and give Amelia the life she deserved. They could start a family...buy their own house, even. He'd have to make sure he and Father were equal partners. And if Father put up a fight, then he'd go to the bank himself. He pictured a vellum business card reading *Ernest Gallo, winemaker.*

That night Ernest neatly transcribed all his calculations in a ledger he had kept from his accounting class at Modesto Junior College. He carefully removed the pages with a razor blade and placed them in a folded piece of thick cardboard. He then sorted through all the articles he had saved from newspapers and journals and separated those that pertained to repeal and the wine business. He taped them on loose sheets of paper and added them to his makeshift folder. Best that Father go into the bank armed and ready.

Joe hadn't been able to get an appointment at the bank until the following week. For Ernest, those seven days felt like seventy. Father had shot down his suggestion that he come to the meeting and shooed him away when he tried to rehearse his proposed presentation. "I've never needed you before and I don't need you now," Joe had barked. But Ernest worried. They couldn't have picked a worse time to try to borrow money. The Depression was at its nadir and Father was in arrears on his other loans.

The day of the appointment, Ernest drove over to his parents' house certain that Father would still be at the bank—he wanted to be there for the news as soon as Joe got home. To his surprise, Father's truck was in the driveway. The meeting must have been really short. *Good news or bad news?* Ernest wondered. He landed on the porch with two quick strides and burst through the front door.

Joe was in his usual spot in front of the fireplace, unshaven, and wearing his usual work clothes instead of his suit, to Ernest's instant distress.

"Well? What happened?" he asked fearfully.

"I didn't go," Joe shrugged.

"What?! Why the hell not?" Ernest shouted.

"Get off my back!" Joe barked. "You and your ideas. You think you're so smart. *L'avvocato.* That's right, you try to trick me with your words."

"But I told you—"

"It's a terrible idea. Just terrible," Joe interrupted. "I learn no amendment has ever been overturned. Ever! So if they keep

Volstead? What then? Then we have worthless equipment. And if they do repeal? You no know how to make wine. Italian Swiss Colony. Roma. They still make wine. But more than that, no one cares about wine in this country. The whole wine business here is just so they don't waste the grapes they can't sell. Americans don't even know how to drink wine with their meals. They want their cocktails…their beer and—"

"But that's not true, Father. That's not how America works. There's always—"

"*Don't interrupt me!*" Joe bellowed as he stood, a sudden reserve of strength inflating his shrunken frame. "You! You have it so easy growing up in this country. You don't know what hard work is. You don't know what I went through to get here. I never forget that boat. Packed like sardines. The vomit. The waste. I should have stayed in Fossano. You and your American ways. Don't you understand? I can't take any more risks!" Father stormed.

"Listen to me. I can get us out of this mess. I'll learn how to make wine. I know I can sell it. I can sell anything," Ernest pled.

"Leave me alone. It's no use. Everything is useless! You don't know what it's like!" Joe screamed. "The stupid telephone rings all day. 'I want my money.' 'You owe me money.' 'We come for your house.' They whine. They insult me. They won't leave me alone. How can I go to the bank and ask for more money?! I never should have listened to you…believed in you."

"You," Ernest pointed. "You need to pull yourself together and stop feeling sorry for yourself. These are hard times for everyone. You need to think of Mamma and Joseph and his future. I'm telling you wine is the answer."

"How *dare* you talk to me like that. Your own father. *Get out of my house!*" Joe growled through gritted teeth. "*Get out before*

I kill you." Father stepped a few inches closer to Ernest as he delivered his threat.

"With pleasure," Ernest spat as he brushed past his stunned mother and stomped onto the porch. He wasn't there to see Joe double over in pain, clutching his stomach and gasping for breath.

Ernest shook with outrage and the unjustness of it all. Father had said yes! Father had given him hope. He had given him permission to imagine a future. Ernest had promised his wife he would provide for her. He had even shared his plans with her father and teased her brothers that his winery would give theirs a run for their money. How could he face any of them now? He redesigned a new business card in his head: *Ernest Gallo, fool.*

Chapter Nine

DREAMS

Any hope of salvaging a morsel of respect for his father was gone. Dead. Buried. Try as he might, Ernest couldn't forgive him for the pain and embarrassment he had inflicted. He scolded himself for his own culpability. He should have known better. Father was unstable and untrustworthy. If it weren't for Mamma, Ernest would be long gone—back in El Centro or any place Father wasn't. Not only had Father capitulated on the winery, but he still hadn't given Ernest the land he had promised. At twenty-three years old, Ernest had a wife to support and not a penny to his name.

He adroitly managed to avoid his father for weeks at a time. Julio fell into the role of intermediary and relayed instructions and messages between father and brother. The family was broken, but everyone did their part—anything to keep the peace. Ernest saw how the rift wounded Mamma and did his best to make it up to her. He dutifully attended Mass every Sunday and tried to be civil to Father whenever the trio's paths converged.

Despite his debt and demonstrable lack of motivation, Joe somehow managed to obtain a loan in the spring of 1932 to buy Fruitvale Ranch, a troubled raisin farm in foreclosure. The forlorn property was in Fresno, a hundred miles to the south. No one could understand how Father pulled it off or why. With little notice or preparation, he and Mamma threw a few necessities into the Packard and drove off with a confused Joe Junior waving goodbye to his brothers from the back seat.

Ernest suspected it was Mamma's idea—a desperate attempt to relieve the tension in the family and give her older sons the independence their father refused them. Whatever the reason, it was welcome news. Ernest and Amelia moved into the family's Modesto ranch. A year later, they were joined by Julio and his new bride, Aileen Lowe, a girl he had known in high school. The two had run into each other at an American Legion dance and eloped in Reno a year later.

Though his parents were only a little more than two hours away, Ernest never visited them. It wasn't completely by design—more like things just seemed to work out that way. Every time Father needed to use a tool or machine from the Modesto farm, it was Julio who made the delivery.

The brothers continued to work fourteen-hour days, but it was on their terms and that made all the difference. Though optimistic by nature, Ernest was still surprised at how buoyant he felt—as if he had been behind a dirty window all his life and someone had suddenly come along and wiped it clean. He felt invincible and ready for anything. For the first time the white stucco house on Maze Road was full of cheer and offered a welcome embrace after a long day's work. Money was tight, but the two couples were in it together. Amelia taught Aileen, the first non-Italian in the family, how to make gravy and risotto and the foursome spent many a late night on the back porch enjoying a glass or two of wine, sharing old memories and new hopes.

Ernest hadn't abandoned his dream to start a winery. He knew the timing was almost perfect and he was confident he could pull it off. Millions of Europeans had immigrated to the United States since 1919, meaning there would be millions more consumers eager for a taste of home. Someone had to quench their thirst. Why not him?

It was a given that Fruit Industries, Roma, and Italian Swiss Colony would resume their roles as the industry's behemoths. All three were still in business, having been granted licenses during Prohibition to supply the sacramental and "medicinal" wine market. Rumor had it Italian Swiss Colony had made much more wine than it could have possibly sold and had a million gallons in storage. But even if that were true, there would still be room in the market for other competitors. After all, before Prohibition there had been seven hundred wineries in California, and though most had gone under, it seemed reasonable to expect the demand would return or maybe even grow. It was as if the industry had been in a thirteen-year coma, utterly oblivious while time and progress marched ahead. Equipment had been abandoned and fallen apart. Coopers had stopped making barrels. Seasoned viticulturists had passed away, changed professions, or moved back to Europe. Even some of the oldest vines, brought to California in the 1850s by Hungarian Agoston Haraszthy, the "Father of California Viticulture," had been wrenched from the ground and replaced by melons and onions.

On March 21, 1933, three days after Ernest's twenty-fourth birthday, Congress passed the Cullen-Harrison Act, legalizing the sale of low-alcohol beer and wine. Upon signing the legislation, the country's new president, Franklin Delano Roosevelt, quipped, "I think this would be a good time for a beer." Ernest was ecstatic. He didn't have the capital to start a winery, but for little more than a monthly lease he could start with a storeroom in San Francisco—a way station where Napa and Central Valley wineries could hold barrels ordered by the city's shops and saloons. That June, Ernest applied for a permit from the San Francisco Prohibition Office, but to his chagrin, it was rejected. The law stated one couldn't open a storeroom unless one owned a winery.

And Ernest knew all too well that one couldn't own a winery unless one owned his own vineyards. He fumed. He couldn't remember feeling so angry. If Father had kept his promise and put just one measly acre in his name, he would be in business. It was as if Father had fused a bit in Ernest's mouth upon his birth and still held the reins in his fists. Anytime Ernest picked up any kind of momentum or veered off the approved course, Father would yank back, stopping him in his tracks.

Frustrated but undeterred, Ernest considered his options. It was possible the requirements to open a winery would change. The bureaucrats certainly would be busy creating new laws and regulations. Whatever they came up with was sure to be unnecessarily complicated. But right now that was irrelevant, for he would still have to deliver Father an ultimatum to give or sell him a parcel of land. He wouldn't—he couldn't—take no for an answer. Trying to think of the best way to approach his father, he realized that if he and Julio acted together, he might fare better. His younger brother had a knack for stepping in at the perfect moment when things got too heated between him and Father. Plus, whatever arrangement Ernest made with Father, Julio should get the same.

As Ernest strategized, a new idea came to him. He'd always imagined starting his business alone, but if he had a partner, it would make it easier to manage the vineyards and make and sell the wine. After all, who would watch the vineyards and wine while he was out of town making sales calls? The wine wasn't going to sell itself and he imagined he'd be on the road a lot. He wouldn't be able to handle everything and he wouldn't be able to hire any help. At least not until he turned a profit. Julio was the only person he knew who worked as hard as he did. And the only person he truly trusted. For the first time, it struck him that his brother was his best friend. And his brother would be a perfect business partner.

It had been four years since Ernest and Julio's waterlogged round-the-clock effort to groom the acreage across from the house. After the heartbreak of losing their first crop to the soil they had ruined, they tenderly nursed the new cuttings they had planted in the spring. At first the one-year-old canes clipped from their Zinfandels and Carignanes looked like a stick farm. But now they had grown taller and sprouted bright green, three-lobed, notched leaves.

Ernest and Julio crossed Maze Road at sunrise with a roll of chicken wire, two pairs of wire cutters, a thermos, and two blue speckled enamel cups. Each had a pair of worn work gloves hanging from his back pocket. A doe and her two fawns startled at the pair's arrival and darted away.

"Looks like we're too late," Julio said, nodding his head toward the retreating animals. The brothers were there to place protective sleeves of wire around each plant to prevent deer and rabbits from pillaging the vines. The sun was just rising over the horizon, casting the field in a peach-tinged glow. Ernest unclipped the lid of the thermos bottle and poured some black coffee into a cup. He handed it to Julio and poured some for himself.

"I'm going into the wine business," Ernest announced. "And I want you to be my partner."

"What?" Julio asked.

"I said, I'm—"

"No, I heard you all right. But I thought you were over that after you didn't get the permit," Julio said. "What happened to going back to school and becoming a lawyer?"

"I can't go back to school now. I'm a married man. Amelia and I want to start a family."

"I would have thought you'd have had enough of this business. I know I'd be happy if I never saw another grape again."

"Wine. Not grapes. *Vino.* It's different. I just want to know if you're in."

Julio sighed, searching for the best way to begin. "I can't, Ernest. You know I've been planning on getting into cattle. I'm too far down that road."

"Don't say no. Hear me out. We'll be partners, fifty-fifty. You know how we missed out on having a real hometown and lots of family around? This is our chance to stay together. In Modesto. Our kids will go to the same school. We'll—"

"Hey. I'm not leaving Modesto. We'll still be close. You'll sell wine and I'll sell milk."

"But that's not the same. I really want this, Julio," Ernest pled.

"See, that's the thing with you. What about what I want? Why does it always have to be about what you want?"

"What are you saying?" Ernest asked.

"You're my brother. My big brother..." Julio began. "And...I don't know. I just don't think it's a good idea. I really feel like I need to be on my own. I need some breathing room. Away from this family."

"This family or me?"

"Don't turn this into a fight," Julio snapped with frustration.

"I'm not. Just hear me out. The wine business is going to explode. Michigan, Wisconsin, Rhode Island, Wyoming, and New Jersey have already ratified the Twenty-First Amendment. The rest of the states will—"

"That's great. Do you even know how to make wine? I mean more than a couple hundred gallons?"

"I'm going to start as a distributor, selling other—"

"And compete against Fruit Industries and Roma?"

"Sure. Why not? I'll work harder than any one of them. But I don't want to do it alone. We can start a family business. Pass it down to our children. And grandchildren," Ernest argued.

"You can do that, Ernest. And my children will inherit my dairy. You know I've wanted to do this for a while. It can't come as a surprise."

"I know, but—"

"I've put a lot of work into this. You can't ask me to give up on my dream so you can follow yours." Absentmindedly, Julio started to kick at a rock embedded in the ground, trying to dislodge it.

"Okay. I get it," Ernest said quietly. "Just sleep on it, will ya?"

"Yeah. Sure," Julio agreed, but his mind was made up.

"Just one more thing. Look around. Now they're just sticks. But these vines will be putting out grapes for a hundred years. Think of that. This can be our legacy. We know this business. It's in our blood. It's different when it's just you and me. You've seen how much fun we have without Father. You belong here,

Julio. This is you. This is me. This is who we are. And where we belong."

"Look, I said I'd think about it. Can we get to work now?" Julio barked.

Later that afternoon Ernest went over to the Franzias' home to return a platter Amelia had borrowed. He was embarrassed to have interrupted his mother-in-law, Teresa, and all five of Amelia's brothers in deep discussion around the dining room table.

"Uh, I'm really sorry," he said, standing in the hallway. "Amelia wanted me to return this."

"No problem. Join us," Teresa said warmly. "Giuseppe's out of town. So you can be the deciding vote." She placed two small glasses of wine in front of Ernest.

"Try the one on the left first," she advised.

Ernest looked around at all the expectant faces and took a slow and deliberate sip from each glass. In an affected manner, he lifted his nose in the air, raised his pinkie, and crooned, "This one reminds me of grilled cherries. It's accessible, but not too forward. The second one finishes like a Wagner opera. Perfectly herbaceous."

Once everyone stopped laughing, Teresa addressed him again, "Seriously, what did you think?"

"You know me. My tastes are simple. If I'd drink a second glass, it means I like it. And I'd have another glass of both," Ernest shrugged.

The family broke out in groans and pleas, both sides advocating for their preferred wine. Good-natured jibes led to laughter and an invitation to stay for dinner. Ernest reluctantly declined knowing Amelia and Aileen would be expecting him.

As he drove home, he wrestled with his emotions. He loved being with Amelia's family. There was a warmth and ease he'd only recently come to know. He did his best to shut out whispers of envy over their commitment to each other and their new venture. Franzia had already bequeathed land to his sons and now they were all involved in their new winery. They were a team through thick and thin.

Julio had to agree to be his partner. That's all there was to it. Together they could create a stability their family had never known. They were a good team. Always had been. Julio challenged him and understood him in a way no one else ever did. Joe Junior could join them after college. He had asked Julio to sleep on it, so he couldn't bring it up when he got home. He'd just have to be patient.

The next morning, the two set off for the vineyard, chicken wire and coffee in tow. Another glorious sunrise greeted them as they set to work.

"Well?" Ernest queried.

"Look, I thought about it and I just can't. It's too risky. No one knows what the repeal of Prohibition is going to look like. And I've already got a lead on a cattle ranch that's going up for sale. Sorry. I really am."

"Wait. I thought about it some more. I almost forgot about Joseph. He can join us too. He can study viticulture in school and add to what we already know. By the time he graduates we'll be ready for him," Ernest added.

"That's a nice idea, but I still can't do it," Julio said as he held his ground.

"What are you afraid of?"

"It's not that I'm afraid. Look, I'm a farmer. You know how much I hate traveling. I couldn't bear another season in New

Jersey or Chicago. I want to be home. With Aileen. I want to be around for my kids when we have them," Julio explained.

"No problem. We can work that out. This…" Ernest said as he swung his arm toward the vineyard, "this is where you're happy, Julio. You stay here and grow the grapes. And I know you'll love making the wine too. I'll do all the selling. I'll do all the traveling. You'll never have to leave home. Leave all that to me."

"I appreciate that, but—"

"Tell you what. One year. Give it one year. The cows will be there. But wine…we need to get in early. If you don't like it after one year, then okay, we tried. You buy your dairy farm and we both live happily ever after," Ernest proposed.

"Ernest. Don't."

"Don't what?" Ernest asked.

"Don't do this. Don't work me. I'm saying no."

"But—" Ernest started to protest before he caught the look on his brother's face. He couldn't quite sort out if it was resolve, frustration, animosity, or hurt—or maybe a mixture of all four. No matter. He respected Julio's request and dropped the subject.

The disappointment Ernest felt over Julio's refusal was profound. It was just a refusal, he reminded himself, but it still felt like rejection. He couldn't blame Julio. He had been talking about the dairy business for months. It was no secret. And he wasn't surprised at Julio's stubbornness. He respected it. But at the same time he wished Julio could share his vision. He would never want anyone to give up on his dreams, especially his brother, but he sure hoped Julio would come around.

Ernest's mind never found a moment's rest. Even in his sleep he was creating balance sheets and negotiating with lenders. Because he had no assets, he knew his chances of getting a loan were slim. But he had faith in his intellect, work ethic, ingenuity, and salesmanship. All he needed was someone to believe in him. Someone to give him a chance. He wouldn't let them down. That, and he had to find it within himself to go to Fresno and finally demand what he needed from his father.

With Father a hundred miles away, Ernest had at last been able to prune the vines the way he wanted, following a new technique recommended by the University of California, Davis, the leading expert in American viticulture. If he had stopped to analyze his feelings, he would have been embarrassed at the twinges of satisfaction he felt knowing how upset Father would be to see him snipping off the clusters of green pea-size berries. With each squeeze of the shears he felt father's emotional bondage loosen its grip.

Alone in the field behind the house, Ernest paused to take in his surroundings. With the lavender and blue mountains as a distant and glorious backdrop, the sun's rays broke through the impossibly white cumulus clouds in streaks from above. Viewed from a distance, the vineyard sated man's hunger for order—the vines aligned in perfect, evenly spaced lines, as if drawn by a draftsman's straight edge. But closer inspection revealed a formidable opponent. The gnarled, twisted trunks told of the vine's vigor and might; its will to stretch and curl and find its own path to sun and water. Without man's guiding hand, the vineyard would be a tangle of woody stalks, canes, and leaves that starved the fruit of the sun it needed to prosper.

Ernest closed his eyes and let the warm air fill his lungs. He swelled with humility and gratitude. An old prayer rippled through his head: *Altissimo, Signore onnipotente, tue sono le lodi, la gloria e l'onore, e tutte le benedizioni.* Most High, all powerful, good Lord, Yours are the praises, the glory, the honor, and all blessing.

He opened his eyes, sensing a stir in the air behind him. He turned to see his sister-in-law hurrying toward him down the grassy path between the vines.

"Ernest, there's a reporter from the *Bee* on the phone. You need to come in," Aileen said breathlessly.

Chapter Ten

TAKE CARE OF EACH OTHER

Ernest arrived at the Fresno funeral home at three o'clock in the afternoon on June 21, 1933. Deputy Coroner William Creager was already there waiting for him. The Prairie Box house had been built by one of the city's founders. Children had once played hide-and-seek in the curtains, holidays had been celebrated, guests had come to visit. But now the only guests who visited were either dead or in grief, shock, or denial. Other than the occasional grim attempt at dark humor, the house was devoid of the laughter that had once filled its rooms.

The bespectacled coroner led Ernest to the back parlor. Ironically, it looked like a tastefully decorated room for the living rather than a place to greet the dead. There was a fireplace and a pair of upholstered wingback chairs. Still-life oil paintings, all by the same artist, lined the papered walls. Someone with an eye for color, design, and texture had carefully appointed the room to create an old-world sense of solemnity and security. But the best of intentions couldn't atone for the two metal gurneys, each mounded with a body-like form draped in a white sheet, in the center of the parlor.

Creager pointed to the two chairs, encouraged Ernest to sit, and tried to prepare him for the gruesome sight that awaited him. No one should have to go through this; losing any family member was tough enough. The deputy coroner was fairly new to the job and this was by far his worst responsibility to date. He apologized for the necessary deed and encouraged the bewildered young man to wait until he was ready.

Ready? The word looped through Ernest's brain. Was he ready? Would he ever be ready? He needed to get ready. Get steady. He exhaled, stood, and walked toward the center of the room. He needed to get it over with. Get out of there. Get home to Amelia. He nodded his assent.

Creager walked to the head of the furthest table and straightened his arms to pull back his suit coat's sleeves ever so slightly. Ernest couldn't help but notice how gingerly the large man pinched the edge of the sheet between his thumb and forefinger, raising it just a few inches.

"That's him," Ernest whispered from the side of the gurney.

When the coroner shuffled a few feet to his right to the other table, his leather-soled shoe kicked one of its metal legs. The table rolled forward a few inches. The surrounding brocade curtains and plush furnishings politely swallowed the clang that rang out, quickly returning the room's sobriety.

"My apologies," Creager whispered.

Ernest turned away as the coroner gently lifted the edge of the other sheet. But he wasn't ready. How could anyone be ready for this? He willed himself to look and assured himself it would just take a second. He could do that. One second. He stared back at Creager and looked down.

The shattered young man opened his mouth, but couldn't form a single word. He dropped his head and squeezed his eyes shut. Mamma. And this is how her life ended. How could this be happening? Her smile. Her embrace. Her love. All gone. Just like that. Snuffed out. Ernest's body shook as an ache he had never known loosened from the bottom of his soul and escaped in a mournful cry.

There was an inquest that afternoon at the sheriff's station. Two men who worked for Father were also there to answer questions. One of them, Max Kane, explained what had happened. After having breakfast that morning with Mr. and Mrs. Gallo, he and a temporary field hand had made two trips into town to get hay. After pitching the second load into the barn, Kane had noticed a bright blue printed cloth in the dirt outside the hog pen. He thought it was a rag, but then recognized it as Mrs. Gallo's dress. He ran over to find her facedown in a pool of blood. Her straw hat lay next to her, a bullet hole through its brim.

Kane couldn't find Joe. The Gallos didn't have a telephone, so he drove to the nearest gas station to call the sheriff. Fifteen minutes later, a sheriff's deputy found Joe on the dining room floor, a bullet hole in his temple, a revolver by his side.

As the story unfolded, Ernest found himself drifting into a detached state. Almost as if Kane were talking about someone else's parents. He glanced around the utilitarian room. One of the sheriffs was taking notes while the other interrupted Kane with an occasional question. Ernest wondered if this was where they took the bad guys. For a fleeting moment he wondered if Uncle Mike had spent any time in this room.

"Your father…did he have any enemies?" the sheriff asked Ernest. "Anyone you can think of who would want to cause him harm?"

Ernest shook his head. "No. No one."

"What do you think happened?"

"Well, I think it's clear what happened," Ernest answered somberly. "My father took my mother's life…and then his own. Did anyone find a note?"

"No, I'm afraid not. Why do you think your father would have done this?"

"He was having financial problems. I can't think of any other reason."

"Did they have marital troubles or anything like that?"

"No."

"They got along okay?"

Ernest thought of telling them about Father's temper. His mood swings. His melancholy. His violent tendencies. About the times he whipped Ernest with his belt buckle. The time he shoved Mamma into the doorjamb. The time he picked Julio up and threw him across the barn. But he knew Mamma would have been deeply embarrassed and heard her familiar admonishment, almost as if she were sitting in the empty wooden chair next to him. *"What happens in the family stays in the family."* The authorities didn't need to know about any of it. Father was gone. Mamma was gone and that was that. Nothing he could tell the sheriffs would bring her back.

"Yes. They loved each other," Ernest answered, believing it to be true.

"So you're confident the situation is a case of murder and suicide?" the sheriff asked.

Ernest's stomach churned and his eyes filled with tears. He pulled a handkerchief from his shirt pocket and wiped them quickly. "Yes," he said softly. "He killed her. He killed himself."

After the inquest ended, Ernest and Kane stayed in the lobby long enough to finish a cigarette. Both in shock, the men exchanged few words, but found some solace in each other's company before parting ways. Weak from the assault on his nerves, Ernest held on to the railing as he made his way down the outside steps of the station. He planted each foot with deliberation before moving ahead. *What now?* he wondered. What did he need to do? Who did he need to speak to first? What would happen to the bodies? How would they get back to Modesto? Thank God Julio had brought Joe Junior up to Modesto the day before, but what would happen to him now? He was still just a kid. Before he could think of a single answer, he was ripped out of his jumble of thoughts.

"Mr. Gallo? Mr. Gallo? I'm with the *Fresno Tribune*. Were you surprised your father murdered your mother?"

The question landed like a baseball bat swung at the side of his head. He even jumped as if he had been struck. Hearing his personal hell phrased so succinctly and matter-of-factly stung more than everything he had already been through.

"Leave me alone," he growled, pushing the brim of his hat over his brow.

"Mr. Gallo, I just wanna ask—"

"Get out of my way!" Ernest yelled, making a beeline to his parked truck, the reporter on his heels. Did everyone already know the horror he was going through? Even this stranger who didn't know him, didn't know Mamma, didn't know Father? How did he even know who Ernest was? How dare he sneak up on him and invade his privacy! Was nothing sacred?

Ernest stopped and spun, bumping into his pursuer and throwing him off balance. "My father murdered my mother!" he screamed. "I saw her. And I saw the devil. *And you want to ask me a question?* Have you no shame?"

He reached the truck, jumped in, and slammed the door shut. He had planned to go to straight to the ranch, but feared the heartless reporter might follow him. He drove in circles until he was sure he was alone and then got a room at the Hotel Fresno on Broadway. The night was long and lonely. Sleep was no match for Ernest's torment and offered no escape. He drove to the raisin farm the next morning. He'd only been once before and was still jarred by the state of the land. He'd never been able to understand what had gone on in Father's mind that had led him to buy such a miserable piece of property. Though he knew both his parents had worked the vineyards tirelessly and hired help when they could, the place looked even more decrepit than it had the year prior. The weeds were taller, the porch lower, and more chips of paint lay in the dirt below the termite-eaten and weatherworn shingles.

Ernest didn't want to visit the scene of the crime, but he felt he owed it to Mamma. Why should he be protected from the horror she had endured? He trudged over to the pen where his father had shot her in the back of the head as she fed the hogs. Ernest looked down at the dark mark by his feet. Her blood. In time the winds of the valley would cast layers of dust over the stain and her last trace would be gone. Why had Father taken her with him? And why here? Slaughtered next to a pigsty. What had happened? Ernest looked at the animals, safe and oblivious on the other side of the pen. The tale they could tell.

Again, the words Mamma had spoken to Julio just yesterday pealed in his head: *"Don't worry about me. I just want you boys to get along and take care of each other."* Why had she said that? Had she known? How could he have saved her? How much of this was his fault? If he had tried harder to get along with Father, maybe they wouldn't have moved to Fresno. And maybe Mamma would still be alive.

Inside the farmhouse Ernest avoided the room where his father had taken his own life. He sat down at the kitchen table and cursed Giuseppe Gallo. He had been a sick, tortured man, but how could he have taken Mamma from them? Sweet, gentle Mamma. Ernest willed himself to hear her voice. Calling his name. Laughing. The singsong way she would say, "Oh, Nino," when she ruffled his hair. He buried his head in his folded arms and wept. He wept for Mamma. For Joe Junior. For Julio. For himself. For the grandchildren who would never know their nonna. For the hard life she had endured. He tried to soothe himself that she was in a better place. With her Lord and Savior. But it didn't help.

He lifted his head and noticed the crucifix on the wall next to the back door. He knelt it front of it, made the sign of the cross, and prayed aloud. "...Holy Mary, Mother of God, pray for us sinners, now and at the hour of our death. Amen." He prayed for Mamma's soul and for strength and guidance. He berated the God who let this happen. And yet he prayed to the God who let this happen. None of it made any sense.

Suddenly he realized it was all on him now. He was the oldest son. The new head of the family. And he had to take care of everything. The funeral. The estate. His little brother, Joe Junior. Modesto. The vineyards would be his. The ramifications of that and the opportunities it would provide simmered in his mind, but he pushed the thoughts aside. He thought of Julio. Sensitive, kind, hardworking Julio. They would get through this together, just like always. Family was everything. Especially now.

Ernest stood to remove the brass cross from the wall, almost stepping on one of Father's orphaned boots. He ignored it and lifted the crucifix in his calloused hands. He kissed Christ's crown of thorns and left Fruitvale Ranch for the second and last time.

Chapter Eleven

FIRST CRUSH

Though the cause of Joe and Susie Gallo's deaths was plain, state regulations regarding homicide autopsies were not. The necessary formalities gave Amelia and Aileen a week to plan the arrangements for their mother- and father-in-law. The closed-casket funeral was held at Saint Stanislaus, their Catholic church in Modesto, with a wake held immediately afterward at the family home. Ernest had moments of lucidity, but mostly felt like he was sitting in a theater watching someone else's tragedy unfold. The day of the funeral rolled by in a somber blur. It was as if someone else were in control of his movements and the words that slipped from his mouth. He knew he must have talked to many of the few hundred mourners, yet he couldn't remember a single face or conversation.

After their wives and visiting family had turned in for what remained of the night, Ernest and Julio sat down on the enclosed back sun porch with a jug of wine and a pack of Camels. For the last week they had focused on acute issues and had agreed to delay any discussion about the future until after the funeral. The only commitment they had made was a pact to never discuss "the troubles" again. What else was there to say and what good would it do? The emotional turmoil and harrowing discussions of the last week had been excruciating and neither wanted to relive any of those feelings again. Best to build a fortress around their sorrow, shame, and anger. Ernest feared a mere whisper of *the troubles* could crumble his emotional wall and spill all the pain anew.

"So..." Ernest exhaled a lungful of smoke into the warm night.

Julio sighed. "Our brides did a nice job. I kept thinking how much Mamma would have liked to see everyone."

"I felt her there. All day. I hope she saw how much she was loved. All those people were there for her. I keep thinking how happy she must be to be with Nonna and Nonno and Our Lord. I know He had His reasons for taking her so soon, but..." Ernest's voice trembled until sobs overtook his words.

Julio put his arm around his brother's shoulder and pulled him close until he stopped shaking. When his breathing evened out, Ernest straightened up and poured two glasses of wine.

"Listen...let's talk about Joe Junior," he said quietly, handing Julio a glass. "I'm going to see what we need to do to become his legal guardians. He'll go to Modesto High and then I'm going to make sure he goes to college. We'll give him the chance we never had."

"I agree," Julio said. "He's a smart kid. Aileen and I will do everything we can to take care of him."

"I can't stop thinking what Mamma said to you: 'I just want you boys to get along and take care of each other.' How did she...?" Ernest took a deep breath and shook it off. "Never mind...I want Joe to go to UC Davis and study viticulture and enology and join me in business when he graduates. By then—"

"Just a sec," Julio interrupted. "I've been thinking about that."

Ernest heard an awkward catch in Julio's voice and wondered if he had been too presumptive. Maybe Julio wanted Joe Junior to join him in his dairy. Though he was the eldest, Ernest didn't want to make family decisions without Julio's input. He respected and valued his brother too much.

"I'm sorry," Ernest said quickly. "I didn't mean to assume that—"

"Ernest, I'm in. I want to be your partner," Julio smiled.

"What? Really?" Ernest stumbled. "Are you serious?"

"Yes."

"But...your cattle ranch? *Your* dreams?" Ernest asked.

"Family comes first. I've been thinking of Mamma's words too. It's what she would have wanted. And it makes sense. The vineyards are ours now, and like you said, wine is in our blood. As long as you do the business side, like we talked about before. I'll take care of the vineyards and the wine. If it doesn't work out, then I can look into cattle. But given—"

"Oh, it will work out. I promise you that," Ernest said with confidence. He stood, stubbed out his cigarette, and raised his glass. Julio rose, lifting his glass in kind.

"To Mamma," said Ernest.

"You know I'm going to make more wine than you can sell," Julio added good-naturedly.

"Ha. I'll sell more wine than you can make. Just watch," Ernest countered.

With that, the brothers clinked glasses, launching the E. & J. Gallo Winery.

As the wine ran over his tongue, Ernest noted it had started to turn. Fitting, he thought. It was as bittersweet as the moment. He renewed his vow to close the door on the recent past. God had opened another door and nothing was going to stop him from charging through it. He would clean up the mess Father had left, take care of the family, and honor Mamma's dying wish.

Ernest made a list of tasks. His first chore was to settle his parents' estate. He couldn't sell Fruitvale Ranch fast enough. He never wanted to see a document with that Fresno address again. Mamma had left a will transferring her modest inheritance to her three sons. But Father had no will. In fact, the only thing he had left behind, besides $1,000 and three motherless sons, was a $30,000 debt. He had never sold his devalued Transamerica stock. Instead, it was still held by the Bank of America as collateral. When Ernest met with the banker later in the week, he was informed that the bank wanted the land back immediately. Only then would they release the stock so he could settle the rest of Joe Gallo's accounts. If he didn't comply, the banker warned, he risked losing everything, including the family home.

The thought of any more loss was an insult Ernest wouldn't consider. He and Julio had worked too hard on that land. They had inhaled its soil. It had worked its way under their fingernails into their bloodstream. They had given each other life. He knew every inch of those one hundred and sixty acres and he was damned if anyone else was going to touch a single grape he had grown, let alone take over any of their vineyards.

Ernest knew the bank would be hard-pressed to find a solvent buyer. Last year—1932—had been the worst year of the Depression to date and there was little sign that 1933 would finish any better. He convinced the banker that they had nothing more to lose by giving him and Julio a chance. The new vines were healthy, and the least risky move for the bank would be to leave the crop in the Gallo brothers' very capable hands.

Ernest's original business plan had been to start with a warehouse in San Francisco and store other people's wine the first year. Then he would invest his profits into making his own wine the next year. No sooner had his application to open a warehouse been rejected than he had begun working on an alternative plan. But on June 21, 1933, all the rules had changed. He was now a vineyard owner, which made him qualified to skip the warehouse step and dive straight into making his own wine. Julio agreed, welcoming the distraction and the focus on moving on with their lives.

Amelia and Aileen encouraged their husbands to slow down. They could start next year. They had no permits, money, facilities, or equipment. It was crazy to think they could get everything they needed in order by the August harvest. Perhaps they should take their time to grieve and heal from the tragedy. That may have been the safe, sensible route. But Ernest's confidence was only outweighed by his impatience. He knew he could pull it off. To any circumspect outsider, however, the odds of the Gallo boys producing a single drop of wine that year seemed insurmountable.

"I can't wait," Ernest explained to Amelia. "Next year will be too late. Everyone will have an advantage over us. I can't—no, I won't—let that happen. It's good for me. Good for Julio. I need to keep busy. I need to push *the troubles* out of my head. I just can't think about it anymore."

But his dreams and plans would remain just that without money. They needed capital—fast. Ernest started with the largest coffer: the Bank of America. The loan officer didn't know if he should laugh at the young man's audacity or scream at him for wasting his time. Hadn't they just let him hold on to his family's land? And now he wanted more? Ernest had known it was a long shot, but also knew there was no harm in trying. He could handle rejection.

Next on his list: family. Ernest went to Oakland to appeal to Aunt Celia. Her response? "Your brother Julio was here last week. I'll tell you the same thing I told him. Your father died owing me $4,000 and I just filed papers with the probate court to get my money back. I wish you boys all the luck your father never had."

Ernest then went to see Aunt Tillie in San Francisco. Her response was a little softer, but the message was the same. "I'm sorry, Nino. I just don't have the money to lose."

Julio joined Ernest to see if their neighbor Claude Maze, for whom their street was named, would give them a small loan. Maze, the wealthiest man in Modesto, was the only person they knew who always seemed to be one step ahead of everyone else. The ridicule in Maze's voice was the unkindest of all. "A *winery*? Now? Boys, it's the Dirty Thirties. You'll end up worse than yer old man. Take my advice: Don't do it. Stick to what you know."

I'll show you, Ernest thought. Rather than letting Maze's cynicism undermine his confidence, he would use the old man's scorn as motivation. He knew he could do anything he set his mind to, and he would prove it to Maze and anyone else who ever questioned him.

Nevertheless, Ernest was running out of options and running out of time. The grapes were getting riper every day. They wouldn't slow down so Ernest Gallo could get all the equipment he needed to make wine. Julio pledged his life's savings of almost $1,000 to the business.

Amelia's belief in her indefatigable husband never wavered. Pained by Ernest's growing frustration, she appealed to her financially savvy mother. Mamma would be a softer touch than Papà. Plus, it had been Mamma's idea to restart the Franzia winery.

Teresa came through and loaned her son-in-law the $5,000 he needed for the Bureau of Alcohol's licensing fees. As much as she cared for him, Teresa was also a shrewd investor. Ernest knew she wouldn't have loaned him the money unless she believed she would get it back. Her confidence bumped the number of people who believed in him to three. He was barreling west along US 48 to San Francisco with his application to manufacture fifty thousand gallons of wine before the ink on Teresa Franzia's check had dried. On the drive, he evaluated his present state.

Experience in producing commercial wine: none.

Experience in marketing wine: none.

Available cash: $900.23.

Borrowed funds: $5,000.

Confidence: Unbounded!

On July 24, 1933, California became the fourteenth state to repeal Prohibition, stoking the fire that burned inside Ernest. Nothing could stop him and Julio now.

Although the Gallos had plenty of land, some of which was still bare, they didn't have the capital to build a winery or a storeroom. A real estate broker showed Ernest an empty ten-thousand-square-foot warehouse for rent just a couple of miles from the home ranch. Conveniently, there was a rail spur that led to an outside loading dock, meaning they could roll wine barrels directly onto the railcars and save money on trucking the barrels to the station. They could even pump it directly into tank cars. The space was perfect. Ernest stood outside the freestanding ivy-covered building with George Beard, the building's manager.

"How much?" Ernest asked, trying not to sound too eager.

"It's a hundred a month."

"That's kind of pricey, don't you think? I've been driving by this corner almost my whole life. This place has been emptier than a banker's heart. How about fifty? That's fifty more than you've been getting."

"Fifty? Can't do that." Beard shook his head as if to underscore his words. "Lowest I can go is seventy-five," he countered.

Ernest pursed his lips and puffed his cheeks. This was only the third property he had looked at. He still had other options and he needed to watch every penny. He released the built-up air from his mouth in a long exhalation. "Sixty and we'll take it," he said at last.

Beard placed his hand on Ernest's shoulder. "Ernest, I feel just terrible about what you boys have been through. Jane and I wanted to help and a beef stew just didn't seem like enough. Sixty it is." Beard took a step back and stretched out his hand.

Inwardly cringing at the reference to *the troubles* and the blatant charity, Ernest accepted Beard's hand with gratitude. A deal was a deal.

The following day Ernest met with the owner of Rossi Machine Company in San Francisco. Rossi had made crushers and presses before Prohibition. Like Ernest, he had predicted the demise of Prohibition and was preparing to capitalize on its death. In the seven months since Roosevelt's victory, Rossi had traveled all over the state, as far south as Los Angeles, the birthplace of the California wine business, looking for neglected equipment he could restore and sell. He sold Ernest a reconditioned grape press and crusher on extended terms.

"We need to talk," Julio said as he sat down across from Ernest at the kitchen table.

"What about?" Ernest replied.

"About the elephant in the room...remember your balance sheet? Your list?"

"What list?" Ernest asked, as confused by Julio's accusatory tone as he was the question.

"Item number one. Experience in producing commercial wine: none. We have the permit, the warehouse...pretty soon we'll have everything we need. We've spent over five thousand. Including most of my nest egg. And guess what? We don't know how to make wine! I mean, two hundred gallons, sure. But remember what it tastes like by June? Vinegar! *Fifty thousand gallons?!* Where do we even begin?"

Ernest rose from the table, clasped his hands behind his back, and began to pace. He looked down at the green and yellow checkered linoleum floor he and Julio had helped install, and remembered how pleased Mamma had been with her new kitchen.

"I know. You're right," he agreed, willing himself not to get swept up in his brother's panic. "We need to figure that out. You know I've been asking around. I've talked to everyone I know."

"I know. Me too. I was thinking of going to the library. I don't know where else to turn. Maybe I'll find something there. I'm running out of options. And time," said Julio.

"Not you. *We.* Let's both go," Ernest suggested. He wanted to make sure Julio understood they were in it together. They had divided their responsibilities, but if they didn't make any wine, there'd be nothing for Ernest to sell.

Julio pushed the narrow drawer back into the quartersawn oak cabinet. "Now what?"

"Let's see if she has any other ideas," Ernest suggested.

He went back to the main desk. The elderly librarian looked up at him and shrugged. "No luck? I didn't think so. No one's come looking for anything like that in over a decade. Now that I think about it, I seem to recall officers coming in and taking all our books about wine and liquor. Sorry, boys."

"Do you have a storage area? Anywhere else we can look?" Ernest pressed.

"Well, you're welcome to look down in the basement. That's where we put the damaged books and things we don't have room for. It's a bit of a mess, but you can take a look."

"Thank you," Ernest replied, before turning to Julio. "How about I check the stacks one more time and then meet you down there?"

Though there had been no books in the card catalog that sounded promising, Ernest retraced his steps through the shelves of books, scanning the spines again, hoping to find a misplaced volume—anything with the words *grape, wine,* or *fermentation* in the title. When he was certain there was nothing there, he joined Julio in the basement.

"How can you even see anything down here?" Ernest asked. The basement had no windows and only two of the ten pendulum lamps had working light bulbs. Julio was bent over a cluttered table under one of the dim lights. "Should I go see if they have a flashlight or a lantern we can borrow?" Ernest offered. "Or even some new bulbs?"

"I already asked. No luck. I've been carrying stuff over here where I can see better. I just finished that section," said Julio, pointing to two neatly organized shelves on the closest bookcase.

Ernest took stock of the room. At some point the library had run out of shelving and the librarians had just started stacking books, journals, and newspapers on any flat surface, including the floor. On the other side of the ceiling, everything was ordered in almost military precision, but down here, behind the scenes, everyone had just given up. Years ago. There was no method. Only madness. Ernest turned to the bookcase behind him to find the US Geographic Board's *Correct Orthography of Geographic Names* sandwiched between *Knickerbocker's History of New York* and *Sons and Lovers* by D. H. Lawrence. He picked up a spilling jumble of musty paper and dropped it on Julio's table, found a stained stool with one short leg, and got to work.

Neither man was wearing a watch, and with no natural light, the day slipped by. Side by side, they silently and methodically sorted through the tangle, both certain they would find something useful. Before Prohibition, wine had been a significant part of the local economy, and surely the prohis hadn't scoured the basement to this extent.

"Eureka! I think I struck gold!" Ernest whooped.

Julio jumped at the sudden outburst.

"Look at this!" Ernest gushed. "*The Fundamentals of Fermentation* and *The Fundamentals of Clarification.* Frederic T. Bioletti of UC Davis." He handed his brother two dusty, yellowed pamphlets for his perusal, adding, "I've heard of him. This is great!"

They leapt up the stairs two at a time. The library had filled since they arrived, but they managed to find two available chairs at a communal table. Each brother carefully read one pamphlet, then switched and read the other one. And then they switched and read them again. And again. They both took copious notes.

"Boys, I'm afraid we're closing now and you need to leave. But you take those old things with you. No one's going to miss them," the librarian whispered over their shoulders. "And when you make your wine, you make sure you bring ol' Mrs. Henderson a bottle."

Waiting for the grapes to ripen, Ernest and Julio began to outfit the empty warehouse. Pacific Redwood was one of the only cooperage companies to survive Prohibition and was struggling to keep up with the sudden demand for barrels. They certainly didn't need the Gallos' business. Yet they had accepted Ernest's handshake and his word as a down payment, trusting he would pay them in full after he had sold his wine. The coopers trucked bundles of precut redwood staves to Modesto from San Francisco and assembled the four three-thousand-gallon fermenting tanks right inside the warehouse. Ernest and Julio tag-teamed between their new winery and vineyards, their ears needing relief from the craftsmen's hammers striking the steel hoops in place.

Once the tanks were finished, Ernest went back to San Francisco to buy the rest of the equipment they needed—a must pump, a wine pump, an ebulliometer to measure alcohol levels, a saccharometer to measure sugar levels, and a basic old-fashioned thermometer. While he was gone, Julio built shelves to hold the new tools and prepared the space. If Amelia was going to be in charge of shipping and tax stamps, she needed a desk for her typewriter. He grabbed hold of one of the fifty-gallon barrels that Pacific Tank had delivered and rolled it to the back corner of the warehouse—as far away as possible from the noisy electric destemmer/crusher. Ernest later brought her a matching stool from the family barn—a ten-gallon cask.

In order to reach their fifty-thousand-gallon goal, Ernest had calculated they would need more grapes than they could possibly grow. Though they owned 290 acres of land, only a small fraction had productive vines. One acre of seven hundred vines yielded an average of four tons of grapes. So considering it took a ton of grapes to make 120 gallons of wine, one acre would yield approximately 480 gallons of wine.

Like any commodity, grape prices could swing significantly from year to year. In 1933, the going rate was fourteen dollars a ton. The Franzias and other wineries had already made deals with local grape growers guaranteeing them payment upon harvest. But the Gallos didn't have that kind of money. The irony and frustration was that Ernest expected to sell his wine for at least twice what the grapes would cost. But by the time he had the cash, the vineyards would be picked clean.

On the drive home after his first meeting with Pacific Tank, Ernest wondered if any growers would agree to a similar deal and sell him their grapes on consignment. The first couple of farmers turned him down once they figured out what he was proposing. They couldn't take that kind of chance. Why should they wait until the end of the year for his money when everyone else was going to pay them at harvest? In addition, who knew if his wine would be any good or if anyone would even buy it?

Realizing he needed to sweeten the pot, Ernest came up with an irresistible offer. He called it a "share deal." It still involved no payment up front, but in return, he would give the growers two-thirds of the profits on the wine he sold. Although he couldn't make any hard promises, he predicted they would earn thirty dollars a ton, more than twice what they were getting from other wineries. Ernest began to hear more yeses than nos. The growers were a tight-knit bunch and word quickly spread about the promising young kid—"one of us"—in the old corner warehouse. Ernest knew his offer was appealing, but he also understood the farmers' blight and the desperation of the times firsthand. Few were in a position to turn down an easy buck and most were at the ends of their ropes.

That first year, Ernest and Julio started what would become an annual tradition. Their deal with each grower was contingent on them visiting his vineyards before dawn on the first day of harvest—before he had clipped a single cluster—to ensure the grapes they were promised were fully mature and had no mold. The Gallos' intolerance for the slightest inferiority would become legendary.

Ernest had been so focused on equipping the winery and shopping for grapes that he had given little thought to their own vineyards. It suddenly occurred to him that he had forgotten to factor in their newly bearing vines. They would need more pickers than usual, and on top of that, he and Julio would be tied up at the winery. He couldn't imagine how they would manage for they had no money left for extra wages. He found Julio having a smoke outside the warehouse and started to explain the situation.

"That's what I've been saying for *weeks*!" Julio barked, throwing his hands in the air, flinging the ash from his cigarette. "I *knew* you weren't listening! Your head has been stuck in the clouds. I've brought this up so—"

"You're right. You're right. I'm sorry. Let me think. Let's not worry. There's a solution. We just have to find it," Ernest said, holding up his palms, as if to stop time and needless panic.

"This whole thing has been such a mistake. We should have stuck to what we know—growing grapes. Who knows if we'll even be able to make wine? Or if it will be drinkable? You know what? *You* figure it out. The grapes behind the house will be ready tomorrow. See you at dawn." With that, Julio strode over to the truck they shared and drove home. Ernest could hoof it for all he cared.

A cascade of guilt flooded over Ernest. He never should have involved Julio. He could abide his own failure, but he couldn't bring his brother down with him. Not after their experience in El Centro and everything else they had been through.

Julio was asleep by the time Ernest got home and out of the house before he had risen the next morning. Ernest dragged himself out of bed and into the kitchen. Through the window, he made out his brother's shape and some full lug boxes at the end of the row he was working. Even from fifty yards away Ernest could tell he was still mad. He decided to start at the opposite end of the field, but couldn't find a knife and still had to talk to Julio. Maybe, he reasoned, it was better to apologize now anyway.

As he approached his brother, Ernest noticed a solitary hulking figure with a distinct gait coming down the driveway.

"Hey, Julio! Is that your track coach?" Ernest asked doubtfully.

Julio looked up and squinted. The sun was still just a promise and all matter was ill defined and tinted the same bluish-gray. "*Coach Marquam*?" Julio walked toward him.

Ernest followed his brother to see what was going on. It was indeed Coach Marquam, but he wasn't alone. Whether he was aware of it or not, he was followed by a trail of people—alone, in pairs, in large groups. Some carried baskets. Others were empty-handed. But all were there to help the family so recently struck by unspeakable tragedy. Parishioners from Saint Stanislaus, old classmates and teachers, members of the Modesto Italian-American Club, even Mrs. Henderson from the library…all in overalls and old farm dresses. With hearts eager to do as much as they could for those poor Gallo boys, they carried hearty stews, homemade treats, and harvest knives.

As much as they didn't want anyone's pity, Ernest and Julio were grateful for the kindness and willing hands, especially when most had so little to give. Julio assumed that Ernest had enlisted the town's help after their disagreement the previous day. But in truth, there hadn't been enough time to spread the word, so Ernest had prayed—to Jesus, Mary, and Joseph, and all the saints. He had asked for forgiveness, humility, grace, and a miracle. And his prayers had been answered.

The temperatures and rainfall had been optimal that year and the vines showed their appreciation by bearing abundant, full, and heavy clusters. When the grapes were trucked to the warehouse, Ernest and Julio carefully sorted through each lug box, discarding any rogue berries before dumping the rest into the crusher. Intending to make blended wine, they didn't separate the varieties. Thompsons, Zinfandels, Alicante Bouschets, and Carignanes...they all went into the crusher together. Then the crushed fruit—or must—was pumped into one of the four fermenting tanks. The tanks were open at the top so winemakers could attend to the pomace cap that always formed. As the must fermented, the crushed stems and skins floated to the top, foaming and expanding like rising bread dough. If the pomace cap dried out, vinegar gnats were quickly drawn to the irresistible odor. So twice a day, one of the brothers would balance on two-by-twelve planks that ran across the top of the tanks and punch down the pomace with a long, blunt-ended paddle.

Ernest and Julio cared for their first crush like new parents—equally nervous and vigilant. They took turns sleeping next to the fermenting tanks, setting an alarm clock to break the pomace cap at regular intervals. Because Amelia was helping with the books, Aileen managed the household, sending Joe Junior over with meals and hot coffee throughout the day.

Julio checked the hydrometer with increasing frequency, carefully noting the Brix levels for sugar content and the wine's potential alcohol level. He wanted a dry wine, meaning the added yeasts had turned almost all of the sugar from the grapes into alcohol. By the seventh day he was taking readings every hour.

"Ernest, come here. I think it's ready!" he shouted.

"How is it?" Ernest called back, hoping for the best and fearing the worst.

"I'm not going to try it without you! Get over here."

Ernest had been painting numbers on the barrels in a system he had devised for keeping track of their stock. "Just a sec!" He placed the paintbrush in a jar and wiped his hands on his dungarees. "We forgot to get glasses!" He rummaged around in some boxes to no avail and at last dumped the pencils and pens from the battered tin cup on Amelia's desk. He wiped it out with his shirttail and handed it to Julio.

Julio climbed the ladder next to the vat and dipped the cup through the pomace into the rich, aromatic nectar. He leaned down to offer it to his older brother.

Ernest politely declined. "You first." He scrutinized Julio's face as his brother lifted the cup to his lips. It was as if Ernest's palate and his brain were connected to Julio's. His brother's slightest expression would inform his opinion of the wine as much as if he had tasted it himself. To his relief, he detected a glimmer in Julio's eyes before his brother even opened his mouth.

"*Salute*! We did it, my brother! It's good. It's really good!" Julio praised.

"To the E. & J. Gallo Winery and the first crush of many," Ernest added. "Now hand me that cup!"

It happened that 1933 was a bumper year. The grapes kept coming, and twenty-four-year-old Ernest and twenty-three-year-old Julio kept making wine.

"Last barrel," Julio announced one afternoon. He reached over and turned off the pump and then tapped the stopper into the bunghole. "We're done," he said with a sigh of satisfaction.

"Not necessarily..." Ernest said cryptically.

"Not sure what you're getting at. But look around. They're all full. No more storage," said Julio. In just three weeks they had filled the warehouse with rows of barrels stacked four high.

"But there's five weeks left of harvest," Ernest stated. "We can make more. That truck I turned away yesterday? I lay awake all night thinking about those berries in someone else's crusher."

"But our permit's for fifty thousand gallons. We've already exceeded that. And like I said, we have no more room."

"I know. But...remember those underground storage tanks Father and Uncle Mike built? We can use them. No one will be any the wiser. We'll barrel it after we sell everything here. I'll apply for another permit so it will all be on the straight and narrow."

By December they had made 177,847 gallons of red table wine. But they hadn't sold a drop. Ernest and Julio had been so busy getting ready for their first crush, they hadn't had time to find bottlers and distributors.

~

Ernest briefly released his death grip on the armrest to wipe his brow with his crumpled handkerchief. He stuffed the soggy square back in his pocket and reclaimed his handhold. This was not the glamorous ride of the future that the airline had advertised, and he braced himself for the next landing. As if to demonstrate just how much terror it could inflict, the aircraft tossed its thirteen occupants like a salad throughout the flight and then threw them back in their seats with each landing. Ernest wondered just how many more times they would need to refuel before they reached Chicago.

He prayed it would be worth the abuse and extravagant expense. He had called Western Union and bought the ticket yesterday as soon as he had received Charles Barbera's letter. It was a bold move. Barbera had sent a form letter and Ernest knew he would have sent a copy to everyone he knew in California. The man Ernest had met while buying his first Chicago hot dog was getting into the bottling and distribution business and needed bulk wine.

Days ahead of his competitors who would all be arriving by train, Ernest was waiting outside Barbera's office, conveniently located across the street from the rail yards, when his old friend arrived for work.

"Hey, it's Ernesto from Modesto! This is a nice surprise," Barbera smiled as he unlocked the door to his office. "We missed you on the yards this year. Come in."

He opened the door to a small office as practical and guileless as he was. The walls were bare but for a promotional calendar commemorating the Chicago World's Fair, now in its seventh month. Arms outstretched overhead, a muse in a flowing skirt was perched atop a globe, the words "Century of Progress" in a banner above; "Windy City Insurance" below.

"Have you been?" Ernest asked, nodding his head at the calendar.

"You bet. You?"

"Nah. No time. See, my brother and I started our own winery. That's why I'm here. You're looking for juice to bottle and I've got juice to sell. I brought some samples with me."

"No kidding. Good for you. Let me try them."

Ernest took a "tenth"—or split—from his case and poured Barbera a taste, glancing at it quickly to be sure it looked all right. After he had bottled the samples, Ernest had noticed the wine was cloudy. It was to be expected given its young age. So before leaving Modesto he had run it through diatomaceous earth to remove small particulates, and to his relief, it was still clear.

"Hmm. Not bad. It tastes just like the stuff I make. Would you be able to set me up with six thousand gallons?"

Ernest's heart pounded and an uninhibited grin spread across his face. He shook Barbera's hand, and just like that, E. & J. Gallo Winery had made its first sale. Not a moment too soon, Ernest thought, considering the first payments on the equipment were due that month. He closed the deal at fifty cents a gallon.

While he was in Chicago, Ernest hit the pavement looking for more buyers. It wasn't easy. After thirteen years of Prohibition you couldn't just go to the telephone book and look up "wine distributor." Bottlers had dried up in lockstep with their West Coast suppliers. The industry no longer had any infrastructure and Ernest would have to be creative. Knowing that churches had been buying wine for the sacrament, he thought a priest might be able to refer him to the parish's supplier. It would be a starting place, anyway. After he had exhausted that avenue, he called glass factories to see who was ordering wine bottles.

By his second week in Chicago, the young wine had turned increasingly cloudy. At the end of every day Ernest would pour each bottle though a paper filter over the bathroom sink in his hotel room until it was clear. He'd hang the filter to dry and roll the bottles back in newspaper for safekeeping.

On his last day in the city, he followed a lead from the hotel manager, tramping through fresh fallen snow for blocks until he finally reached a nondescript brick tenement. He checked the address twice before walking down the cement steps and knocking on the basement door. When there was no answer, he tried the handle, surprised to find the door unlocked. He pushed it open and was greeted by a familiar fruity and musty aroma. The small room was a hub of activity and filled to capacity. Around twenty aproned women stood behind rows of tables, filling bottles from wine barrels and applying labels with their gloved hands.

One of the women stepped forward to see what he wanted. Her question left her mouth in a puff of crystallized air. It was almost as cold inside as it was outside.

"I want to see your boss," Ernest told her.

"He's not here. Why do you want to see him?" she asked, her eyebrows furrowing as she looked the stranger up and down, making no effort to hide her suspicion and distrust. Ernest wondered if she could be any less friendly.

"I want to sell him some wine."

"Wait a minute," she said before ducking her head to fit through the small door at the back of the room.

She returned wordlessly and went back to her work. Soon a bearded man wearing round tortoiseshell spectacles shuffled in from the same door.

"Do you have any samples?" he asked in a thick European accent Ernest couldn't place.

Ernest unwrapped one of his bottles and poured a small taste. The man held the glass up toward the small filthy window just below the ceiling, as if a ray of natural light could somehow break through the grime and reveal the wine's color and clarity. He spun the liquid around the sides of the glass and stuck his nose inside as deep as it could possibly reach. At last he took a sip. Ernest studied the man's face as he swished the wine around his mouth before swallowing, but couldn't read his reaction.

"How much?"

"Fifty cents a gallon," Ernest replied.

"Och. I can't be bothered with cheap wine. I have a reputation," he said, his voice full of insult.

"I understand," Ernest said, surprised by the man's answer, his mind scrambling for a way out. "And I think I can help. Could you afford wine that was ninety cents a gallon?"

When the man nodded his assent, Ernest reached for his second bottle, drawn from the same tank as the first, and poured another sample.

"Try this one," Ernest urged. "This is my special blend for discriminating buyers. Not everyone can appreciate its finer qualities."

The man repeated his tasting routine. "This…this is good stuff," he enthused, unable to tell he was drinking the exact same wine. "Can you send me a hundred barrels?"

Before returning home to Modesto, Ernest went to New York and sold the rest of their wine—all 177,847 gallons. From some buyers he got fifty cents a gallon; others, ninety. He was still in the city on December 5, 1933, the day President Franklin Delano Roosevelt formally ended Prohibition. It was the first time in history an amendment to the United States Constitution had been repealed.

Grateful the year was over, Ernest spent New Year's Eve alone in a crowd of thousands and watched the lighted ball drop over Times Square. Yes, 1933 had ended well and marked the founding of the E. & J. Gallo Winery and the realization of Ernest's dream, but the year would forever by contaminated by Father's heinous crime.

"You *must* say yes," Ernest urged. "You just *must*."

"I'm sorry, Mr. Gallo. The bank's position on this is intractable," the manager said grimly.

"You've got to be joking," Ernest replied. He could not believe he was in this spot. He had committed buyers for *all* of their wine, but still needed more than two thousand barrels to ship his product. "Do you not understand that I've already *sold* the wine? As soon as the wine is received on the other end, I'll have payment. Your loan will be repaid *immediately*."

"I understand your predicament, but my hands are tied. I'm sorry," said the manager. "These are tough times for everyone."

"You think I don't know that? I'm telling you the wine is *sold*," Ernest repeated, his voice rising with his frustration. "You'll be repaid in no more than two weeks. I'll be getting checks for close to a hundred thousand dollars and you're telling me the Bank of America can't loan me *five hundred* dollars?! How do you expect us to pay you *any* of the money we owe you if we can't deliver our product?"

The manager excused himself. Ernest had been sitting in his office for two hours and he needed to clear his head. He called the regional loan department from the assistant manager's phone to explain the situation and got approval to issue the loan. He took his time cutting the check, though, quite happy to exert some power over the unapologetic force in his office. *Let the fireplug sweat a little more,* he thought.

"Sign this and don't come back to borrow any more money this year," the manager gruffly warned before handing Ernest a check for $500.

Although the negotiation had been frustrating and taken much longer than it should have, Ernest didn't hold on to any of his angst or begrudge the bank manager. The man was just trying to do his job. Ernest had gotten what he wanted and that's what mattered. He put the morning behind him and moved ahead with his day, thinking about his next steps.

"What in God's name are you fellows doing?"

Ernest and Julio continued rolling the five-hundred-pound barrel up the ramp and pushed it into the railcar.

"What does it look like we're doing?" Ernest grunted at the stranger.

"Hey, it's Jack!" Julio exclaimed. "Ernest, remember I told you about Jack Riorda from the New York auctions?" Julio walked over to shake his friend's hand. "You still with Italian Swiss?"

"Not anymore. Just opened my own winery. In Napa. I was driving through town and thought I'd stop and say howdy. Met your bride. Congratulations, by the way. She told me I'd find you here," Riorda smiled. "Seriously, though. What are you doing?"

"We're sending it to Chicago…our first press," Julio added proudly.

"Tell me you're joking. That wine is too new. It will never make it. It's still fermenting! Why, it'll blow those barrels clear apart!" Riorda warned.

Ernest looked at Julio's friend. Italian Swiss Colony in Sonoma was one of the oldest and most successful wineries in California. If Riorda had worked for ISC, then he was no slouch. He knew his stuff. Besides, Julio had always spoken highly of him.

Ernest felt his heart race. The pamphlets from the library had said nothing about waiting to barrel. What if Riorda was right? That would be the end of the E. & J. Gallo Winery. They'd be out of business before they had even left the gate. All their work would be for naught. They could say goodbye to the family's land they had struggled to save and hello to bankruptcy. He would have let everyone down. And no one would trust him again. His word would mean nothing.

To make it worse, Riorda continued his doom and gloom. "You boys have gotta be patient. Our wine? We're aging it for at least a year. Then we'll get a dollar a gallon. That's how you make money."

"Well, our buyers want it now and we need the money. We're already getting ninety cents," Ernest shrugged, his voice less assured than usual.

"You'll regret it. Even if it makes it to Chicago, they'll send it right back on the next train after they taste it."

"Well, it's too late to do anything about it now," Julio shrugged. "We don't have a choice at this point."

Ernest counted the days, mentally tracking his future obliviously chugging along through Nevada, Utah, Colorado, Nebraska, and Iowa. He knew every landmark, every station, and was haunted by images of his barrels bursting apart at the seams, his precious wine sloshing back and forth in the railcars, spilling out the sides and coating the tracks, forming pink ice. On the fifth day, he waited for Barbera's angry call informing him of the mess he'd found when he pulled open the doors of the railcars. Ernest scolded himself for his ignorance. But the phone never rang. Instead, Barbera sent a wire, congratulating his young friend on his success. All the wine they shipped that year arrived intact. After expenses, the winery made $30,000, almost the exact amount of debt Joe Gallo had harnessed on his sons.

Rather than quenching Ernest's drive, the taste of success only left him thirsty for more. The following year, E. & J. Gallo sold 450,000 gallons of wine and doubled that figure in 1935. Within two years Ernest paid off the last of his father's debts. Against all odds, he had held on to the family's property during the worst fiscal crisis in US history. Though the son couldn't atone for his father's sins, he had at least cleaned up the mess the man had left behind—or at least the financial part. No mortal could clean up the emotional damage Joe Gallo had wrought.

Chapter Twelve

FRESH AIR

Though his boast had been good-natured and without any serious intent, Ernest actually was selling more wine than Julio could make. While he spent five months of the year on the road—focusing on Southern California and a few East Coast markets—it was up to Julio to ensure they could fulfill the incoming orders. They shipped barrels of wine directly to regional bottlers who would bottle it and distribute it to storekeepers. Each bottler printed his own labels with no regard to winery, grape varietal, region, or year. Wine was considered a commodity. So if Julio couldn't make enough, he could buy it in bulk from other wineries and blend it, or not, in Modesto. He cultivated relationships with vintners in the Central Valley and as far away as Lodi to the north and Sonoma and Napa to the northwest.

After their first year in business, the brothers agreed on a mission that would inform every decision they made and determine the trajectory of their company. To distinguish E. & J. Gallo from every other winery, they would focus on two goals: to escalate Americans' consumption and appreciation of wine by introducing increasingly sophisticated beverages as their palates matured; and to give American consumers the highest quality product at the most affordable prices. Let those in Napa make the varietals, the fancy Cadillacs of wine, and compete against the French.

Buying wholesale and surplus wine from others to fulfill their orders gave the Gallos less control over their prices and the quality of their final product. They could keep their costs down by making all, if not most, of the wine they sold. But they had utilized every square inch of their rented ivy-covered warehouse and there wasn't room for the equipment they needed to make the volume of wine they knew they could sell, not to mention space to store all the barrels.

Because Ernest was rarely in town and the vineyards were in winter dormancy, Julio spearheaded the search for land they could develop. He settled on ten acres on Dry Creek just north of the Tuolumne River, not even half a mile from their current location. By 1936, Ernest and Julio had collateral, bulletproof financial statements, stellar reputations, and an optimistic but achievable business plan. And after carrying their documents into the bank, they walked out with the half-million-dollar loan they needed to build a state-of-the-art winery.

Julio consulted with experts at the University of California's Berkeley and Davis campuses to make sure they installed the most efficient and technologically advanced equipment. Plans for the assembly line–like winery included conveyor belts that led to two rotary centrifugal crushers that could process sixty tons of grapes an hour. The wine would be pumped through an elaborate filtration system and network of pipes to forty-thousand-gallon concrete fermenting tanks, which could be built much larger than redwood tanks and were leak-proof, more hygienic and easier to clean, and offered better temperature regulation.

No expense was spared on the equipment needed to produce better-tasting, vast quantities of wine. The shipping dock and office buildings were almost an afterthought. The modest one-story concrete and wood structures were rudimentary, but serviceable. Neither brother planned on spending much time behind a desk and couldn't see any reason to squander funds that could be better used elsewhere.

"The front desk told me you called," Ernest said into the receiver. "Everything okay?"

"No, it's not," Julio snapped. "I got a call from John this morning. He said you told him to go ahead and install two more tanks."

Ernest sat on the edge of the phone booth's small mahogany seat with a sigh and pulled the bifold door closed. He felt like he was coming down with something and wrapped his scarf snugly around his neck. He hadn't been able to tighten the broken valve on the radiator next to his bed and had been blasted by a dry inferno all night. He'd cracked the window open for relief, wrestled with the bedcovers for hours, and woken up shivering.

"I did talk to John. Are you upset?" Although he phrased it as a question, Ernest already knew the answer. He could tell when his brother was troubled, even over a two-thousand-mile-long crackling phone line.

"You'd better believe I'm upset! We're partners, right? Fifty-fifty. And I'm here. You're not. Darn it, Ernest, you can't make a decision like that without me. And then for me to hear it from John?!"

"We've got the money. What's the big deal?"

"It's not about the money. It's about the commitment. That's eighty thousand more gallons than we discussed. Eighty thousand gallons I have to make. We're getting too big too fast. I can't keep going at this pace. It might be what you want, but it's not what I signed up for. I want to be home with my wife and baby. I'm already missing out on too much," Julio complained.

"I hear you. But look at it this way. More tanks mean more income. We can hire more people and you'll be home with your family. I'll be home soon and don't have any trips planned for the next few weeks. I'll be able to supervise the construction. You can take some time off."

"Sure. But then you'll want more. And more. I think you need to ask yourself how big is big enough? And at what cost? I know you, Ernest. Maybe better than you know yourself. I think we need to be more circumspect. Maybe not in such a hurry. And you can't just call Cahill and order more tanks without talking to me first. If you're not going to treat me like a partner, maybe you should just cross out 'and J.' and leave me out."

Ernest shook his head, exasperated by his brother's caution. As much as he tried to see things from Julio's point of view, he found his worries unwarranted and frustrating. They had doubled their production each year they'd been in business and hadn't missed a step. There was no indication they couldn't make or sell another eighty thousand gallons. But he wasn't going to risk losing the partnership—or, more importantly, his relationship with Julio. They had survived too much together. They needed each other. He knew that and he believed Julio did too. Maybe Julio was more upset that Ernest had made the decision without him than about the extra tanks.

"Hey, I'm really sorry. It won't happen again," Ernest apologized. "I just want to be the best at what we do. I can't turn my back on an opportunity. If we don't do it, someone else will. We'll talk more when I get back. Meanwhile, don't worry! Everything will be all right."

Ernest hung up. He couldn't remember ever feeling so fatigued and wondered if maybe he was pushing himself too much. Perhaps Julio was right and they both needed to slow down. He made a note to see the doctor next week if he was still feeling poorly.

"Ernest, this isn't a death sentence," the aging Dr. Maxwell assured, putting his stethoscope back in the pocket of his white coat. Though most doctors of the day dressed like bankers, Ernest was always struck by Dr. Maxwell's preference for all white, down to his oxford shoes.

"Heck, I know that. What kind of thing is that to say?" Ernest bit back. "You don't think I can beat this thing? Just watch me." He was taken aback by the physician's thoughtless statement. Certainly, tuberculosis was a common killer, but the thought of him being one of its victims? Well, that just wasn't going to happen. Yes, the news was unwelcome and a bit of a shock, but it was just another bump in the road. If he couldn't drive around it, he'd drive over it or though it and handle whatever came at him.

"So, do you have something you can give me here or do I need to go the pharmacy?"

"Come on, you know there's no medicine I can give you," the doctor smiled.

"There's nothing new? Something people just don't know about yet?" Ernest urged.

"No, 'fraid not. The sanatorium's the only option. And you don't want anyone else to catch this. You know how contagious this thing is."

"Nope. Can't do that. I have my own business. My brother…I can't just take a couple of months off," Ernest panicked.

"A couple of months? Six if you're lucky. Sorry, son. It's the only way you'll beat this. Rest. Fresh air. Healthy living. There's a place I like just north of San Francisco. I'll call ahead and tell them you're coming."

"But—" Ernest protested.

"Do you want to get better? Live to have children? Be there for your wife and brothers? Then you'll go," insisted Dr. Maxwell.

The next day Julio drove Ernest to the sanatorium in St. Helena in Napa County.

"I'm so sorry," Ernest lamented. "I can't believe this is happening. I wanted to take the pressure off you, not put more on."

"I'll be okay. I can handle it. The important thing is that you get better," Julio assured, hoping to disguise his nervousness. He was already overwhelmed from supervising the vineyards, the wine, and the construction of the new winery. And now seconds and thirds had been piled on his plate.

"You know nothing's going to change. I'll get my own phone line and make all the sales calls. Amelia can bring me the books and all the orders. You and I will talk every day. I just wish I could take over the construction right now and give you a break. Please look after Amelia—and of course, Aileen and your two little ones. And remember, outside the family—"

"Nobody knows where you are. I know. Relax," Julio reassured.

Preferring not to waste any more of his brother's time, Ernest insisted Julio drop him off at the building's front entrance.

The disease was in its early stages and other than passing fatigue and an occasional cough, he felt healthy and able. In fact, he felt a little silly to be checking in to a hospital at all.

He pulled his suitcase from the trunk and looked up at the impressive four-story monolith set against the green hillside. It reminded him of the Shelburne Hotel in Atlantic City, except for the outdoor porches that wrapped around each floor. If only he were checking into the Shelburne with Amelia by his side for the vacation she was overdue.

A young nurse rushed down the front steps and insisted on carrying Ernest's suitcase. He protested, to no avail, and was practically pushed into a wheelchair by another nurse waiting for him on the porch. "Doctor's orders," she chirped, her sing-song tone incongruous with her no-nonsense attitude.

Ernest continued to object as she wheeled him into Dr. Krinsky's first-floor office. The lanky doctor rose from behind his desk to greet his newest patient. Everything about the man was angular and sharp—from the creases on his pants to his nose, jaw, shoulders, and elbows. His pencil moustache punctuated his presentation.

"Dr. Krinsky, I presume," Ernest guessed as he stood up from the wheelchair and pushed it aside. "First of all, I'm not that sick. Second of all, I didn't have time to call before I came... but I need a phone line installed next to my bed as soon as possible. My wife will have my newspaper subscriptions sent here. I like to read them with my breakfast. What time is your mail delivery? If not—"

"You must be Mr. Gallo," the doctor spoke slowly. "Welcome. Now, let's not get too far ahead of ourselves. Am I correct that you've never been to a sanatorium before?"

When Ernest nodded, the doctor continued. "I think I need to clear up any confusion. While we want—no, while we *strive* to keep our patients comfortable, I'm afraid we do have some rules. All for your own good, of course. Nurse? Could you please give Mr. Gallo a copy of Krinsky's Commandments?"

Ernest cocked his head as the nurse handed him a typewritten numbered list that continued on three stapled pages. He put on his glasses and looked at the document. At first he read silently, but as his agitation increased, he began to mutter.

"...no using profane or indecent...must be in bed...refrain from all conversation until Doctor...the toilet without...*Krinsky's Crawl*?!"

"Ah. That one. I've noticed that our patients...particularly those who can afford full payment like yourself...tend to do everything too fast. Talking. Walking. Fresh air and *rest* in particular, Mr. Gallo, are the focus of our treatment. To encourage our patients to slow down, we help them by insisting they say, 'I am getting stronger' between each step they take. I like it more than 'one Mississippi.' It also reinforces a positive state of mind. Of course, that's after you graduate from the wheelchair and—"

"*Graduate from the wheelchair*?! I can't stay here! I can't live like this! This is ridiculous. This—" Ernest wasn't able to finish his sentence. His increased heart rate had created an urgent need for more oxygen. When his diseased lung tried to carry out the autonomic act, he was overcome by an ill-timed coughing fit. He couldn't stop.

Dr. Krinsky patiently waited while Ernest struggled to recover his breath. "It may seem ridiculous now, but we have the lowest mortality rate of any sanatorium in the country. I can help you get better. But you have to agree to do things my way. You do want to live, don't you, Mr. Gallo?"

"Of course I want to live," Ernest grumbled once he'd recomposed himself. "Where do I sign?"

Ernest soon recognized that everything he needed to do to get better went completely against his nature. Not only was he confined to bed most of the day and forbidden from talking, but he also had to accede complete control over every aspect of his being. His opinions didn't matter. He wasn't in charge. He hated everything about it.

Ernest finally vowed to himself to make the best of the abrupt change in his lifestyle. Though his body was in custody, his mind was free. He read everything he could get his hands on—the *Wall Street Journal,* the *San Francisco Chronicle,* the *Napa Register, Wines & Vines,* and the *American Wine Journal.* On Tuesdays Sister Xavier came by with the library cart. The erudite nun always had something special for Ernest, guiding him through all the best literature he'd never had time for. He even read the Bible all the way through—something he'd always wanted to do.

The radio became a good friend. With Dr. Krinsky's permission he would gather with the other patients in the recreation pavilion for *Kraft Music Hall,* the *Carnation Contented Hour, Coke Time, Lux Radio Theater,* and *General Motors Concerts.* Maybe in the next couple years he'd be introducing the *Gallo Opera Hour.* Or, better yet, Julio could. He was the more outgoing of the two and would perform better in the limelight.

Thankfully, his daily regimen included long hours spent outdoors. Though still prone under blankets on a deck chair on the enclosed porch, he was grateful for the sunshine, fresh air, and view of Napa's rolling vineyards with the Mayacamas Mountains in the distance. Ernest especially enjoyed the late-afternoon marine breezes and noted the changing climate and how the *ter-*

roir—the region's inherent natural attributes—differed from that of Modesto, just over a hundred miles to the southeast. Even though Napa's soils were less fertile than those of the Central Valley, its more moderate climate made for a longer growing season. So although its vineyards generally produced a third of that of its southern cousin and its grapes were much smaller, the fruit was more intense in flavor. Napa couldn't compete with the Central Valley in regard to quantity, but its natural topography and variety of microclimates and soils meant it would always yield more complex and venerated grapes.

During his months at the sanatorium Ernest abided all but two of Krinsky's Commandments: no alcoholic beverages and no work. Amelia had been his accomplice. She bought an oversized purse and on visiting days would fill it with wine samples from Julio as well as correspondence, invoices, orders, and the office books. She would share her husband's opinions and thoughts with Julio upon her return to Modesto. She assured each brother the other was well and managing under the far-from-ideal conditions.

Despite adhering to most sanatorium rules and remaining optimistic, Ernest felt he was in decline. His body had less energy than when he'd been in New York. His cough had more blood. He was easily winded and the recent stabbing sensation in his chest was getting worse. An X-ray confirmed the disease had remained in just one lung, but fluid had leaked into his pleural cavity.

Ernest knew death lay in wait under each patient's bed. He would say goodnight to the man next to him, never knowing if he'd still be there at sunrise. Though Krinsky's Commandments forbade patients from discussing the details of their treatment with each other, they couldn't hide their physical deterioration or the troubled looks on the attending nurses' faces. Though he tried, Ernest couldn't expunge the mortality tallies that ran in his head. Nor could he stop inwardly predicting who would make it and who wouldn't. Some of these men had become close friends and he wanted to see them get better.

When Dr. Krinsky suggested a pneumothoraxic procedure to collapse the infected lung, allowing it to rest and heal, Ernest made an unconscious sign of the cross as an expression of relief. The injection of Novocain and the syringe to suction the fluid and oxygen from his chest were far more appealing than the barbaric-sounding thoracoplasty he had heard of, in which the surgeon would permanently remove seven of the patient's ribs.

After six months of confinement, Ernest was finally discharged. His infected lung had cleared and he was symptom-free. He was warned not to overdo it and to eat well and get regular, moderate exercise. Julio picked him up at the sanatorium, and rather than driving straight home, Ernest had insisted they first stop at the almost-finished winery.

The three-hour drive had given them time to discuss what was next for E. & J. Gallo. Julio wanted to branch out from only producing red wine. Fortified wines like brandy and sherry were outselling table wine five to one. The country had a sweet tooth when it came to fermented grape juice. Ernest wanted to focus on bottling. California was one of the only states left to permit sales from barrels, and consumers seemed to be adjusting to the new idea. Plus, the government was pushing the whole industry in that direction because bottles were easier to regulate and tax.

Worried about his brother's stamina, Julio parked as close as he could to the cluster of new concrete tanks. Each of the twenty-four was almost the size of a house. Ernest stepped to the closest one and brushed his hand along the smooth surface. He put his cheek against the cool finish and looked up to the bright blue sky overhead.

"The sketches didn't do it justice. This is overwhelming. I am in awe," Ernest crowed, meandering between the tanks, looking up at the arteries of metal piping that formed a manmade circulatory system. "I wish you had given Joseph more to do. This was too much for one person."

"Oh, Joseph helped. But you and I agreed that school would always come first for him. I kept my word."

Ernest circled around to a vertical ladder attached to one of the tanks, gripped the sides, and stepped on the first rung.

"You probably shouldn't. Wait until you're stronger, why don't you?" Julio worried. "These tanks aren't going anywhere. Ever. It can wait."

"You kidding me? I've been dreaming of this day for months! I'm fine!" Ernest shouted as he ascended. "Just a little slower than I'd like."

Julio followed in case Ernest slipped, lagging a few rungs behind as he watched his brother climb the thirty-five-foot ladder. When they reached the top, they stood side by side on the catwalk and looked out for miles. Yosemite, the pride of the Sierra Nevada, lay due east, and the Coastal Range, to the west—with vineyards, orchards, and crops in between that filled the country's kitchen pantries.

Ernest was infused with joy as he looked down at the tanks, winery, and framed office building. He took a deep breath in, using both lungs to their fullest, and let the air out in a long sigh of satisfaction. "Thank you for doing all this. You did a great job. I know it wasn't easy," he said as he put his arm around his brother's shoulder.

"This?" Julio joked. "Oh, this was nothing."

"Look. You can see Father's fields from up here."

"Nice straight rows. Not bad for two little squirts, huh?"

"No one can say we didn't work hard," Ernest said. "Father was a tyrant. But he made us who we are today. For that I'm grateful."

"Me too. Before we climb down, look down there. You can see the arch," Julio said, pointing to the Modesto landmark built in 1912 to welcome motorists to the seat of Stanislaus County.

Though the inscription was too far away to be legible, Ernest remembered the motto that stretched over I Street and repeated it: "'Water, Wealth, Contentment, Health.' Amen to that. Yes, indeed. Amen to that."

Chapter Thirteen

BOTTLED UP

In anticipation of Ernest's discharge Amelia had rented a two-bedroom house in town. She worried that the old family home would be too hectic for her convalescing husband. Though Julio and Aileen's son, Bob, was adorable, he was entering the terrible twos, and their daughter, Susann, was just a week old. Amelia knew Ernest would be crisscrossing the country as soon as the doctor gave his approval—if not before—but at least she could ensure he would return to a quiet sanctuary.

While Julio focused on producing brandy and fortified wines, trying to catch up to the American public's new preference for higher proof and sweeter wines, Ernest returned to the road, traveling around California and up and down the East Coast. Each state had approached the Twenty-First Amendment differently. Some opened the tap statewide while others left it up to their counties to decide, and some were quicker to grant liquor licenses than others. Eighteen states created monopolies in which they were to be the sole wholesaler and retailer of alcoholic beverages. Wine was sold in forty-four states under forty-four different regulations regarding bottle sizes, labeling requirements, pricing controls, and state taxes. For this reason and others, Ernest focused his efforts on just a few states.

In 1940 there was virtually no universally recognized national brand of wine. Vintners simply made and shipped their wine and left the rest to independent regional bottlers with whom they had contracts. Bottlers serviced liquor manufacturers and multiple wineries and arranged delivery with retailers. They had no interest in promoting one wine over another. A consumer could travel the United States and buy the exact same Roma wine under seventy different labels. But Ernest wanted to do for wine what Coca-Cola had done for soft drinks and make Gallo the first national brand of wine.

Because his resources were limited, he decided to start in one market. California liquor regulatory laws gave all power to the state government, meaning the entire Golden State was wet. San Francisco was close to home, but in wine country's backyard. Loyalties with older wineries were longstanding and hard to break. So he decided on Los Angeles. It was convenient enough. Plus, he liked working with bottler Sam Watt, co-owner of Distillers Outlet.

From the start Ernest had felt his job wasn't done until the consumer twisted the cap off the bottle. With that in mind, he wanted to see the world through the consumers' eyes. Watt had given him a list of L.A. retailers that carried Gallo wine. With a Hertz rental car and a map, Ernest explored the city, stopping at new self-service chains like Vons and Ralphs as well as independent cigar shops, liquor stores, and drugstores. He had made sure Watt listed all their retailers, not just the largest. He could learn as much from the guy who sold a few bottles a month as the one who sold hundreds.

As the Ford coupe descended the Cahuenga Pass into the San Fernando Valley, Ernest felt the heat rise. It was November, for God's sake. He worried about the cases of wine in the V8's roomy trunk, but there was little he could do. He consulted his map until he reached the Burbank Market, a simple, lonely building on the side of the road advertising groceries, meats, beer, and ice cream. It was his twenty-sixth stop since leaving his motel room that morning.

A bell rang above his head when he opened the door, and he was greeted by a young man in a bow tie and white apron, standing behind a tall counter. The store was lined with wooden shelves holding cans, jars, bottles, and dry goods. The once-open floor plan had been filled with additional shelving. Some cans were still in their shipping boxes, others arranged in pyramid-like stacks. The storekeeper had utilized all available space in an orderly fashion.

"Can I help you find anything?" he asked.

"I'm looking for a bottle of wine," Ernest said, playing the part of a regular shopper.

"All our wine is over in that corner next to the beer. We've got fortified wine and some dago red."

Ernest bit his lip. He knew the man meant no harm. The term had become synonymous with red table wine. Perhaps it could be taken as a backhanded compliment to the hardworking Northern Italians who had built and still dominated the California wine industry. Simi, Petri, Sebastiani...the list was endless. It galled him nonetheless. Too many bad memories of hate-filled epithets spoken to demean and hurt. To put Italians in their place.

"Ah. Red table wine. That's what I'm looking for," Ernest said casually, a new habit he had cultivated as a subtle and polite correction. He continued toward the shop's dim back corner but couldn't see any table wine. He bent down and moved a box of Pabst Blue Ribbon beer and found two dark olive-green bottles of Good Samaritan Grape Brandy. Behind them he found a bottle of Roma Estate California Burgundy. Reaching deeper into the shelf, he pulled out a bottle of "California Wine." The plain multipurpose label had two columns listing alcoholic contents by volume. Under 19.5 to 21 percent: port, sherry, muscatel, Tokay, white port, and Angelica; and in a second column, 12 to 14 percent: claret, burgundy, Zinfandel, sauterne, and Riesling. The box next to "claret" had been checked off with a pen. On the dark bottom shelf, it may as well have been a bottle of molasses.

He picked up the bottle of Roma and ran his right hand along the top of his scalp through his slicked-back hair. Sure, he was annoyed that the store didn't have any of his wine. Yet even if it had, who would have seen it? He wondered how he'd ever managed to sell a single bottle.

He almost tripped over a cardboard box on his way back to the front of the store. The top flaps had been ripped off, exposing two dusty mismatched bottles and a discarded tissue. He bent down and grabbed a bottle by the neck. The tissue was stuck to the label of the familiar glass, but even before disdainfully pulling it away, he knew what he'd see: Gallo Port. As if to clinch the insult, a piece of hardened chewing gum was glued to the bottle's heel.

Ernest flinched as if the wad had been hawked at his face. It felt personal and utterly dismissive—like a mockery from the universe just to make sure he knew his place. He blushed in humiliation and his fists clenched, wanting to strike back at the long-gone offender. He brushed his palm across his cheek in an unconscious effort to wipe away all traces of the affront as he tried to assess his surroundings from a different perspective.

He removed himself from the equation and assumed a new identity: Ernest Gallo, proprietor of the Burbank Market. He stood in place imagining he had just received a delivery of spirits, beer, and wine. Turning 360 degrees, he thought of where he would place the new bottles. Soft drinks and beer already filled the cold case. Gin, whiskey, and vodka would go prominently and conveniently behind the cash register like wallflowers hoping to be noticed on a whim and passed to the hands of an impulsive shopper. And the wine the distributor had added to the order? Some of it would fit on the shelves. The rest would have to stay in the shipping carton for there wasn't any extra space in the cramped storeroom. Might as well put it on the floor near the rest of the wine. Clearly the proprietor hadn't given the box high regard.

Then he changed hats and became Ernest Gallo, consumer. He pictured himself walking into the store, hungry and thirsty, but with no clear agenda. He retraced his path through the store, and soon became aware that he was only focused on items at eye level. There he saw familiar brands: Campbell's Soup, Heinz, Kellogg's, Ritz. Household names. If he wasn't already a wine drinker, he probably wouldn't have paid any mind to the unfamiliar dark bottles in the unlit corner. And if his Wrigley's had lost its flavor and elasticity, why not spit it out into the almost empty cardboard box at his feet?

Before leaving the shop, Ernest quizzed the shopkeeper. "I'm curious why you don't have more wine. I had a heck of a time finding this." Ernest placed the bottle of Roma on the counter and pulled a dollar bill from his billfold.

"Well, it's not much of a seller, and as you can see, we don't have much room to spare. Some folks like the sweet stuff, but most of our customers prefer the spirits," the man answered as he handed Ernest his change.

"Why do you think that is?" Ernest asked.

"Oh, I dunno. I suppose they like a bigger kick."

"Are you the owner? Do you decide what items to carry?"

"I am. And yes, I see what sells and tell my suppliers what I need. With wine, I just carry whatever they bring me…You sure ask a lot of questions, Mister—"

"Gallo. Sorry. I make wine and I'm trying to find out how to attract more customers."

"From what I see, Mr. Gallo, when it comes to wine, most folks just want a cheap nip. They're not fussy about what they buy. As long as it's sweet."

"Got it. Thanks for your time," Ernest said as he left.

Though the store had been stuffy, at least there had been a fan by the cash register. He opened the Ford's trunk, trying not to burn his fingers on the scalding metal, and grabbed a complimentary two-ounce cobalt blue jug of their new Gallo port. He gave the miniature piece of pottery to the storekeeper and told him he'd be back soon.

He had time to visit a few more stores before his dinner with Sam Watt. Sam's wife, Anne, was an excellent cook and Ernest always looked forward to evenings in their home. On the scenic drive to Pasadena, he strategized about ways to sell more wine. Roma, Italian Swiss Colony, and Cresta Blanca had begun to advertise in newspapers and on the radio. Clearly they were also aiming to go national. But he and Julio had just invested everything they had into production. He would just have to think of another way to get Gallo noticed.

His mind was so full of schemes and dreams, it wasn't until he saw the signs for Santa Anita Park that he realized he had driven straight through Pasadena and past the Watts' home. He doubled back, making it there just in time for dinner.

"You know, Anne, you're the reason we're trying to make a name for ourselves in Southern California," Ernest charmed, cutting another bite of chicken fricassee.

"Oh, you just like it because she used your wine," Sam joked.

Ernest chuckled. "You just brought up my favorite subject."

"You mean your *only* subject," Anne teased.

"Fair enough, Mrs. Watt. Touché. Excuse me one second," Ernest said as he went to his briefcase by the front door. He returned with a new blend Julio had been developing and the bottle of Roma he had bought in Burbank. "Taste test?" he asked as he returned to the small dining room.

"Why break tradition?" asked Sam.

Ernest opened both bottles while Anne placed some extra glasses on the table. He poured about an inch of wine in each glass, pleased that his wine was a deep garnet compared to the Roma's pale ruby hue.

"Hey, Sam, I've been thinking. Why do we use brown and green glass?" Ernest questioned.

"I'm not sure. It's just what everyone's always used. Probably because it's the cheapest. Why do you ask?"

Ernest held up the glass of Gallo wine. "Just look at this beautiful color. Who wouldn't want to drink this? It's rich, warm, inviting...See how much darker it is than the Roma? But when you look at the bottles, they both look the same. All afternoon I've been thinking about how Gallo can stand out from the crowd. I think clear bottles would be a good start."

"I'm sure we can do that," Sam added, liking the idea. "I'll call my guy at Owens-Illinois."

"I want to come up with a new bottle shape and labels too. So consumers will recognize Gallo wine with one glance. And at some point, bigger bottles. I have a feeling people will pour more generously that way."

Ernest savored his last bite of chicken and used a piece of bread to sop up the remaining sauce. He took another sip of wine. "Americans don't know what they're missing. No good meal is complete without a nice wine."

"Well, you've got your work cut out for you," Sam smiled.

"I have an idea," Anne said. "What if you put a recipe on each bottle? Something like this chicken? Then more housewives would buy it."

"Oh, I don't know, Anne," her husband said. "It's usually men who—"

"I think it's a fine idea," Ernest interrupted. "Ink is cheap. And my brother and I have always wanted our wines to be enjoyed with food. Do you have more recipes? Ones that use different types of wine?" She nodded as Ernest continued, "Would you be willing to write them down?"

"You bet. More than you can use. I'd love to help!" Anne glowed.

He could almost see their new bottle in his hand. Ernest knew Sam would be on the phone with the glass factory first thing in the morning. The pieces were coming together, but there were still too many missing.

On the drive to his motel, Ernest mentally retraced his day, revisiting each store, picturing its layout and wine selection. His heart sank as he imagined his innovative clear bottles relegated to the shadows of a bottom corner shelf behind a six-pack of beer.

Ernest felt like he was on the cusp of solving the riddle. Just out of reach, but oh so close, it almost felt like déjà vu. He went to bed, but knew it was just a charade. His brain was too busy for sleep. The gaps in synergy closed sometime between 2:00 a.m. and 4:00 a.m. He arose, made some sketches, did his morning calisthenics, showered, and scoured the yellow pages for the closest hardware store. After a quick breakfast at the coffee shop across the street, he drove to Crown City Hardware. He quickly gathered everything he needed and made a beeline back to the motel. He pulled a case of wine from his rental car's trunk, informed the front desk he'd be staying another night, and hurried back to his room. Removing his shirt and tie, he stripped down to his undershirt and got to work.

About two hours later, Ernest heard a knock on the door. *Housekeeping,* he thought. "All good!" he shouted. "Can you come back later?" But the knock persisted. He put down his tools and opened the door to the rotund front desk clerk, flushed and sweat-drenched from his hike up to the second floor.

"I'm sorry, sir…but we've had…some complaints," he said, trying to catch his breath. "The noise…our other guests…"

"Oh, that. I'm almost done. No more hammering," Ernest explained. "See?" He pointed to a tall wooden rack that already held a dozen bottles of wine and had space for 108 more. There was a recessed niche on the top that held a single bottle of red wine.

"Come in. Look at this," Ernest beckoned. He found the cord behind the rack and plugged it into an electrical outlet. He flipped a switch, turning on a concealed light bulb that illuminated the highest bottle.

"Um…that's swell, but…" The bewildered clerk searched for an appropriate response.

"See, you can almost see the wine, and that's through a green bottle. Imagine when it's clear. Also," Ernest added, picking up a measuring tape, "the footprint is no bigger than a case of wine. It doesn't take up any room. Well, not much at all."

Six months later, Sam Watt called Ernest to tell him he was going out of business. Too many bottlers had sprung up post-Repeal and there simply wasn't enough work to go around. There was a pandemic sweeping the country, taking out bottlers one by one. The Gallo bottler in New Orleans had gone belly-up a year earlier.

"I can't lose you, Sam. If you go under, I'll be back at square one."

Ernest had always struggled with the winery/bottler partnership. It was like being a shipwright, selecting and felling the strongest oak in the thicket and lovingly planing the planks to velvet perfection. After painstakingly caulking the seams between each steamed and twisted board and building a watertight showpiece, the craftsman then handed the tiller to someone else, someone who might make it to the next shore or just as easily head straight into a hull-crunching reef. Every time Ernest lost a bottler, he lost any progress he had made building his brand in that market and his competitors would swoop in and claim his customers as their own. If he had any hope of succeeding, he'd need to captain his own ship.

Sam and Anne Watt were good people—people Ernest trusted and wanted to keep in his life. He proposed a solution similar to the one that had saved his share in the New Orleans market. E. & J. Gallo bought 51 percent of Distillers Outlet and Sam stayed on to manage the operation. As majority owner, Ernest restructured the company. His first order of business was to sever the bottler's relationships with all other wineries. Distillers Outlet would be exclusive to Gallo and both parties would benefit from the arrangement. He was confident that he understood the bottling and distribution business better than most bottlers. Because federal law prohibited him from selling directly to retailers, this vertical expansion was the only way he could get closer to the consumer.

He began by training a sales team to tackle the Los Angeles market. Wire bottle racks were made from his wooden prototype. Salesmen would encourage storeowners to place the racks in premium locations. They would cultivate a personal relationship with their retailers by visiting each store every week or two. While there, they would dust unsold bottles, restock the rack, and hang "Gallo" bottle collars on each neck for extra exposure. If a store wouldn't accept the Gallo rack, a salesman would personally organize its shelves, moving Gallo bottles to a higher position.

Ernest was counting on storekeepers' "silent recommendation." His idea was that shoppers would notice Gallo wines' prominent position and assume it to be the storekeeper's favorite. He gave his sales force strict orders, from how they dressed to the jokes they could tell. Before going on to their next stop, salesmen were instructed to ask themselves, "How did I improve Gallo in this store as a result of this call?" Everything was outlined in the "Big Red Book," a training manual given to all company salesmen.

Joe Junior had graduated from high school in 1937 and dropped out of Modesto Junior College a year later. Ernest was bitterly disappointed. Since becoming his guardian he had encouraged his little brother to get the education he and Julio had been denied. Both had been counting on Joe Junior to transfer to the University of California at Davis and study enology and viticulture. His technical expertise would have given them a significant advantage over other wineries. The family was having Sunday dinner at Julio and Aileen's when Joe Junior dropped the news.

"What do you mean you're quitting school?" Ernest said, his voice tight with shock.

"I can't do it," Joe Junior sighed. "It's not for me."

"But what about Davis? Getting your degree? Joining us at the winery?" Julio asked.

"That was your idea. And his," Joe Junior said, nodding his head toward Ernest. "You never once asked me what I wanted."

"But we talked about this…for *years,*" Ernest protested.

"You talked. I listened. I can't do all these math and science classes. I barely got by in high school and now they're even harder. I'll go from part-time to full-time at the warehouse, but I'm done with school."

"Why don't you just take a break? Take a semester off?" Ernest suggested. "You can always go back. Think about it."

"Sure. I'll think about it," Joe Junior agreed, but everyone at the table knew he was just trying to end the uncomfortable conversation.

Ernest left the table in frustration as Amelia got up to clear the dishes. He needed to sort out his feelings and was afraid he'd say something hurtful. He and Julio had assigned Joe Junior chores over the years, expecting him to help around the house and the winery, but they had agreed to go easy on him. They remembered how difficult it had been for them to complete high school with the amount of work Father had doled out. He couldn't help but think Joe Junior simply hadn't applied himself. He hadn't tried hard enough. If he didn't care about school, then at least he could have been more helpful to Julio when Ernest had been in the hospital. Maybe they had made things too easy for him. He began to regret giving him the new car for graduation.

The thirties ended on a high note with the births of Julio and Aileen's second son, Philip, and Ernest and Amelia's first, David. Ernest felt blessed he was able to provide for his family. He knew Amelia would be a loving mother and was grateful she rarely complained about his never-ending business trips. He never worried about her and the baby because his brothers and sister-in-law were so close. By working hard now, he reasoned he'd have more time for his son later.

After adding a distillery in 1937, Ernest and Julio realized they needed to grow more Thompson Seedless grapes. The versatile fruit was ideal for fortified wines, and should the country's preference swing back to table wines, any unused Thompsons could be dried and sold as raisins. They found 440 acres in Keyes, eight miles south of Modesto. Though only eighty dollars an acre, the property had an infestation of nearly impossible-to-kill morning glory that had deterred other buyers. It was some of the most fertile land Ernest had ever seen. He estimated that they could buy two mules and a weed cutter and hire a man to plow the land over and over for a year until the weeds conceded defeat, and the purchase would still be a steal.

So while Ernest continued his campaign around the country, Julio held down the ever-expanding fort. He divided his time between the vineyards, the winery, and the distillery. He spent more time than he would have liked in his car as they were still buying grapes and wine from others to meet their needs. Fortunately, his travels kept him relatively close to home. He never had to go further than Sonoma and he did that as little as possible. He couldn't believe how quickly his children were growing and didn't want to miss a second of it.

Julio and his team were forever trying to improve their repertoire and expand the company's offerings. Ernest paid acute attention to their competitors' products and Julio tried to replicate their best-selling wines. He experimented with different yeasts, grapes, temperatures, and blends, ever mindful of E. & J. Gallo's mission to make the best-tasting, best-selling, and most affordable wines while introducing the drink to more and more Americans.

When Ernest was in town, he would join in the daily tastings, always excited to see what his brother had come up with for him to sell next. After spending a productive spring morning behind his desk reviewing orders, he made his way over to the production room for the 11:00 a.m. tasting. Julio always led the review, keeping track of the numbered bottles and glasses to ensure a "blind" tasting and unbiased results.

Ernest sat down and waited for his brother to explain what they would be sampling. The always crackerjack-sharp Julio seemed to be having difficulty finding the right words. His speech was stumbling and awkward. Ernest noticed the dark circles under his brother's eyes and the unmistakable tremor in his hand when he poured the wines. He made a mental note to check in with his brother after the meeting. But once they started discussing the samples, Julio seemed revived, writing down everyone's thoughts and consulting the lab reports to compare opinions to the chemical analyses. Ernest left for lunch certain he had misread Julio at the beginning of the session.

After lunch he looked for Julio in the room that housed his experimental blends. The walls were lined with steel racks holding barrels in perfectly spaced symmetry—almost like precisely stacked timbers in a lumberyard. Ernest wanted to discuss building a bottling plant in Modesto. He found Julio leaning against a barrel at the end of the row, jotting notes on a clipboard, a wine thief in his left hand.

"Do you have a minute?" Ernest asked.

"Sure. What's up?"

"I'm thinking it's time to build our own bottling plant. Here in Modesto. It will give us more control of our product. We know it will be completely sanitary and we'll be in charge so nothing will get messed up. We'll save money and we can reduce our prices," Ernest explained.

"Oh, I don't know. I think we should stick to what we know and what's working."

"We can learn. Just like we learned how to make wine. Sam Watt can help us get started."

Julio placed the clipboard and glass pipette carefully on top of the barrel. He put his hands in his pockets and faced his older brother and said one word. "No."

"What do you mean, 'No'? Sleep on it. We'll come to a compromise. Figure out how we can both be happy. Like we always do."

But Julio just stood in place, slowly shaking his head from side to side. His chin was on his chest, his eyes avoiding his brother's. His shoulders fell and his body began to tremble.

"You okay?" Ernest asked. When his brother didn't answer right away, he demanded, "What's going on? Julio?!"

But Julio continued to shake without saying a word.

"Is this about the bottling?"

No answer.

"Julio! Answer me!" Ernest was confused and his concern was escalating rapidly.

"I can't…I just can't," Julio lifted his head and slowly shook it from side to side, his eyes looking past Ernest, fixed, but not focused on anything.

"Can't what?"

"I just can't. It's too much. The vineyards. The wine. The distillery. I don't even know what my children look like. I'm off to Napa at three in the morning and they're in bed by the time I get home at ten. How can I keep this up and still be a good father? And a new plant…Bottles?" Julio's breath grew shallow and fast.

"It's okay. Don't worry about it," Ernest assured. "Why don't you go home? Get some rest. You look really tired. A good night's sleep and everything will look better in the morning. Don't worry about the bottles. It was just an idea."

Ernest was rattled by Julio's strange behavior. He may as well have taken the rest of the day off himself considering how little work he got done. Was a bottling plant really too much? They had hired plenty of really great people and could always get more. Maybe Joe Junior could even run the plant and it wouldn't be any more work for Julio. If he wasn't going to stay in school, it could be perfect for him. If they could bottle all their wine right there in Modesto, it would actually mean less work in the long run. It would pay for itself in time and money. He reassured himself that Julio would come around once he got some rest. They had always been able to work out their differences.

The next day Julio wasn't there for the eleven o'clock tasting session. Ernest had never known his brother to miss a single appointment. Even when his appendix had burst, he had tried to convince the doctors to postpone the emergency surgery until Ernest had come back from the East Coast so he could take over.

Julio's secretary told Ernest he had called in sick. An alarm went off in Ernest's head and he drove straight to the home ranch, where he was greeted by Aileen.

"I wanted to call you, but he insisted," she said defensively.

"What's happening?" Ernest asked.

"To be honest, I don't really know. He won't get out of bed and he can't stop crying." Aileen's shoulders were raised, her arms crossed, each hand on the opposite elbow as if she were trying to physically hold herself together. Ernest noticed a pile of dishes in the sink and a basket of yet-to-be-ironed clothes. Aileen was wearing a dressing gown and two-year-old Philip was still in his Dr. Denton's.

"Maybe he'll talk to you," Aileen hoped. "He won't let me call the doctor. He's been having trouble sleeping for months. I think he's exhausted. But you go in. I'll stay here."

Ernest walked into the couple's bedroom, where he found Julio curled up on the queen-size bed. His head was cradled in his arms as if trying to shut out the world.

"Hey, what's going on?" Ernest said gently as he sat at the edge of the bed.

But the only answer he got was muffled sobs. He rubbed his brother's back and tried to soothe him.

"It's going to be okay, Julio. Whatever's going on, I'll fix it."

Ernest kept asking questions, but Julio wouldn't—or couldn't—talk. Ernest examined his brother's body language for any sign, no matter how slight, that he was getting through. Julio would stop crying for a minute and Ernest would feel like he was making progress, but then his brother would start shaking and the tears would flow again.

"It's okay. You get it all out. I'll be right here," Ernest comforted. He lay on the bed behind his brother, wrapped his arms around him, and held tight. But as strong as he wanted to appear for Julio, Ernest was shaken to his core. Julio's eyes were full of fear. Ernest had seen that look before—in Father after the Crash. He waited for Julio to fall asleep before gingerly rising from the bed to talk to Aileen.

"He's had moments like this, but it's never lasted this long," she confessed. "I tried to hide it from the children, but they know something's not right. I don't know what to do."

"He needs help. He has to see a doctor. I don't care what he says. It's not up to him." Ernest was emphatic. That look in Julio's eyes had cut a chink in the fortress he had built around the past. He'd learned to accept the regret he felt for not seeking help for Father before it was too late. But he wasn't going to let anything happen to Julio. He wasn't sure what kind of help he needed, but he was going to find it. Though Julio was his own man and was no sap, Ernest felt responsible. He was the one who was always pushing for more. Maybe he had driven his brother too hard.

Julio willingly checked into an asylum near San Francisco where he stayed for the spring of 1941. He scolded himself for letting his brother down and abandoning his family, but knew something had to change and he hadn't been able to do it alone. He couldn't spend the rest of his life like this. He slowly regained his mental fortitude and began to recognize the adjustments he needed to make to maintain his stability and former good cheer.

Three weeks after Julio began treatment, the doctor believed he was ready for visitors. Ernest waited on a park bench in a eucalyptus grove on the hospital grounds. He tried to sort out the conflicting feelings of dread and longing that were waging a war inside him. Though the hospital had carefully been chosen, mental institutions were scary places. He wondered if Julio would be different. And if so, how? What kind of drugs had they given him? He'd read about the new electroconvulsive shock therapy doctors were excited about. Would they have tried that? Would Julio be angry? Distant? Or even catatonic? Could he be turning into their father? Though scared to see him, he had missed Julio terribly. Ernest ached to reconnect and apologize for his role in his brother's collapse.

When he saw Julio coming down the grassy slope, Ernest's fears all but vanished. His brother's head was high, his gait confident and swift. Ernest stood, reached out his arms, and pulled his brother close. They held on to each other tightly in a tearful, wordless embrace.

"I'm so sorry, Ernest. I don't know what happened," Julio apologized when they sat down. "I guess it just got to be too much. The pressure. The hours. The traveling. I just don't know..." he trailed off.

"No. I owe *you* an apology. I pushed you too much. I never took you into consideration," Ernest said regretfully. "*I* put you here."

"I'm letting everyone down. I feel so weak and so ashamed," Julio sighed.

"Nonsense. I love you. Your wife and children love you. And no one thinks any less of you. I've been so focused on growing the company, I didn't quite appreciate how much you were taking on. It's too much. We're going to hire as many people as we need and—"

"Thanks, but I just feel—" Julio interrupted.

"No more apologies, okay? You just get strong and healthy for your family. You come back to work *if* and when you're ready. On your terms."

Ernest drove back to Modesto, feeling inordinately better than he had on the way to the hospital. He literally counted his blessings, thinking of all the things in his life for which he was grateful. Julio was going to be okay. He wasn't turning into Father. He would be his old self soon enough. Amelia had recently given him another healthy son. And to his wife's astonishment, Ernest had wanted to name his second son after his father, Joseph. It hadn't been an easy conversation.

The couple had been seated in a movie theater on a rare "date night" and were waiting for the picture to start when Amelia, eight months pregnant, said it was as good a time as any to settle on a name for their second baby.

"If it's a boy? I'm thinking of Joseph. After my father," Ernest had suggested.

Amelia's response had been quick and from the heart. "Are you kidding me? You want to name our son after that man?"

"He was my father," Ernest said softly.

"And a…a…monster," Amelia said, after searching for just the right word.

"I'm trying to move past that."

"Well, I don't know if I can. And what about your brother Joseph? He might have a son someday and he might want to give his son his name. If there's going to be another Joseph in the family, it should be his. I don't think we can do that."

"Nonsense. First of all, we don't know if he'll ever have a son, and if *we* do, he could be the last boy in the family. And besides that, *I* should have been called Joseph anyway. I'm the firstborn and my father should have given *me* his name. Not his *third* son. I think it's perfectly okay to name my son after my father."

In a failed attempt at discretion, the middle-aged woman sitting in front of them twisted slightly in her seat. This was turning into a very interesting conversation and she didn't want to miss a word.

Ernest nodded his head toward the eavesdropper and slowly lowered his open palm to Amelia in a gesture to mean they should soften their voices.

"But what about David? Then shouldn't we have named him Joseph?" Amelia whispered. "This doesn't make any sense to me."

"I can't really explain it. I don't fully understand it myself. But naming our son after my father feels like the right thing to do."

"Tell you what, if it's a girl, I pick the name. A boy…it's up to you," Amelia whispered.

With that, the house lights began to dim and an angry "Shh!" hissed from a few rows aft. The red velvet curtains parted as an image faded in on the black screen. The camera panned up a "No Trespassing" sign attached to a chain-link fence and the conversation was over. A few weeks later, Amelia gave birth to their second son. He was christened Joseph Ernest Gallo.

Julio was getting better, and Ernest, at thirty-two years old, would be pulling into the driveway of the new house he had helped design, right across the street from the Maze Road family home where Julio still lived with his family. The $14,000 house was nestled in the once-godforsaken land he and Julio had leveled in the rain. Their brother Joseph was earning his place in the winery and all the Gallo boys were together as Mamma had wished. E. & J. Gallo was on its way to becoming a known brand, holding a steady and propitious trajectory. There seemed to be no limit to what they could achieve, thought Ernest.

And then came a conflict of such magnitude, his world was completely turned upside down.

Chapter Fourteen

PITCHING IN

Julio had been back at work for four months. Per doctor's orders he was spending less time in the winery and distillery and more time outdoors in the vineyard. He left most business and legal decisions to Ernest as he found such matters too stressful. But on this mild winter morning he had placed his straw Stetson on the hat stand by his front door and donned his fedora. He and Ernest were going to San Francisco to meet with a contractor the following day to talk about building a bottling plant in Modesto. Gallo wine was selling so well in Los Angeles that it was time to tackle other markets. Julio had agreed that bottling their wine at a plant they owned and controlled in Modesto would be a brilliant move.

It was the kind of December afternoon when Californians boast to each other about their state, convinced it's simply the best in the nation. Ernest and Julio had spent enough winter months in Chicago and New Jersey to empathize with those less fortunate—those buttoning their heavy coats to the neck, tramping through coal-blackened snow, exposed ears stinging, red noses dripping.

"How did we get so lucky?" Ernest asked. The seasonal rain had left the rolling grasslands and plateaus of the Diablo foothills green and lush. The cirrocumulus clouds looked like the rippled sand left by a retreating tide. A flock of starlings seemed to be following their car, clumping like a magnetized mass and then stretching apart, dipping and soaring in purity and freedom.

"I forgot to tell you I talked to Joseph again," Ernest said. "He's still stuck on raising cattle."

"Even after you told him about the bottling plant?" Julio asked, shaking his head.

"Yup. Said he can't stand working for us. That we've been telling him what to do his whole life," Ernest shrugged.

"Have we?"

"Who knows? I mean, we were his guardians, so it was our responsibility to tell him what to do, right? But he was pretty emphatic. I'm disappointed. We could really use his help and I don't see why he doesn't see what a great opportunity it is."

Julio felt his heart rate quicken. He had become skilled at recognizing early signs of stress and learning how to divert his anxiety. "It's time for the news," he said. "Mind if I turn on the radio?"

Ernest reached over and pushed the button to tune in KQW and cringed when he heard the Campbell's Soup jingle. He immediately knew that "Mmm, mmm good" would be looping through his head the rest of the day. But the following announcement abruptly and mercilessly derailed any train of thought he might have had.

"The Japanese have attacked Pearl Harbor, Hawaii, by air, President Roosevelt has just announced. The attack also was made on all naval and military activities on the principal island of Oahu..."

"Good God!" Julio exclaimed, looking over at his brother in shock.

Without a word, Ernest steered over to the road's shoulder in a spray of dust. His heart was pounding and he had pins and needles in his hands. A quick glance at Julio told him he was in a similar state.

"What do you think this means?" Ernest asked.

"It means we're at war," Julio said stoically.

Ernest sat with both hands on the steering wheel, trying to come to terms with the unimaginable. He had prayed the United States could somehow stay out of World War II, but now that would be impossible. Afraid of losing the AM radio signal if they drove any further, he and Julio stayed in the car, dumbfounded, anxious for the slightest bit of news about the attack. Ernest turned the volume up, as if by making the broadcast louder it would make the unreality of the news more real.

"We need to go home," Julio said. "Maybe those rumors of Japan attacking California weren't just rumors."

To their regret, Ernest's battle with tuberculosis and Julio's recent hospitalization meant neither could enlist in the armed forces. Both pledged to do all they could for their country and were surprised to find how many ways they could help through the winery, distillery, vineyards, and the undeveloped farmland they owned.

Though World War I had been just twenty years ago, no one knew exactly what to expect. Times had changed and this war had two fronts. The wine industry was in a panic. They were just getting traction after the repeal of Prohibition and now this. Who knew what kind of sanctions the government would decree and what the ramifications would be? Ernest managed to keep everything in perspective. He had weathered plenty of storms. He'd get through this one too.

The first hit E. & J. Gallo took was the loss of some good workers—young men, including Joe Junior, who clamored to enlist to fight evil a world away from the comfort of California's Central Valley. First and foremost, Ernest was an American, but his Italian side was just as much a part of him. Like a blended wine, you couldn't separate the Zinfandel from the Carignane. And now the two sides were avowed enemies. In the paranoia of war, would others question his allegiance? Would they see him as an American or an Italian? And what would happen to Joe Junior? Would the army send him to Fossano, Father's hometown, to kill his own cousins?

Upon the outbreak of the war in Europe, President Roosevelt had established the Office of Price Administration to prevent wartime inflation. A month after Pearl Harbor, he created the War Production Board, which prohibited nonessential production and oversaw the conversion of industries to meet needs the war had created. Gasoline, heating oil, metals, rubber, and plastics were rationed. Railroad tank cars were requisitioned. Both agencies had a significant impact on many businesses in the country, and the wine industry was no exception.

With America's supply of natural rubber from Indochina cut off by the Japanese, the War Production Board ordered distilleries to stop production of spirits as industrial alcohol could be used to manufacture synthetic rubber for tires, footwear, and equipment. Unable to make whiskey, gin, and other hard liquors, distillers developed a sudden taste for wine and brandy and the sales they could generate. National Distillers bought Italian Swiss Colony and Seagram acquired Paul Masson. With the purchase of Cresta Blanca and Roma, Schenley became California's biggest winery. Ernest and Julio predicted the distillers' foray into the wine business would be short-lived. Wine was practically a crop. It couldn't be made without a deep knowledge of agriculture or managed from an office on the other side of the country.

Ernest couldn't conceive of selling E. & J. Gallo. It was akin to some stranger coming in and offering to buy one of his children. There was simply no amount of money that could ever make it acceptable. He couldn't imagine answering to a board of directors. He'd had enough of someone telling him what to do by the time he was twenty. He wasn't in it for the money. His needs were simple and fully met. After all, he could only live in one house, drive one car, and wear one suit at a time. What more did he need? The winery gave him purpose. It was exciting and each day was different. He liked to share the adage, "Choose a job you love and you will never have to work a day in your life."

He reached out to the Defense Supply Corporation to see if it needed more ethyl alcohol. It would be a way the company could pitch in and might also alleviate some of the frustration he felt at not being in the trenches. The government said yes, but wanted him to dismantle the stills and ship them to Kentucky. Ernest suspected that once the stills left Modesto they'd never make it back. He was on the phone with Washington, DC, when Julio came into his office.

"Heck no, we won't," Ernest exclaimed into the phone. "We'll do it here. I'll call you tomorrow with the details." He hung up, clearly perturbed.

"What was that about?" Julio asked.

"They're still pestering me to take apart our stills and send them to Kentucky. You gotta know it's the distillers' idea. Just another way to mess with us. I told them if our stills are going to make ethyl alcohol for the government, why should we let someone in Kentucky do it? We'll do it ourselves. That way we can continue to make brandy three months out of the year," Ernest said, the frustration still ringing in his voice.

"That's what I'm here to discuss," Julio said. "The guys and I are almost done. We converted an old boiler into a grain cooker and made a mash tub from other scrap. Then we can—"

"Hold on. It's moot now," Ernest interrupted.

"What do you mean?"

"They just told me there's not enough grain to make industrial alcohol. They want us to use molasses instead."

"You're not serious. Molasses?"

Ernest caught a hint of distress in his brother's voice. Julio had been tinkering with the stills for weeks, jury-rigging them to process grain instead of wine. Ernest had just hurled him back to square one. Though Julio had seemed stable since his hospitalization, Ernest always simmered with worry about his brother. He had missed the warning signs before, so he was trying to be more attentive to Julio's mannerisms.

"Well, what can you do? The guys and I will figure it out," Julio assured.

Watching Julio leave his office, Ernest breathed a sigh of relief. Julio had taken the news well.

The winery soon received regular shipments of blackstrap molasses from Hawaii and distilled it seven days a week in three daily shifts. In addition to making what they called "torpedo juice," Ernest implemented a tartrate recovery program. Argol, an unrefined form of tartar that coated the sides of the tanks during fermentation, could be scraped off and converted into calcium tartrate, an essential ingredient for manufacturing gunpowder. The company also helped feed the troops with hogs they had inherited in a prewar land purchase and by making raisins.

Americans sacrificed its sons and fathers, cheer and comforts. Those at home needed a tonic, and because their favored spirits were less available and more expensive, they turned to wine. Though Ernest's efforts to build a national brand had been hamstrung by the war, sales remained strong and Americans were beginning to discover wine.

Blueprints for the bottling plant were taped to the wall behind Ernest's desk and were a daily source of frustration and motivation. Construction materials weren't available, but Ernest refused to let it go. Bottlers had continued to go belly-up, leaving conveyor belts, pumps, corkers, and labelers to oxidize and decompose in empty warehouses. The government had no use for the equipment. So when Ernest heard a New York bottler was taking down his shingle, he offered him a distributorship in exchange for the bottling equipment. For the cost of shipping the assembly line piece by piece to Modesto, Ernest finally got his bottling plant, and a new market to boot. Somehow he was managing to grow his company during these extraordinary times. All while doing his part for his country.

But in Ernest's experience good news and bad news always seemed to go hand in hand. Julio suffered a setback and was readmitted to the hospital. And Joe Junior was a constant source of worry. Though he had been stationed in Colorado, he could be sent to the front any day. Without either brother at home, Ernest felt adrift. He wondered if he would be haunted by Mamma's last words until his dying day.

Thanksgiving 1942 was a muted affair. Ernest, Amelia, and Aileen did their best to be cheerful for the young children, but all were pained by Julio and Joe Junior's absence. But on Christmas

Eve, the enthusiasm of five children under eight years old was irresistible. Per tradition, everyone gathered at the home ranch, still Julio and Aileen's home, for *bagna cauda*. Amelia placed the cast iron skillet on the table, warning the children not to get burned and to wait until after grace before dipping their pieces of crusty bread and vegetables in the fragrant garlic and anchovy dip. Ernest poured wine for the adults and added a splash to each child's water glass according to their age.

"How come Bob always gets more?" four-year-old Susann griped while shooting her older brother the most scornful face she could muster. "It's not fair."

"Wine is healthy and Uncle Ernest is teaching you how to respect it and drink responsibly," Aileen explained. "You will get more when you get older. Drop by drop, as your body grows and your palate…er, your tongue can taste more flavors." Though from a German family, Aileen had adopted her in-laws' traditions and come to appreciate their culture's respect for alcohol. Wine was had with every meal, but she had yet to see any one of her family drunk.

Ernest cleared his throat. "Yes. Listen to your mother. Now please bow your heads." He clasped his hands in prayer and bowed his head. "Dear Lord, please look after Joseph and keep him safe as he continues to serve our great country. And please keep Julio under your watchful gaze and help him get stronger and healthier every day. We pray for courage for our troops and wisdom for our leaders. Thank you for this meal and for your son, Jesus Christ. Amen."

"Can we please say a prayer for the Falasca family too?" Amelia asked.

"Of course. But why?"

"Maria's brother Antonio was declared an enemy alien. Soldiers came and grabbed him. They sent him to a camp in Montana," Amelia explained. "It's because he's Italian. They think he might be a spy or doing something to help Mussolini."

"That's ridiculous. The Falascas are a good family. Don't they have two sons serving in the Pacific? They're as American as anyone. It's terrible what they're doing to the Japanese. Now Italians too?" Ernest said angrily.

"Even Joe DiMaggio," Aileen added. "You know his father was declared an enemy alien. They confiscated his fishing boat and he can't even go to his own son's restaurant in Fisherman's Wharf because he can't travel more than five miles without permission."

"And Joltin' Joe's *in* the US Army!" Ernest exclaimed. "It's outrageous!"

He felt sick inside. As proud as he was of his Italian heritage, America came first. His grandparents and his father had barely scraped by in Italy. And now he and his brothers were living the American Dream. He couldn't imagine anyone questioning his loyalty. To be taken from your home and family and placed in a camp? They called them camps, but he knew better. They had imprisoned the Japanese and now they were going after the Italians. He remembered the times he was called a wop, a guinea, and a dago, and the classmates who teased him about the lunches Mamma made. He looked around the table at the children's faces. Innocent. American. He caught himself exploring their features: their skin, dark hair, brown eyes. Did they look Italian? Would they be singled out too? How far would it go? Wasn't that why they were fighting Hitler, after all?

He resented the Chicago and New York gangsters for unfairly saddling Italians with a reputation for brutality and barbarism. A few vile thugs had made it harder for everyone else. And now *Mussolini*?! Italians revered family and God. Contrary to the criminals in newspaper headlines and Hollywood's exploitation of their deeds, Italians were some of the gentlest people he knew. Their generosity was unmatched. How could others not see that?

"We must be careful. Warn your brothers and sister. And especially your parents. Tell them no more Italian in public. They're the most vulnerable…the elderly, if you can imagine that," Ernest said to Amelia. "Now, enough politics. It's Christmas! We can't let the *bagna cauda* get cold. Mmm, it smells so good. Children, tell me, what did you ask Santa Claus for? Bob, you first."

Chapter Fifteen

A GREAT BLEND

Thankfully, both the business and family survived the war. Joe Junior had seen some action in the Philippines, but returned home unharmed. Shortly after he had enlisted, Julio had bought him 160 acres in Turlock, halfway between Modesto and Livingston, and planted it with grapevines. Joe planned to go into the dairy business when he was discharged, but also wanted to grow grapes—though on a much smaller scale than his older brothers. Once more Joe refused to join the winery as a partner, but agreed to manage the winery's newly acquired vineyards in Livingston until his plans fleshed out. Ernest and Julio had also hired a viticulturist to oversee the four hundred different varieties of experimental grapes they had planted. They had built a small pilot plant on the four-thousand-acre property to make small batches of trial wines. They were determined to dissect every stage of the winemaking process to learn how they could make wine better and cheaper than everyone else.

As soon as the war ended, Ernest went back to building his brand. By 1947 Gallo was the top-selling wine in California, the state with the highest per capita wine consumption. Ernest attributed their success to the sales techniques he had implemented in Los Angeles and continued to apply them to other markets. He single-handedly tackled one region at a time and didn't advance to the next until Gallo was outselling all its competitors.

One day, a man named John Frieberg approached Ernest. Frieberg had left a lucrative job on Madison Avenue to start his own ad agency. He had experience and an imagination that knew no bounds, but no clients. He tracked Ernest down after literally bumping into a toga-clad Bacchus wearing a sandwich board reading "By Golly, Be Jolly, Buy Gallo" outside a Vons market in Los Angeles. Inwardly appalled at the lowbrow slogan, Frieberg diplomatically assured Ernest he could do better. Impressed by the young man's moxie, confidence, and willingness to work with a shoestring budget, Ernest decided to give him a chance. He was trying to launch in the Midwest where no one had heard of Gallo before and needed to make a strong first impression.

"*Life* magazine?!" Ernest exclaimed. "How in the world are you going to pull that off?!"

"I'm still working out the details. You just do your part," Frieberg told him.

"Let me use your phone," Ernest said, reaching across Frieberg's desk to dial home. "Amelia, get ready to throw the biggest party Modesto has ever seen."

With no capital for a broad advertising campaign, Frieberg had concocted a scheme to get the country's most popular magazine, *Life*, to do a feature on the winery. Of all the national publications, *Life* had the highest advertising rates, but if everything went according to plan, Ernest wouldn't spend a penny. Well, at least no more than the cost of throwing a swell "vintage party."

Ernest had never seen his wife so focused and at the same time so scattered. Amelia left no stone unturned as she prepared to throw a *Life*-worthy bash. She had first launched into full-blown spring-cleaning mode, going as far as commandeering the family's old toothbrushes to tackle crevices she seemed to unearth on a daily basis. Then she took two trips to San Francisco: the first to make sure the children would be appropriately attired on the big day; the second to the elegant City of Paris department store to find just the right outfit for herself.

She commanded the vineyard workers around her backyard like a five-star general, overseeing the placement of every arbor, barrel, trough, paper lantern, and streamer. Barrels had been delivered from the warehouse for the men's barrel-lifting contest. She had driven to five Woolworths to get all the baskets she needed for the grape-picking race, only to find she had to go back to San Francisco to find a suitable tiara for the "Queen of the Crush." When she wasn't running errands or arranging the backyard, Amelia joined Aileen in the kitchen to prepare food for the four hundred guests they anticipated.

The family had invited everyone they knew. Frieberg had volunteered to scout the area for attractive, photogenic young ladies. He knew what would capture the magazine photographer's eye. And in a cliché straight out of Hollywood, he found the perfect "Queen" at a Modesto soda fountain. With the promise of appearing in *Life,* the comely young girl eagerly agreed to "bathe" in a barrel of foaming sauterne must on the big day.

Though the townspeople quietly snickered at the "annual tradition" and the "bacchanalian harvest custom" that *Life* was coming to capture, they gamely showed up at the Gallo family home for the fun and games, free food and drink, and the chance of seeing themselves on the same pages that had featured Greta

Garbo, Rita Hayworth, Ted Williams, and Bob Hope. For all anyone knew, Hollywood movie stars or producers could be at the Gallo party that night. In truth, no one knew what to expect.

Ernest proudly placed his arm around his wife's shoulder after refilling the punch bowl for the third time in half an hour. Four hours in and the celebration was still in full swing. "You did it. You pulled off the party of the century. Having fun?" he asked, pulling her in closer.

"Darling, I am. You?" Amelia smiled up at her husband. "Look at them," she said pointing to a few barefoot couples linked in a circle inside the largest vat. "Weren't those grapes already crushed?"

Her husband chuckled. "I think those six are the reason I've had to refill the punchbowl so many times. I suspect it was the fellas' idea. Anything to get a doll to hike up her skirt."

"Ernest…" Amelia giggled.

"This party's a gas, Mr. Gallo."

Ernest turned to see a man chewing a cigar, inches away. He looked down and noticed a camera in the man's right hand, hanging near his knee.

"Glad you're having fun. Get some good pictures?" Ernest asked, trying to hide his embarrassment. He hadn't known the magazine had sent *two* photographers. Frieberg had only introduced him to one. He'd need to talk to him about that later.

"Sure did."

"How much does that thing weigh?" Ernest pointed to the rig in the man's grip.

"About six pounds...without the strobe." The photographer lifted the camera in a bicep curl to demonstrate its weight. "So, how many years have you been having this party?"

"Oh, not that many," Ernest hedged.

"And the Queen? She's a secretary at your office?"

Not wanting to lie, Ernest looked for a diversion and noticed the man's empty left hand. "Been too busy working to have some wine? Let me get you a glass."

"Thanks, but no. I don't drink. So, rumor has it you had quite the childhood. You grew up right across the street, right? With your mother and father?"

Ernest didn't like where the conversation was heading and looked to Amelia for a lifeline, but she had been drawn into a circle of women and her back was turned. Maybe he was being overly suspicious. Over the course of the evening he'd had more wine than usual, but he definitely wasn't drunk. He always got a laugh when he told people that he'd only been drunk once in his life—and that was when he was five years old.

"I thought you were a photographer. You sound more like a reporter," Ernest tried to joke.

"I do a little of both. Wherever I can find work," the man shrugged. "It must be a great disappointment that your parents couldn't be here tonight...did they throw annual crush parties, too? Are you continuing the family tradition?"

Ernest's jaw dropped. Who was this SOB and what did he want? Had he been set up? Was the whole party a sham? A ruse? Were these guys really with *Life*? Had he been naive to think that the prestigious magazine would come all the way to his house for a photo op when they could have easily gone to Martini's or Petri's—winemakers that readers would recognize and admire?

"Excuse me," Ernest mumbled, fighting the urge to run. He needed to get to Frieberg and find out what the hell was going on. Was he in on it too?

As he weaved his way through the crowd, smiling glad-handers patted him on the back and held out their palms for a quick shake and an expression of gratitude for having been a part of the night Modesto would never forget. One "Excuse me" after another slipped from the fake smile he managed to maintain until he found Frieberg charming a pretty girl, his hand propped on the trellis behind her.

"Please excuse us," Ernest said tersely to the freckled girl, who scampered away. "What's this about?" he demanded of Frieberg.

"What's what about?"

"This. All of this," Ernest said, waving his arms at the party behind him.

"This is free national publicity, Ernest. This is three pages in *Life* magazine," Frieberg smirked, wondering what had happened to his boss's customary equilibrium.

Ernest scanned the crowd, trying to see if the man with the cigar had followed him. "That second photographer, the one you didn't introduce—"

"What second photographer? How much have you had to—"

"*I'm* asking the questions." Ernest pointed to his own chest for emphasis.

"Slow down. I'm not following anything you're saying," Freiberg said calmly.

After Ernest relayed his encounter, Freiberg assured him the event was legitimate. The whole town knew about the night and clearly some slippery reporter had gotten wind of it and crashed the party. The ad man urged Ernest to relax and enjoy the rest of his evening while he looked for the intruder.

With the benefit of time Ernest forgot about those ghastly ten minutes of what was otherwise one of the best nights of his life. With a little legwork Freiberg had learned the uninvited guest was a well-known Fresno nut job who had been showing up at random functions pretending he was famed street photographer Weegee. There hadn't even been film in his camera.

With a little pressure from Ernest, the magazine agreed to give him advance copies of the article scheduled for the October 8, 1945, edition. He personally delivered the tear sheets to as many stores as he could. He assured them customers would be drawn to the not-quite-scandalous photographs of the bikini-clad "Queen of the Crush" and the barefoot girls holding their skirts over their knees while they stomped the grapes. He kept a list of stores that agreed to let him hang the tear sheets in their windows to see how sales compared to those that didn't display the story. As he predicted, the former sold twice as much wine.

Gallo began to advertise via print, billboards, radio, and eventually television. No part of the process was too small for Ernest's scrutiny. He gave everything his utmost effort and expected everyone else to do the same, no more, no less. Well…maybe more because he was paying them, after all.

Frieberg had convinced Ernest to bury Bacchus once and for all and return to the more sophisticated rooster logo. He had arranged for a series of billboards to be staged throughout the Midwest markets they were trying to enter. But Ernest wouldn't sign the contract Frieberg presented him with until he had personally approved the location of each sign. The billboard agency explained that their placements were graded on a scale—the ones with the best exposure and traffic were considered As; those tucked away on less traveled roads were Ds. All their contracts included a mixture of grade A through D billboards.

"Nope. Definitely not paying for any Cs or Ds. I'm not sure about Bs yet. I wouldn't sell a sub-par bottle of wine. Why should I pay for a sub-par billboard that no one will see? What kind of way is that to do business?" Ernest argued. "How do people get away with such things?"

Ernest's logic was difficult to refute. So Frieberg checked in and out of five different motel rooms across the Midwest with his indefatigable boss. They would leave their shared room at 5:30 a.m. and drive until nightfall, following the route the billboard agency had highlighted on the map it had provided. Frieberg drove so his boss could x out any location that didn't meet his uncompromising standards.

They were considering two different designs for the billboards. One featured a bottle of wine and the slogan, "Gallo Wine: Something to Crow About." The other campaign would deliver a one-two punch. It began with a teaser and no mention of the product, just a collage of red-lipsticked women's mouths and the words "On everybody's lips…" Two weeks later, the words "Gallo Wine" would be added. Ernest wondered if anyone else would see the irony. For just over a decade ago, women in the temperance movement were waving signs that read, "Lips that touch liquor shall not touch ours."

Chapter Sixteen

DROP BY DROP

"*Paisano*? Really?" Ernest scrunched up his nose in disdain. "I don't like it. I don't like it at all."

"Hear me out," urged his sales manager, Al Fenderson.

The two men were at one of their favorite lunchtime haunts, which happened to be Modesto's finest bistro, Café Provence. As Fenderson was about to explain his position, the waitress came by to take their orders, starting with her best customer.

"Mr. Gallo?"

"I'll have the filet au poivre."

"Um, I'm *so* sorry. You're a little later than usual today. That gentleman over there just ordered the last filet. Do you want to look at the menu again?"

Ernest decided on the coq au vin after Fenderson placed his order, and then turned the conversation back to finding a name for the new wine Julio was developing using Roma's best-selling Vino da Tavola as a taste to replicate. Fenderson argued that to most Americans "paisano" sounded exotic and authentically Italian. It rolled off the tongue with a sophisticated ease. Only Ernest and a small minority of native speakers would make the association with *paesan,* a Mediterranean peasant.

Though his circle of trust was harder to get into than the Bohemian Club, Ernest knew there was no point in hiring the best if you didn't listen to them—especially when they went as far as disagreeing with the boss. He distractedly watched the restaurant's last steak pass him by en route to a more fortunate diner. The vested waiter balanced the round tray on his fingertips like the professional he was and placed the meal in front of a well-heeled gentleman. To Ernest's astonishment, the fat cat held an empty Coca-Cola bottle in his hand and signaled that he wanted another.

"Will you look at that?" Ernest blurted out.

The blond sales manager turned his head toward his boss's gaze and was greeted by a big smile and a waving piece of meat impaled on a silver-plate fork, held in either a friendly gesture or maybe a signal of surrender.

"That's the guy who got your steak, boss."

"Yes, but look what he's drinking," directed Ernest. "Sugar. And bubbles. No tannins to soften the fat and release the flavor of the meat. No acids to help digestion. It's a travesty. A waste of a fine cow."

"Want to ask David to pour him some Gallo?"

"I don't think he'd get it," Ernest shrugged. "Right there. Take a good look. Because that man there? He's our problem. He's the customer we need to win. And I think I just figured out how to do it. How we change this country. We do it drop by drop. Just like we do with our children. But instead of adding wine to the water, we add sugar to their wine. When they develop a taste, we can offer more products, slowly reducing the amount of sugar until their palates appreciate the nuances of a complex Petite Sirah or Zinfandel. We need to train them. Coax them into understanding the flavors my brother and I grew up with.

"That's why Vino da Tavola is so popular. It's light, fruity, uncomplicated. Julio added some muscat to his blend to match its sweetness. Maybe this is how we steer the country from sweet fortified wines to table wines. Through wine *beverages*. Drop by drop."

Released in 1952, Paisano was a national success. Gallo was soon trucking in 50 percent of all the wine produced in Sonoma and Napa counties from wineries such as Frei Brothers, Beaulieu Vineyard, and Mirassou to Modesto for blending with the wine they made from their less complex and more abundant Central Valley grapes. Ernest was pleased, but not truly content, with the sales figures for Paisano. Although there were no hard statistics, he estimated that 15 percent of the population was drinking 85 percent of the sold wine, and in his book, that wasn't good enough. Not at all. Somehow he needed to create more wine drinkers.

A latent image of the soda-drinking fat cat from Café Provence was never far from his mind. The philistine appeared like an unblemished daguerreotype, uncannily crisp, fork midair. Ernest had to reach him. Now that he was a leader in the field, he had taken a more active role in the Wine Institute, the industry's political arm. He used his position to lobby the federal government for new laws regarding alcohol regulation, including changes in taxation, permissible alcoholic content, and the addition of natural flavors. Julio was already experimenting with new wine beverages that might soon be legal. When the government approved the proposed changes, Gallo would have a head start on everyone else and be able to claim the new market as their own.

~

The lanky young man shifted uncomfortably in his seat. He had never been west of Dodge City before. Just that morning he had been doing his rounds when his boss reached him at Katz Drug Store and told him he was wanted in Modesto. Now here he was seven hours later, waiting in an empty office for his boss's boss, Mr. Gallo. In an unsuccessful attempt at self-distraction he tried to decipher the meaning of the plaque on the wood-paneled wall. "Wine is food. Treat it with respect." Maybe if he understood what it meant he'd be back in Kansas City instead of wondering how badly he had erred to warrant an urgent summons west. Surely he wasn't here for good news. He wondered if the sweat he felt dripping down his biceps could leach through his gray serge jacket and regretted not buying the black suit his mother had suggested.

"Mr. Johnson." His name was delivered as a statement with no overt undertones, neither friendly nor challenging. He stood and turned to greet the raspy-voiced speaker. After shaking hands with the shorter man twenty years his senior he was encouraged to return to his seat.

Ernest wiped his browline spectacles with his tie while he addressed his nervous salesman. "Procter and Gamble. That's where Fenderson found you?"

"Yes, sir."

"Recognize these papers?" Ernest held up a sheaf of handwritten notes.

"Yes, sir. Those are my daily reports and route sheets," Johnson answered.

"How many accounts do you manage?"

"Three hundred and twenty-four, sir."

"You sure about that?" Ernest's right eye narrowed when he asked the question.

"Gosh, sir. You're right. Katz just opened another store. Three hundred and twenty-five."

"How many retailers are there in Olathe who don't carry our products?"

"Um, I'm not sure, sir."

"What about Lawrence?"

"I apologize, sir. I don't know," Johnson replied, unaware that his right leg had started to jiggle at an alarming rate. Ernest could feel the floor shake beneath his feet.

"Here's what you need to do, Mr. Johnson. Identify them. Identify them by name and address."

"How do I do that?" The young man regretted the question even before the foolish words had slipped from his dry mouth. But a savior in the form of Al Fenderson came unknowingly to the rescue.

"Ernest?" Fenderson asked from outside the doorway. "Oh, sorry. I didn't know you were…Hey, it's Danny from Kansas City!" But after quickly reading the panic on the salesman's face, he added, "Everything okay?"

"It is," Ernest stated. "Johnson's our best man in Kansas. He's going to set up a program and open accounts in Olathe and Lawrence." He stood and addressed the not-yet-relieved salesman. "Do it as quickly as possible. Then we'll expand our sales force and increase our pressure. This is still a primitive business, but it's not going to stay that way. Now go play it straight."

Johnson quickly shook both men's hands and made a swift retreat.

"I think I made him nervous," Ernest shrugged.

"Yes, you can have that effect on people," the sales manager agreed good-naturedly.

"Well, you know what they say in Italy. *Il vinaio è un guerriero.* The winemaker is a warrior. What can I do for you, Al?"

"So you know Bleiweiss and I went to L.A. to try to figure out what's going on with our white port."

"And you figured out why it's not selling?" Ernest guessed, impatient for the unadorned facts.

"Not exactly."

"Folks still prefer that Santa Fe stuff?" Ernest asked.

Fenderson couldn't figure out how he could do it. Without missing a beat, Ernest Gallo could name every product in every market and how their sales compared to his now, six months ago…two years ago.

"Yes, but that's not the point." Fenderson held up both palms as if to slow his boss down.

Ernest now heard the notes of excitement in Fenderson's voice that had eluded him before. "Well, what did you figure out then?" he snapped.

"Watch this." Fenderson pushed some papers and the marble clock/pen set on Ernest's desk to the side to clear a small space. From a paper bag he withdrew a half-empty bottle of Gallo white port, and to Ernest's confusion, a bottle of concentrated lemon juice. Ernest watched as Fenderson carefully poured the lemon juice into the bottle of port, swilled the concoction around, and poured a glass.

Ernest raised his bushy eyebrows in doubt. But Fenderson hadn't steered him wrong yet. He sipped the mixture and was immediately struck by how refreshing it was. Not too tart. Not too sweet. He took another sip to make sure and nodded his head.

Fenderson explained that after visiting one of their retailers in downtown Los Angeles, he and Bleiweiss had noticed bottles of concentrated lemon juice incongruously placed next to the white port. Though both thought it odd, neither said anything until later in the morning when they discovered the same setup in store after store. A shopkeeper explained that he didn't know how the trend had started, but people were drinking half of the port straight out of the bottle and refilling it with lemon juice.

"You need to show this to Julio," Ernest enthused.

"I thought you might say that. Already told him I was coming."

Julio was also impressed with the unlikely mixture and instructed his winemakers to put all other projects on hold. The Gallo production team worked closely with the sales department to create their first fortified wine/citrus beverage. As they finessed the recipe, the consensus was that it tasted best when chilled. They decided to market it as an alternative choice for cocktail hour and emphasize its lower cost and alcohol content compared to hard liquor. Ernest was sure the man he had privately come think of as Fat Cat would approve of this unsophisticated entry-level wine beverage.

Ernest suspected they had a massive hit on their hands, but to everyone's frustration, he held off production until they could come up with a fitting name. Nothing like it had ever been sold and the product deserved a unique name. It couldn't sound like any other wine. It needed to sound American. Radical. Prestigious. And as powerful as its 42 percent proof. Ernest turned to Fenderson, who had discovered the port and lemon juice phenomenon and proven his marketing instincts with Paisano. The two were flying back from a market survey in Texas when the pale blond turned to his boss and uttered three syllables.

"Thunderbird."

~

That year—1957—was a turning point in Ernest's life. Thunderbird sold an astronomical nineteen thousand cases in its first month—in Los Angeles alone. The potion was magical and seemed to jump off the shelves of its own accord. It was such a hit that even its jingle had wormed its way into the public's psyche. That summer, Ernest and Fenderson sat in a rental car at an Atlanta intersection waiting for the light to change. On a whim Ernest leaned out the window and addressed some pedestrians on the sidewalk.

"What's the word?" he shouted.

In unison, the trio of strangers yelled back: "Thunderbird!"

Fenderson whooped in surprise. Thunderbird wasn't even sold in Atlanta yet. The two men spontaneously broke into song.

"What's the word? Thunderbird. How's it sold? Good and cold. What's the jive? Bird's alive. What's the price? Thirty twice."

Ernest was encouraged by the public's enthusiasm for the new beverage, but knew his competitors wouldn't remain idle. There were still more consumers to reach and he wanted them to be his. He scrupulously tracked his competitors' products, advertising, distributorships, market reach, pricing, and sales. Consumers could be fickle and the business was catching up to the times, learning from Coca-Cola and Procter and Gamble. If he let his guard down for a second, a slew of wineries stood ready to steal his business.

Also in that year, Louis Petri, head of Italian Swiss Colony, gave his competitors the fright of their lives. For $7.5 million he had bought the surviving half of a tanker that had been sunk in the war. The purchase enabled him to ship four million gallons of wine at a time through the Panama Canal and maneuver his way around the railroads' steep shipping rates. The train lines had enjoyed a virtual monopoly as a semi-trailer truck full of wine exceeded most state highways' weight limitations. Petri had come up with a cheaper way to ship his wine. He could lower his prices and thereby threaten everyone else's sales.

Petri's bold move was the reason why Ernest and Julio found themselves at a booth in a San Pedro diner waiting for their sandwiches. They had flown down that morning and had just looked at three ships scheduled for the next day's auction. To Ernest's disappointment the ramshackle barges looked like they were one rogue wave away from an eternity at the bottom of the ocean.

"Maybe we should buy them anyway. Right now," he said in desperation.

"What? Were you looking at the same ships I was looking at?" asked Julio, his voice sharp with surprise.

"If we buy them now, we can probably get all three for under a million. If we don't buy them today, we could lose them at auction tomorrow."

"Better that than losing them at sea. Look, I said I'd come with you, but I still think it's a bad idea. There have gotta be other ways we can reduce our costs. Maybe ISC is okay shipping in bulk to regional bottlers, but I don't want any part of that. It would feel like we were going backwards," Julio argued. "I like bottling in Modesto. It's working. We're one of the only ones bottling and sealing our entire output in a sterile environment. Local operations can't provide the same standards of hygiene and I won't compromise on quality control. George Thoukis told me one time their bottler forgot the rinse cycle and almost distributed ISC wine with soap bubbles inside the bottles."

"Yeah, I heard about that one," Ernest chuckled. "Tell you what. I'll do some research into transporting *cases* of wine by ship. That way we keep bottling and we get out from under the railroad's thumb. I'm also going to call Norton Simon over at United Can. They raised the price of their bottles again."

"You're kidding me." Julio shook his head in exasperation. "Didn't they just go up five percent three months ago?"

"Yup. Because the union raised its rates three percent. And before that it was because sand had gone up two percent so they had to go up four percent. And before that? Blah blah blah. Well, Meidel came to see me yesterday. Big smile on his face. Telling me we had taken up so much capacity of their plant they needed to build a new furnace. Meaning they were going pay for their furnace by charging us more!

"I told him I've had enough and said, 'Norton Simon must be making a fortune off us. I want a new contract. I'll pay you a flat ten percent over your costs.' And you know what he said? 'That'll be more than you pay now.' And get this…'We're not even making that much off you. You wanna see the figures? I'll show you any time.'

"You know what? I'm going to hold off on calling Simon. First I'm going to Meidel's office to call him on his bluff. I'm gonna look at their books. He said I could. Then I'll talk to his boss," Ernest stated.

The Gallos returned to Modesto that night without buying the barges. At nine o'clock the next morning Ernest was already waiting for Meidel when he arrived at work. The plant manager was surprised to see him and reluctantly pulled out the spreadsheet as promised. Ernest could quickly see that United Can was making a killing on the Gallo account. After examining the spreadsheet in his hands, he folded it up and put it in his suit jacket's inside pocket.

"Hold on," Meidel protested. "What do you think you're doing?"

"I need to show this to my brother. We're equal partners. Promise I'll bring it back tomorrow."

But instead of heading south toward Modesto, Ernest drove straight across the Bay Bridge to the Bank of America headquarters in San Francisco. There, he met with Fred Ferroggiaro, chairman of the loan committee.

"Fred, I want to borrow four million dollars," Ernest said, quickly showing his hand.

"Come again? I thought I just heard you say you wanted to borrow four million dollars."

"Your hearing is excellent. Always has been," Ernest quipped.

"That's an awful lot of money. What's it for?"

"I want to build a glass factory."

"*A glass factory?!*" Ferroggiaro shouted.

"Calm down. Don't say anything else until you take a look at this." Ernest unfolded the spreadsheet and flattened it out on the manager's desk. "This is how much it costs to make glass. It's not an estimate. This is an actual breakdown. Norton Simon is taking us to the cleaners. Look at the profit margin. How many Van Goghs do you think I've bought him?"

"But you guys are in the *wine* business. Remember? What the hell do you know about making *glass*?"

Ernest bristled inside, but outwardly, he remained expressionless. When would people start believing in him? Maybe he didn't know much about making glass, but he certainly could learn and master anything he put his mind to. All he had to do was talk to as many experts as he could and hire someone he trusted who worked as hard as he did. He had never failed and had paid back every loan he had ever taken out—including his father's, as he sometimes bitterly remembered.

After closer examination of the figures—and perhaps Ernest's vigorous reminder of the consistent growth of his business, his pecuniary track record, and the possibilities further vertical integration would offer—Ferroggiaro agreed to the loan.

The next day Ernest went back to Meidel's office to return the spreadsheet and told him that unless they could supply glass at a much lower cost, he wanted out of his contract.

"You'll have to talk to Mr. Simon about that," Meidel answered tersely, wondering what fate awaited him after his boss learned he had shared private company information with their biggest client—information that could cause them to lose the account.

Ernest didn't know how much time he had before Louis Petri would break a bottle of French champagne against the bow of the SS *Angelo Petri,* christening the ISC tanker to be named after his father. Julio had convinced Ernest to stay on dry land, to wait and see how Petri's experiment played out. Nevertheless, Ernest met with the president of the Santa Fe Railroad under the guise of bestowing a professional courtesy—to give him advance notice that he was looking for a boat like Petri's. ISC had changed the rules of the game and Ernest wouldn't be able to stay in business with the railroad's exorbitant shipping fees.

ISC was one of the railway's biggest accounts in California and the loss was going to hurt. The newly installed railroad president couldn't begin his term by losing Gallo's business too. He agreed to reduce shipping fees for cased goods by 13 percent, not just for Ernest, but across the board. Ernest Gallo was suddenly the most popular man in the wine business. Robert Mondavi, Louis Martini, and August Sebastiani all called to express their admiration and gratitude.

A week later Ernest met with Norton Simon. The curly haired tycoon casually drew the winemaker's attention to the large painting on the wall outside his office—his latest acquisition. Ernest recognized Goliath, prone, with David's foot pressing his head to the ground, the giant's own sword held over the victor's head and seconds away from removing his own. The biblical story was one of Ernest's favorites and he had always identified with the small underdog. Surely it was a good omen for the negotiation ahead.

But Simon wasn't going down without a fight. "I've got a contract with you," he reminded sternly.

"Yes, to make all our *clear* bottles. When your people said they couldn't make the type of green ones we wanted, our researchers got to work and developed a new formula for green glass," Ernest explained, knowing Simon would instantly see the contractual loophole.

After asking a few questions about logistics, Simon was certain the bank wouldn't come through on Ernest's loan, and Ernest didn't tell him they already had. "I'll tell you what," Simon angled. "If you can get financing to build not only the plant, but the warehouse you'll need to store your glass, I'll let you out of our contract."

Bank of America came through as promised and Gallo Glass was born. Their new green glass "Flavor-Guard" blocked the ultraviolet light harmful to wine and quickly gave Gallo a major advantage in the increasingly competitive market. They could promise retailers a longer shelf life than everyone else. Julio had become friendly with Nick Franzen, a plant superintendent about to retire from Simon's United Can. He agreed to get the new factory going and train Julio's twenty-three-year-old son, Bob, to take over the operation.

~

In 1960, after successfully lobbying Congress for changes in the tax law regarding carbonated alcohol, Gallo introduced Ripple and followed their success of Thunderbird with another groundbreaking wine beverage. Made from the cheapest grapes—Thompson Seedless—Ripple was easy on a college student's wallet and straddled the divide between soda and beer. The carbonation was about half that of Coca-Cola, and the alcohol content twice that of beer. It was sold in single-serving green Flavor-Guard bottles embossed with a tactile rippling design.

By the mid-sixties, Ernest felt Americans were ready for a more sophisticated table wine. That, and the success of Thunderbird and Ripple had come with a significant downside. He and Julio had been prescient in creating products that would appeal to the country's taste, but hadn't foreseen the clientele who would become their biggest fans. From New York to California, no scene of urban blight was complete without empty bottles of Thunderbird and Ripple scattered on the asphalt. Gallos' drinks were cheaper than liquor and packed more punch than beer. Ernest wanted people to hear the word *Gallo* and think "wine," but had found "wino" was becoming the more likely association.

He was afraid they were veering off course. He and Julio had succeeded in making quality products at affordable prices, and in doing so, had cracked open a new market and made a small fortune. E. & J. Gallo was the biggest winery in the country. The Gallos were held in the highest regard by their peers, but their name was becoming a punch line.

While vintners in Napa began to focus on estate or vintage wines—those made in the style of the French, using a single type of grape from a certain terroir or area—Julio concentrated on making blended wines. He and Ernest believed that Americans would prefer a consistent product to one that changed from year to year at Mother Nature's whim. Neither man held much regard for barrel-aged wines and maintained the position that wine should taste like fruit, not wood.

Ernest joked that the brigade of UC Davis and UC Berkeley PhDs his brother had recruited to his Livingston labs could put the first man on the moon before NASA. The enologists and chemists worked tirelessly to finesse the red table wine Ernest planned to release as Gallo's entrée into the more upscale market. The blend of Zinfandel and Petite Sirah berries from Napa and Sonoma made a rich, full-bodied red with undertones of cherry jam, licorice, and black pepper. They named it Hearty Burgundy, and soon after extended the line with Chablis Blanc and Pink Chablis, creating the enduring and award-winning Gallo Gourmet Trio.

Chapter Seventeen

CIVIL WRONGS

In 1960 E. & J. Gallo sold thirty million gallons of wine, making it the biggest winery in the United States. To maintain that volume they continued to crush grapes from other growers and supplement their blends with contracted and surplus wine from the Central Valley, Lodi, Napa, and Sonoma. Their standards for hygiene and the quality of the grapes and wines they would accept were daunting. They supervised the production of all the wine they bought to make sure it met their specifications and paid little mind to complaints from their fellow winemakers, who were insulted and exasperated by the process. If they didn't want to comply, there were plenty who would.

Determined to do everything within his means to improve the quality of their wines, Julio approved over four hundred experiments to be conducted in the Livingston labs he managed. Chemists and viticulturists examined fermentation temperatures, yeast strains, clarifying agents, tank coatings, filtration techniques, and more. Findings were published immediately and devoured by both American and European winemakers.

But a wine could only be as good as the grapes it came from. Possibly worse, but definitely not better. Ernest and Julio were frustrated by how not only Gallo, but also the whole California wine industry was being stymied by inferior grapes. So in 1965 they added a Growers Relations Department, the first of its kind in the industry. Twenty men worked under a former California Polytechnic State University professor and visited growers year-round with suggestions on how to grow better-tasting grapes. Two years later the Gallos rocked the industry by offering growers incentives to rip up their healthy, high-yielding Thompson Seedless vines and replace them with fine-wine varieties. Gallo would tell each grower what to plant according his viticultural region and make further recommendations based on what they had learned from their experimental vineyards in Livingston. To compensate for the growers' trust, risk, and initial loss in revenue, Gallo would guarantee a generous minimum price for the next ten to fifteen years.

"Listen to this," said Ernest, reading to Amelia from the *New York Times*. "The Gallo program will probably be welcomed by most of the rest of industry. Gallo is saying, 'We're going to help finance you to convert your vineyard to a good wine variety. It will help you to make more money, help us make better wine, and make the consumers happy.' Couldn't have said it better myself," he grinned. "They got it right—except for the part about the rest of the industry being happy. I guess everyone's accusing me of giving the growers too much money. But you watch. Someday they'll thank me."

Ernest was accustomed to such grumblings. Gallo had always paid its field workers higher hourly wages than other growers. Over the years he had tussled with plenty of his peers upset at the precedent he was setting each time he voluntarily raised his employees' wages. But unlike other vintners, Ernest knew the aches, thirst, and risks that accompanied twelve-hour days in the fields. He had walked mile after mile in the pickers' shoes and had always wrestled with the disparity in wages between the winery workers and those in the field. In his mind there was something inherently wrong with the system when the pickers who endured backbreaking work in the hot sun earned less than the lab-coated bottlers sitting on stools in the air-conditioned factory.

So in 1967 when Gallo grape pickers voted to join Cesar Chavez's fledgling United Farm Workers Organizing Committee—a division of the AFL-CIO and later known as UFW—Ernest and Julio stood behind their workers. The winery employees had been unionized since 1943; those in the glass plant, since the day it had opened. Many of the union's demands for growers had been in place at Gallo for years. They had always refused to hire children, and their permanent field workers already had a health plan, credit union, and regular cost-of-living raises. On top of that, their pesticide exposure was less than the state's allowance. But workers at other vineyards weren't as fortunate. Ernest hoped that by being one of the first big wineries to sign with the union, others would follow their lead. Gallo signed two consecutive three-year contracts with the UFW.

"*Jefe,* we have a problem," the straw boss told Julio when he and Ernest came by on their rounds to see how the harvest was going. "We don't have enough men today. We're not going to be able to get all the grapes."

"José, that's on you. How many years have you worked for us? You should know how many men you need," Julio replied in frustration.

"*Sí,* boss. The problem is that the union pulled ten men this morning and bussed them to Sacramento. They had no choice. If they didn't go demonstrate, they won't get any more work."

"Again? That's just wrong. Those men work for us. Not Chavez!" Julio fumed. "We need to pick all our grapes today. They can't wait another twenty-four hours. This is absurd. Ernest, we have to do something about this."

"We do," Ernest agreed. "I've already had it with their hiring hall."

"*Sí,* Mr. Ernest," José added. "Our people are upset their families are all split apart. I used to be able to see my daughters every day, but now they are sent to other vineyards."

"You're absolutely right, José. Family comes first," Ernest replied.

When their workers elected to join the union, Ernest and Julio lost their right to choose who worked for them. The UFW instituted a hiring hall where members would report for job assignments doled out by the union men who ran the hall. Though decisions were to be made based on seniority, the system was imperfect and highly corruptible. Hardworking men and women spent days with no work watching bribes change hands while others moved to the front of the line. Some of the pickers who had worked for Gallo for decades were now sent to other wineries. Working families with one car scrambled to get everyone to and from vineyards miles apart. There were stories of mothers returning to work asked to pay retroactive back dues they didn't have, and of others who badmouthed the union or skipped a protest and found themselves in bad standing and out of work.

Ernest couldn't imagine an outsider dictating whether or not he and Julio could work together. Shouldn't it be up to them? Vineyard work was grueling and laborious. How could the union say they had their members' best interests at heart while denying them the simple pleasure of working side by side with their loved ones? Most of the field workers were Hispanic or Filipino, and Ernest shared the regard held for family in their cultures. Fathers working next to sons; mothers with their daughters; husbands next to wives. And because Ernest was the one paying these men and women, shouldn't he be the one to choose who worked for him? He and Julio had always hired a tight, loyal group. Now when they went to the fields they saw mostly unfamiliar faces.

On June 26, 1973, after Gallo's contract with the UFW had expired, leaders of the Western Conference of Teamsters informed Ernest that his employees had voted to switch unions. The UFW challenged the results, claiming Gallo had given the Teamsters a sweetheart deal—that the "employees" who voted to switch unions were scabs. Innocent or not of whatever intricate machinations may have led to the change in their union representation, seventy of the two hundred seasonal Livingston farm workers decided to go on strike. The strike lasted three months until civil rights leader Chavez decided the boycott was a more effective tactic in *La Causa,* his nonviolent crusade to improve wages and working conditions for farm workers.

Chavez had learned from the national boycott of table grapes and lettuce he had led from 1967 to 1970. It had proved almost impossible for American consumers to tell whether or not the iceberg lettuce or green grapes at their corner Piggly Wiggly had come from a UFW signatory. Chavez realized it would be more effective if the UFW targeted a brand consumers recognized. So in 1973, he went after the big dog: Gallo.

Chavez was a shrewd organizer and his grassroots effort had drawn passionate young Americans to fight for the cause of oppressed California farm workers thousands of miles away.

Bell-bottomed activists picketed supermarkets across the country, urging consumers to boycott Gallo wines and even the markets that sold them. To Ernest's chagrin, even Catholic priests and nuns had taken an active role in Chavez's campaign.

Ernest was confronted by the boycott at every turn. Full-page ads in the *New York Times* and *Los Angeles Times* proclaimed in bold caps, "THERE'S BLOOD ON THOSE GRAPES," and lower on the page, "Boycott non-UFW grapes, lettuce, and Gallo wine." Every day new stores were pulling Gallo from their shelves. Protestors marched with signs bearing the UFW's graphic Aztec eagle that read, "Don't buy Gallo wines," going as far as listing their other brands—Paisano, Thunderbird, Carlo Rossi, Eden Roc, Boone's Farm, Night Train Express, Ripple, and Andre—to make sure the public knew all the guilty parties in Gallo's greedy domain.

Despite the ugly attention, sales had suffered little and there was no doubt the winery would weather the maelstrom and continue to grow and expand. But Ernest hated the bad-mouthing, the daily pleas from the media, and the unwarranted attention. The three-month strike in Livingston had been especially hard on Julio. Ernest had urged him to stay in Modesto, but his principled brother had insisted on crossing the picket lines every day. How could he expect others to brave the ambush if he wasn't willing to do it himself? Despite Chavez's appeal for peace, protestors across the state had lost their lives—though thankfully none at Gallo. Nevertheless Julio prayed for their souls while he endured the shaking fists and screaming faces outside the Livingston compound—some belonging to people he had known for years. It had taken nerves of steel and profound self-examination.

Ernest was livid about the public shaming and smearing of his name. The name he had managed to disassociate from two names from his past: Mike Gallo and Joe Gallo. And the name he was still trying to redeem from two of his own making: Thunderbird and Ripple. Some activists had gone as far as burning him and sweet Julio in effigy. Dan Solomon, recently hired to combat the public relations disaster, had finally convinced his boss to break his lifelong media silence and actually hold a press conference, but Ernest knew his voice would never be heard. Somehow he had become Goliath and everyone always rooted for David.

March 1, 1975, was a Saturday, but Ernest dressed as if it were a regular weekday—his overalls and work shirts had long been replaced by wool suits and wide-striped ties.

"Ernest, are you sure they won't come here?" Amelia worried.

"Positive. They'll probably holler by the offices on the way to the park, but that's about it. Sheriff's got two cars at the bottom of the driveway for the rest of the week. No one's getting by them," Ernest assured.

"But—"

"Amelia, you're safe. Worst'll happen is you'll hear them shouting out on the road. Now I gotta go. I'm already running late," Ernest said sternly.

Cocooned by vineyards and towering cypress trees, Ernest's home was a stone's throw from everything he held dear: the home his brother had built on the same property, the winery, the bottling plant, the glass factory. His life was here. After a childhood spent moving from town to town, Ernest had no interest in ever leaving. He and Julio had turned Modesto from a cow town into a company town. But when he looked in its citizens' faces he couldn't tell anymore if they were grateful or resentful.

He went out the side door to the driveway where not two, but four sheriff's cars were parked. Two would stay and watch the house. The other two would escort him to his office just three miles away through a town he didn't quite trust anymore.

"New car, Mr. Gallo?" the young deputy asked as Ernest opened the driver's door of the baby blue Coupe de Ville.

"Yes. Well, no. Well…kind of. She's new to me but already a couple years old," Ernest explained as he positioned himself behind the wheel. "Do you have any idea how much a car depreciates the second you drive it off the lot? Crazy to buy a new car."

Ernest hated the routine. It made him feel dirty. Like a criminal. Like he had done something wrong. He had always tried to be honest and fair. He treated his workers the way he would like to be treated and had gone above and beyond any other vineyard owner. Had anyone even heard Gallo spokesman George Frank's correction that the dirt-stained little boy in the now-famous photograph taken in the "Gallo vineyard" was actually pulling an onion out of the ground? Had anyone believed that the conditions inspectors had "uncovered" at their workers' housing camp had been the result of a plumbing emergency that couldn't have happened at a worse time? It killed Ernest that the sewage backup would have been fixed before the inspection if the first plumber had been willing to cross the picket line.

As Ernest turned his Cadillac off Yosemite Boulevard, he wasn't surprised to see that the mob was bigger than usual. And as usual the hands that pounded the hood and trunk of his sedan were soft and white. Hands that had never turned the soil or plucked a single grape. The contorted faces that pressed against his window were red and stretched wide to spew as many insults as possible in the few seconds they had until the Oppressor himself passed. Ernest's heart raced. He was glad he had skipped breakfast. He didn't trust his stomach to keep everything down.

"PIG!"

"CHEAT!"

"MONSTER!"

Ernest kept his eyes straight ahead and focused on the license plate of the sheriff's car. He steered his wide sedan into his parking space in front of the two-story neoclassical administration building Gallo had built in 1963. He never tired of how the sunlight reflected off the ground glass from Thunderbird bottles that had been mixed into the concrete. Peacocks and guinea hens roamed the carefully landscaped and contoured grassy grounds that stretched from the building down to a man-made lake.

Still recovering from the melee outside, Ernest walked into the large atrium that was filled with natural light—what they had come to call the Palm Court. Ferns and palm trees thrived in the open space, reaching up to the balcony that wrapped around the second floor. Expecting his employees to work as long and hard as he did, Ernest had done his best to make the environment as comfortable as possible. Rather than hire an industrial designer per the architect's recommendation, he had given each employee a budget and the freedom to decorate his or her office according to individual taste. The architect had cringed at the idea, but Ernest knew he was right and still appreciated how each man and woman had expressed his or her personality with the choice of furniture, colors, and décor.

He said his customary hellos as he made his way to his second-floor office, which was directly above Julio's. He stopped by Dan Solomon's office and asked Dan to follow him upstairs.

"How soon until they get here?" Ernest asked, hustling down the open hallway.

"Probably around eleven, Mr. Gallo," the former NBC executive replied.

"And how many are there?"

"We're not really sure. As few as six thousand. As many as ten. The line is two and a half miles long."

"Cripes. Really? You know it's because the war's almost over. These kids are just looking for something new to protest." Ernest turned into his wood-paneled office and sat at his desk, taking off his glasses and pressing the heels of his palms over his eyes. "Did someone put up my sign?" he asked, referring to the banner he wanted hung along the side of the road urging the San Francisco marchers to bypass Modesto and go straight to Sacramento. Couldn't Chavez see that his efforts would be better spent urging state lawmakers to support the new National Labor Relations Act that would guarantee farm workers' rights? On top of that, thousands of farm workers across the state still weren't unionized. Chavez should be organizing those workers instead of focusing on Gallo, whose workers were treated fairly and already in a union, just not the one Chavez wanted.

"You know, I respect Chavez and what he's trying to do," Ernest admitted. "Heck, if the circumstances were different, I'd hire the guy. He's a great marketer at heart. That UFW logo would look great on a bottle of Thunderbird," he chuckled. "You know he's even selling belt buckles and jewelry? If only my brother and his team could have perfected that Chavez-resistant grape they've been working on..."

But in truth, Chavez had pushed too many of his buttons. Amelia was scared and now he was scared too. Not just of the boycott, but of the reporters that tagged along. The press conference was scheduled for later that day. The wolves would be waiting for him at the Chuck Wagon downtown and there would be no escape. He had successfully avoided the press ever since that reporter had called from the *Fresno Bee* asking about his parents all those years ago. He couldn't count how many interviews he and Julio had declined over the years. Requests had intensified significantly since Chavez had set his sights on Gallo, but the brothers had remained steadfast in their refusal to grant interviews of any kind, certain any reporter worth his salt would bring up *the troubles* and the past they had worked so hard to protect.

But Solomon had made a compelling argument. Ernest had no choice. The "March on Modesto," due to arrive in a few hours, couldn't be ignored. Ernest simply had to defend himself and his company. The newspaper ads Gallo had placed couldn't possibly stem the tide of public disapproval Chavez's PR machine had generated. Ernest had reluctantly agreed. All he could do, he decided, was tell the truth. Maybe people would come to understand that he wasn't the bad guy.

"Sorry, what was that you said?" Ernest asked Solomon, realizing he had drifted away. "Joan who?"

"Baez."

"Never heard of her. Marching with Chavez? Another hippie?"

Solomon chuckled underneath his breath, silently hoping he'd get a glimpse of the famous folk singer—a secret he'd never share with his buttoned-up boss.

"Excuse me, Mr. Gallo?" his secretary, Ouida, interrupted. "Your wife's on the phone."

Ernest picked up the receiver, but "Hello?" was the only word he got out. His face paled as he slumped back in his chair and listened to Amelia's emotional torrent. He hung up the phone after a few minutes, oblivious to Solomon's worried and curious expression.

"Ouida, I need to talk to Cesar Chavez as soon as possible!" Ernest yelled, unaware that his secretary was still standing in the doorway. "The SOBs threw a rock through David's bedroom window."

Once off the main road, Ernest kept an eye out for the landmarks Chavez had given him, turning right at the fork in the road, left at the old barn, and then taking the third left after the group of mailboxes at the side of the road. He slowed to a few miles per hour on the uneven, twisting dirt road to save his car's suspension. With each switch in the road he wondered if he had taken a wrong turn. Several times he thought of backtracking to the mailboxes, but remembered that Chavez had said it would take a few miles. He had forgotten to look at the odometer and now it was too late.

He finally spotted two men standing by a wooden gate. He pulled his car behind their parked pickup truck and stepped out, recognizing Chavez immediately. The civil rights leader had told him he would be accompanied by the owner of the ranch and no one else. He must have forgotten to mention the two German shepherds.

"Howdy," Ernest said, stretching out his hand, hoping Chavez wouldn't feel the beads of sweat that had been building with each passing mile. Here he was, about to shake the hand of the man who had done his best to tear down everything he had created. The man who had made his family prisoners in their own home. The man who had dragged his good name through the muck, determined to turn the world against him. By the end of the day he would make sure Cesar Chavez knew the real

Ernest Gallo. He'd show him he wasn't an evil capitalist clawing his way to the top on the backs of the unfortunate proletariat.

After he shook hands with both men, Ernest looked down at the dogs. "So these are the famous Huelga and Boycott. Okay if I pet them?"

"I wouldn't recommend it," Chavez smiled.

"Ah. Yes," Ernest nodded, remembering Chavez's highly trained companions were not mere pets. "You know, I should send you the vet bills for the herd of Dobermans I had to get for my house."

Chavez stiffened until he saw the smile on Ernest's face. "We do what we can to protect our loved ones," he said. "I thought we could take a ride around the ranch and talk. John has a spectacular piece of property and it would be a shame not to see it while you're here."

"No one knows about this? You weren't followed?" Ernest worried. Chavez had agreed to keep the meeting confidential, but Ernest couldn't help but look around. The secret rendezvous between the two famous adversaries would be a career-changing scoop for any reporter.

"Just you, me, and John. He won't talk. Neither will the dogs. Or them." Chavez cocked his head to the left.

Only then did Ernest notice the two horses grazing nearby. He followed Chavez and the rancher over to the animals. Each had a bridle and reins, but there was only one saddle at the base of the nearby tree. Chavez handed the dogs' leashes to John.

"I took you for a Western guy," said Chavez, walking over to the hand-tooled saddle.

"I'm okay bareback. Which one is mine?" Ernest asked, referring to the horses.

Chavez pursed his lips and raised his eyebrows in approval.

"Not as young as I used to be, though. Can you give me a boost?"

Ernest placed his left boot in Chavez's interlaced fingers and swung his right leg over the dark seal bay. Ernest knew Chavez to be a master propagandist with an acute eye for detail and optics. It was no coincidence that Chavez had kept the nearly all-white Appaloosa for himself and designated the horses as if outfitting the good guy and bad guy in a Hollywood Western.

The bay followed the Appaloosa up a narrow hilly trail, not leaving any opportunity for conversation between the two men. *Well, this is weird,* Ernest thought. He had come to give Chavez a piece of his mind, discuss their differences, and try to work out some kind of détente and here he was on a horse, half expecting a band of Apaches to come over the ridge to rid Cesar Chavez of his evil nemesis.

Chavez stopped on the edge of a plateau and waved for Ernest to come to his side and pointed. "See that house over there?"

"Yes. Quite isolated, but what a view," Ernest remarked.

"That's where Jonah Meyers lives. Six thousand square feet. Indoor-outdoor swimming pool. Tennis court. And if you look over there to the left…that flat spot…that's the new helipad he just added."

Ernest had never met Jonah Meyers, but he had heard of him. Rumors were he had family money and was aggressively collecting and developing vineyards and planning to build a winery. He knew where Chavez was steering the conversation, but didn't play along. "Well, a helicopter will come in handy living out here," he said.

"Come this way." Chavez turned his head to the left and nudged his horse with his heels. Ernest followed him around a small bend to another overlook.

Chavez drew Ernest's attention to the foothills below and a patchwork of crops dotted with stooped figures casting long shadows in the early morning sun. "These are Jonah Meyers's fields. Where are the toilets? The water? The shade? Here. Look," Chavez said, handing Ernest a pair of binoculars. "How many children do you see?"

"I don't need to look," Ernest said indignantly. "You know we take care of our workers. That kid in the papers? Look at that picture again. He was picking onions. We have water and toilets. My brother even invented a rolling seat so the pickers would be more comfortable, eliminating stoop labor. If you're good to people, they'll be good to you. We've had the same people working for us for thirty years in every part of our business. They stay because we take care of our workers. At least until you came along. Do you know anything about me?"

"Honestly? Not a lot. My life is an open book. Yours? Not so much," Chavez admitted. He had heard a lot of rumors and secondhand accounts about the reclusive wine baron, but didn't know what to believe.

"I run a family business and I don't think what I do is anyone else's business," Ernest explained.

"So, no interviews..." Chavez took a second before completing his thought. "But you employ many people. You have a responsibility to them...to those less fortunate. Those who do backbreaking work so you can hop on your private jet and—"

"Let me tell you who I am," Ernest interrupted, irritated about what Chavez was implying.

For the next hour and a half, the two men rode side by side as Ernest bravely opened up to the man who had given him so many sleepless nights. It was risky, but he knew Chavez was a moral man—a fellow Catholic whose heart, though misguided, was clearly in the right place. His gut told him he was trustworthy and honest.

Though Chavez was only two when the stock market crashed, his formative years had been molded by the Great Depression when his family lost their Arizona farm and relocated to California. The men considered the parallels in their lives—their shared faith, identification with two cultures and the racial epithets they had endured, childhoods spent toiling in fields and always being the new kid, love for their wives and children and the brothers who were their best friends, the pursuit of excellence, and the belief that anything is possible. As they neared his parked car, Ernest implored Chavez to consider that they weren't that far apart when it came to farm workers' rights.

Shortly after the secret meeting, Ernest noticed that the boycott seemed to be losing steam. Two years later, Chavez ended the sanctions against Gallo, pleased with a new California farm labor law that was considered the strongest in the country.

Chapter Eighteen

SOUR GRAPES

A few years later, in 1979, Consolidated Foods, a large national conglomerate, bought the Gallo Salame Company, a local San Francisco salami manufacturer founded in 1941. Ernest was familiar with the label, but with the acquisition he grew alarmed that Consolidated was laying the groundwork to take over his company. At best they were planning to capitalize on the Gallo name, which could create consumer confusion. He couldn't imagine any other reason why Consolidated would have bought such a small operation. Fighting lawsuits, frivolous and otherwise, and taking action against others had gone hand in hand with running one of the most successful companies in the world. In addition to defending the winery from the Federal Trade Commission, Gallo's in-house and outside lawyers had handled grievances from employees and consumers as well as trademark infringement disputes, including one against a Gallo Coffee and even a Gallo Wine based in Ohio.

Ernest told his legal department to handle Consolidated Foods and it took four years for the two stalwarts to come to an agreement. The winery ended up paying Consolidated Foods $2 million for the Gallo Salame trademark and permitted the food manufacturer to continue using the name on processed meats and cheeses. E. & J. Gallo would protect the trademark and their own liability by conducting three factory inspections a year. Ernest had spent five decades building a brand consumers trusted and couldn't risk the damage that might come from a health scare or product recall.

Joe Junior, while managing his brothers' Livingston vineyards until 1967, had built his own empire. By the 1980s he owned twenty-five thousand acres, making him one of the biggest landowners in Livingston's Merced County. His holdings included Joseph Gallo Vineyards, Joseph Gallo Dairy, Joseph Gallo Feed Lot, and Gallo Cattle Company. His eight-thousand-head herd was one of the largest milk producers in California, and at one time he owned the state's biggest dairy replacement herd with thirteen thousand heifers. Besides the income his cattle generated, Joe sold around twenty thousand tons of grapes a year to E. & J. Gallo.

Joe founded Joseph Gallo Cheese in 1983 in an effort to capitalize on a surplus of milk and protect his dairy from a reduction in federal pricing supports. That June, he and his business partner, thirty-two-year-old son Mike, invited friends and family to the cheese plant's ribbon-cutting ceremony. The El Niño weather phenomenon had doused California with record amounts of rain and snow, turning the Golden State into a patchwork of green hues usually found only in the Emerald Isle. The fifty-foot-long white catering tent outside the plant's entrance looked striking against the cloudless blue sky. There, guests found relief from the sun and ample food and wine—Gallo, of course—served by uniformed waiters. A forty-pound block of Cheddar stood as the centerpiece on the long table in the middle of the canopy. Then came the familiar *thwap* of a helicopter, getting louder and louder as it lowered a few hundred feet from the plant. Curious guests as well as parents tugged by their excited children stepped out of the tent to see Ernest and Amelia arrive.

Ernest led Amelia under the six-seater's whirring blades to join the party as she held a scarf to protect her coiffed curls. Most of the guests knew their host's brother and his preferred mode of travel. Julio and Aileen were out of town and had already sent their regrets. Amelia went to catch up with her sister-in-law while Joe Junior introduced Ernest to the Wisconsin cheese maker who had consulted on the plant's construction. As soon as he could pull Ernest away from everyone who kept interrupting to say their hellos, Joe brought his big brother inside the plant, which was right next to the dairy.

The tour began in the pasteurization area. Like the winery, the room's labyrinth of stainless-steel tanks and pipes and digital control panels looked like it could have been transplanted from an ocean liner's engine room.

Joe pointed to a tube. "That's where the direct underground pipe from the dairy comes in. Like I said earlier, no transportation costs. Plus, it's obviously more hygienic this way."

"Nice," Ernest complimented. "I'm proud of you. This is really impressive."

As they entered the cheese-making room, their voices echoed off the 3,500-pound stainless steel vats and mold presses. The plant had been in production before the inaugural party and shelves were already lined with forty-pound blocks of cheese. Ernest noticed a stack of unassembled cardboard boxes labeled "Joseph Gallo Cheese Company" and his heart missed a beat as he instantly thought of his arrangement with Consolidated Foods.

"Um, you're only selling wholesale…right?"

"Yup. Most of my customers are chain stores...supermarkets. They cut up the block and repackage it in smaller amounts."

"So, a customer won't go into a store and see a Joseph Gallo Cheese Company label on a bar of cheese?" Ernest asked.

"No...they won't. What's it to you?" Joe asked, bristling, knowing his older brother wasn't just being curious.

"You know Gallo Salame?" When Joe nodded, Ernest continued. "Well, we've been in court with them for three years now over copyright infringement. We just settled, and under our arrangement they can sell cheese products under the Gallo name. I just want to make sure there's no conflict here and everyone's protected."

"It shouldn't be a problem. I'm a wholesaler. That's okay, right?"

"Yes. That won't be a problem. Our agreement just covers retail sales. Listen, Amelia and I have a thing in Napa tonight so we need to get going. Congratulations again. This is really great. Julio will be impressed too."

At seventy-five years old, Ernest Gallo was a multimillionaire and still maintained a pace that would bring most men half his age to their knees. The company had a few thousand employees and a highly skilled and trained sales force, recruited from the best MBA programs in the country, but Ernest still worked like his life depended on it.

Approximately a year after the opening of Joe Junior's cheese plant, Ernest had one of his frequent lunches with Ken Bertsch and Al Fenderson at Café Provence, during which they discussed marketing their premium line. When Ernest returned to his office, he immediately noticed an object had been placed on the center of his desk. Closer inspection showed it was an eight-ounce package of Monterey Jack cheese bearing the label "Joseph Gallo." Underneath was a note from one of his salesmen: "Found this and Gallo Salame next to our varietal display at the Raley's downtown."

The sense of betrayal that overcame Ernest was like a direct sucker punch to his solar plexus. He began to shake with rage as he recalled his conversation with Joe about trademark infringement and the winery's agreement with Consolidated Foods. His brother was no dummy and Ernest knew he had been clear about his concerns. What on earth was Joe up to? Ernest fought the impulse to call Julio. His brother didn't need the stress. Especially if it was something he could handle on his own.

He called out to his secretary. "Ouida, get me Joseph on the phone!"

Dividing their time between fields, factories, and family, the Gallo brothers were notoriously difficult to reach. Ernest had recently paid $8,000 for two portable phones for himself and Julio, but his only chance of speaking to Joe Junior immediately was if he happened to be in his office. Fortunately, he was.

"Joe! I'm looking at a chunk of cheese that has your name on it!" Ernest screamed into the receiver.

"And?"

"What do you mean '*And*'?! You know you can't do that! I explained it to you. What the hell am I supposed to say to Consolidated? We fought them for four years and now I'm supposed to tell them, 'We wouldn't let you sell under Gallo, but it's okay if our brother does?' I have a reputation. My word means something. I thought yours did too."

"Hey! Gallo is *my* name too! You knew my company was called Joseph Gallo Cheese. It's not like I've been keeping it a secret."

"Yes, but you assured me you were only selling *wholesale.* You've got to stop selling retail," Ernest ordered.

"You can't tell me how to run my business! What makes you think you have the right? I can change my business plan any time I want without your permission!" Joe shouted into the phone.

Ernest's hearing aid squealed and he quickly plucked it out before the feedback became unbearable. Besides, his brother's voice was loud enough for him to hear without the amplification the device provided. "We both know you're just trying to capitalize on the brand Julio and I built."

"What? That's ridiculous."

"Then change the name of your cheese. Raley's is selling it next to *my* wine. Consumers will think it's *my* cheese."

"Well, I can't help that," Joe countered.

"That listeria scare? When they thought those two people died from eating contaminated cheese? If something like that happens, it could kill my business."

"Nothing like that's going to happen. I make a quality product."

"You just don't get it," Ernest steamed. "I've worked my whole life to redeem my name. To build a brand."

"Damn it, Ernest. It's my name too!" With that, Joe ended the conversation with a click and a dial tone.

Ernest placed his elbows on his desk and his head in his hands. What had happened to Joe? Why was he being so unreasonable? He could build his own brand just as he and Julio had. Ernest had never shied away from a confrontation, and normally business was business and he would have been on the phone with his lawyers by now. But this was family—an attack from the inside, from someone he loved and trusted. Ernest closed his eyes and tried to make sense of Joe's position and attitude. A rogues' gallery flashed in his mind: Father, Uncle Mike, the Lady with a Thousand Faces, Dr. Krinsky, Fat Cat, Cesar Chavez, and others—nameless—who also elicited a like sense of unease or betrayal: rail yard thugs, the reporter outside the Fresno sheriff's station, the *Life* party crasher, a slew of loan officers, and all the lawyers he had faced in the cost of doing business. And now, his own brother?

He called the company's general counsel for advice and was reminded that they were obligated to inform Consolidated of any possible trademark infringement. After numerous protracted phone calls and some masterful negotiation, Consolidated said E. & J. Gallo could license Joseph Gallo Cheese Company. Ernest suspected they were content with the Gallo Salame brand and never had an interest in extending the line to cheese anyway. He was thrilled. He was on good terms with Consolidated and Joe could keep his name on his packages. The talks with Consolidated had taken a year. All the while, Joe had continued to market and sell his Gallo-brand cheese. The royalty-free contract the Gallo legal department drew up for Joe was based on their contract with Consolidated, giving the winery the right to inspect the cheese plant to ensure it maintained sanitation standards.

To Ernest's utter shock, Joe Junior refused the terms, balking at the inspection clause, of all things.

"What? The USDA's not good enough for you?" Joe asked sarcastically, referring to the government's routine health and safety inspections of the dairy and cheese plant.

"Look, it's the same deal we have with Consolidated. What's the big deal?" Ernest asked. He had just finished a rare but typically frustrating round of golf at Pebble Beach and had stayed in the cart to call Joe while the rest of his foursome had gone into the clubhouse.

"My lawyer says it gives you too much power. You can just shut me down," Joe explained.

"Now why would we ever do that?" Ernest spoke into the brick-size device he held by his ear. He really couldn't believe he was having this conversation. A kid came over from the pro shop to clean his clubs, but Ernest waved him away with a flick of his wrist.

"I know how tough you and Julio are. Nothing's ever good enough for you. You always find fault with me and it'll be the same with my factory. If you care so much, why don't you have your team build me a new brand?"

"Tell me you're kidding," Ernest sighed, shaking his head. "Look, sign the contract. If you don't, I have no choice but to sue you. If I don't, Consolidated will."

"Go ahead," Joe answered.

Ernest was satisfied that he had done all he could to protect his business and his brother. It was in the lawyers' hands now. But as soon as the lawsuit was announced in the paper, the phone started ringing. Reporters. A feud of this magnitude within one of the nation's wealthiest and most successful families was headline-worthy. Nothing this juicy had hit the wine business since the Mondavi split. The spotlight zeroed in on the reclusive wine baron. Local, national, and even international journalists wanted a quote, a picture, an interview. But Ernest maintained his silence. One of the reasons he had kept Gallo private was to guarantee he'd never have to answer to anyone. As far as he was concerned this was a family matter between him and his brothers. It was nobody else's business.

He found refuge in his office. Sometimes when he heard the peacocks' shrill callings outside he would run to catch the magnificent spectacle. He never tired of the birds' mating dance as they shook their feathers into a colorful array. *Another one of God's many wonders,* he would think. But on the afternoon of July 31, 1986, his reverie was interrupted by a rustling outside his door. He turned to see Ouida chasing a field worker into his office.

"I told you, you can't just…I'm so sorry, Mr. Gallo…I told him not to come in, but he wouldn't—"

Suddenly, Julio tore into the office, angling himself in front of the secretary and the stranger, waving a piece of paper overhead as if stuck in the back of a hall trying to place a desperate bid with a nearsighted auctioneer. "*Did you see this?! Did you see this?!*" he screeched.

"Hold on. What the devil is going on?" Ernest asked, alarmed by the scene that was forming in front of him.

"This," Julio cried, still shaking the document. "This letter from Joe."

"Joe who?"

"Our brother! *That* Joe! He's actually going through with it. He filed a counterclaim!"

"What? Let me see!" Ernest took the letter from his brother's hand, certain he was mistaken, confused. He lifted his eyes as soon as he realized he was holding an attorney's letterhead. "Who are you?" he addressed the stranger. "What do you want?"

"Mr. Gallo, I have some legal documents I'm supposed to deliver to you." The "field worker" handed Modesto's most famous citizen an envelope and left.

"Is this a joke? *Is this a joke?!*" Ernest yelled, searching Julio's face for an answer. An answer he could live with.

But it wasn't a joke. Joseph Gallo had indeed filed a counterclaim against his two older brothers—seeking a third of the E. & J. Gallo Winery. He had been talking about "his share" for weeks, citing mismanagement of their parents' estate. But neither Ernest nor Julio had taken him seriously and didn't think any judge would, either. Joe had been fourteen when he and Julio founded the company, for God's sake. Ernest grabbed his suit jacket and stormed out of the office without another word.

After being redirected from the plant to the dairy to the feedlot, Ernest finally found his youngest brother on the Joseph Gallo Vineyards in Livingston. *The ones we planted for him!* he thought. His rage grew exponentially with every step closer to his brother. An internal alarm reminded him that he was of heart attack and stroke age, but he could do nothing with the thought. Counting to ten was not going to help.

Ernest waved the letter in his hand. "What the hell, Joe?!"

"I just want what's owed me, Ernest. That's all."

"What's *owed* you? What's that supposed to mean?" Ernest yelled.

"My share of the winery. You and Julio used Father's vineyards to get your start. A third of those vineyards were mine." Joe Junior held his posture straight as he faced his eldest brother, holding his stare.

"The winery always paid for those grapes. It went toward the estate and you got your piece when you turned twenty-one. That was, what? *Over forty-five years ago?!*"

"My lawyer looked into the guardianship papers and there are a number of discrepancies. You comingled my inheritance with yours to start the winery. Once I told him about Father's business, he realized that *Father* had started the family winery.

Not you and Julio," Joe explained, taking off his straw hat to wipe his brow with his shirtsleeve.

"Father sold *grapes*. He never sold wine. You can't rewrite history. What is this about? How many times did Julio and I ask you to join the winery? And you always said no. *Every time*. This is crazy. I've always taken care of you and done right by this family. I don't know what bottom feeder you hired, but you're a fool for listening to him."

"C'mon Ernest. We both know you would never have made me an equal partner. You and Julio are thick as thieves. You always wanted it to be just the two of you. You didn't call it Gallo *Brothers* Winery, did you? Neither of you ever had any time for me."

Ernest raised his eyebrows in disbelief. Was this about revenge? An ill-advised reaction to the trademark lawsuit he and Julio had filed? He thought of all the times they had needed and asked for Joe's help at the winery. He had turned down every offer—even when they were struggling through Julio's breakdowns. And to think that Julio had planted the very vineyards they were standing in, tending them so they would bear fruit by the time Joe got back from the war. They had invited him into their tartrate recovery business during the war and offered him and his children shares in Gallo Glass. He had grazed his cattle on their land for years.

Ernest could practically hear the lawyer whispering in Joe's ear. The winery was valued at undisclosed millions and beckoned greedy opportunists like a siren. But Ernest couldn't understand how his brother could have been so easily manipulated and turned against his family—after all they had been through.

"Joe, brother to brother...what's this about?" Ernest asked, trying his best to sound calm or at least as concerned as he felt.

"Look, if you and Julio just pay off my debts I'll drop the suit." Joe broke his gaze and focused on the stripe of crabgrass growing between the rows of vines.

"Is that what this is about?" Ernest heaved. "You know what? I don't know what to say. I'm sorry if you're having trouble. But this wasn't the way to handle it."

With that, Ernest went back to his car. It took a few attempts for his shaking hand to insert the key into the ignition. He wondered if he'd ever talk to his brother again.

It took three long years for the case to be heard. Opening arguments began on November 22, 1988, in a Fresno courtroom. The trademark infringement suit *E. & J. Gallo Winery v. Gallo Cattle Company* would be decided without a jury. US District Judge Edward Dean Price had dismissed Joe's counterclaim back in September, so the focus would be just on the trademark issue. Ernest and Julio weren't seeking any monetary damages; they simply wanted an injunction against their younger brother from selling his cheese under the Gallo name. At seventy-eight years of age Julio still tried to minimize external stressors and decided it best to avoid the rest of the proceedings after attending the first day of session. But Ernest didn't miss a day. He found sitting with his attorneys too adversarial, however. Too close to the conflict. Instead, he sat in the second row behind Joe where their eyes wouldn't meet. The courtroom was cold and bare, nothing like those of his childhood excursions in San Francisco.

The trial grew increasing ugly with the defense implying that Gallo had intentionally targeted the inner city's disadvantaged population with Thunderbird and listing egregious unverified and unfounded consumer complaints. In turn, winery counsel questioned the dairy's sanitation and quality control. The trial even provided fodder for Johnny Carson's opening monologue on *The Tonight Show*. With his customary smirk, Carson asked, "Have you heard about the Gallo brothers' family feud? Ernest and Julio are suing their brother for using the name Gallo on his cheese. What do they expect him to call it? Kraft?" Ernest stewed over the negative publicity. It was embarrassing for the family and bad for business. He still couldn't believe they hadn't been able to settle out of court.

The trial concluded on December 28, 1988, after an expectedly somber Christmas. Joe and his family declined Christmas Eve dinner at Julio's and Christmas Day festivities at Ernest's. Ernest knew Mamma's heart was breaking as she looked down on her fractured family. It took an excruciating six months for the judge to issue a decision. He ruled in favor of the winery. It was a bitter victory. The bottle of Tott's champagne remained caged and corked and Ernest did his best to resume business as usual. But his life, his family, his hometown would never be the same.

On January 18, 1990, Joe's lawyers filed an appeal with the Ninth Circuit Court of Appeals in San Francisco. Because of damage the courthouse sustained in the 1989 earthquake, the hearing was relocated to Pasadena. Approximately two years after the filing of the appeal, the court issued its decision and upheld the district court, prohibiting Joe from using the name Gallo on retail packages of cheese. Judge Betty Fletcher also ruled that Joe's counterclaim to a one-third share of the winery was barred by res judicata, meaning the matter couldn't be pursued further because it had already been adjudicated by a competent court. The legal battles were put to rest on February 7, 1992, but the hatchet would never be buried.

At eighty-three years old, Ernest had fought the hardest battle of his career—of his life. In his heart and much-searched soul, he knew he had only done what had to be done—for Julio, the business to which they had dedicated their lives, their children and grandchildren, not to mention his responsibility to Consolidated Foods. But the casualties and costs were almost unbearable. He could see it every time he looked at Julio. He'd always been the more sensitive of the two and Ernest couldn't deny his frailty or how much he'd aged in the last few years. While Ernest's remaining hair was still mostly dark with gray roots, Julio's was completely white.

Ernest felt the loss of his relationship with Joe every day. The course of the three brothers' lives had been set nearly six decades earlier on the day their father had taken his and their mother's lives. Though Ernest and Julio had never shared their mother's last known words with their younger brother, they had heeded her wish as if it had been a commandment from above. At the young age of twenty-four, amid tragedy and the depth of the Great Depression, Ernest had become responsible for a teenage boy overnight and had done his best ever since. He recognized the mistakes he had made over the years, but none had been borne from malicious intent. He turned to the Lord for comfort and the words, "Forgive us our trespasses as we forgive those who trespass against us."

Chapter Nineteen

THE LEGACY

Ernest never fully recovered from the feud. He hid it well, maintaining his usual hours at the office, entertaining at home, and treating his children and grandchildren to lavish European vacations and a rafting trip down the Grand Canyon. He confided in his beloved Amelia and no one else. He continued going to church, but now went to the eleven o'clock mass so he wouldn't see Joe. He had mastered a quick scan of every restaurant he entered, and when behind the wheel, had learned to look the other way before he approached a roadside sign for one Joseph Gallo business or another. His, Julio's, and Joe's families were all so enmeshed in the community that it took complex choreography to try to avoid each other. Sometimes Ernest felt like an actor waiting in the dark wings for other characters' scenes to end so he could take the stage.

In 1964 Ernest had been awarded the wine industry's highest honor, the American Society of Enologists Merit Award, for outstanding leadership. Julio received the same award eleven years later. In 1983 the brothers were honored together in a rare joint public appearance and presented with *Wine Spectator*'s Distinguished Service Award. A who's who of the California wine industry gathered at the Fairmont Hotel in San Francisco for the black-tie affair. Amelia and Aileen had coordinated ahead of time and each wore a long-sleeve emerald green cocktail dress accented by a strand of pearls.

Ernest spoke into the microphone in his characteristic deliberate manner. "We were lucky as young men we were grape growers at the time Prohibition was repealed. We were lucky that we both felt that the wine business was a natural extension of growing grapes. And we're both lucky that we have fine and remarkable wives." He paused and added, "Therefore, with so much luck, we had very little to do with it. Thank you." The room erupted in laughter and applause as he stepped away from the podium.

On May 2, 1993, Julio—Ernest's brother, his touchstone, his best friend—lost his life in a terrible accident. Julio had been visiting his son Bob's ranch. With his wife of sixty years at his side and two adult granddaughters in the back seat, the eighty-three-year-old had misjudged a sharp turn and his jeep had plunged down a steep embankment. All passengers had survived, but Julio's lung had been critically punctured in the crash. He made it to the hospital, but died soon thereafter.

Ernest was crushed by the news. Julio had always been by his side, through the darkest days and the brightest. Life without him was unimaginable. They had suffered and survived, picking each other up when one had fallen. Their trust in one another was implicit and inexplicable. They could speak volumes with just a slight shrug of the shoulder or shift in stance.

How could it be that he would never hear Julio's voice again? His laugh? His counsel?

Seven months after Julio's death, Ernest said goodbye to his first and only love and wife of sixty-two years, Amelia. Ernest hadn't thought his heart could break any more, but then their son David, co-president of the winery, died suddenly from a seizure four years later, in 1997. He was fifty-seven years old.

The year of Julio's and Amelia's deaths, the winery broke into the industry's super-premium category with its introduction of Gallo Estate Wines, followed a year later by Gallo of Sonoma. In 2000 it was named Best American Wine Producer at the International Wine and Spirit Competition and would make history in 2005 as the first US winery to receive the International Organization for Standardization's ISO 14001 certification in recognition of the high environmental standards it maintained. The latter might have been Julio's proudest accomplishment and Ernest was aggrieved that he hadn't lived to see his lifelong dedication to conservation and sustainability validated. He remembered how his brother had loved strolling through all the new wetlands they had created and the riparian habitats Julio had fought to protect.

Italian winemaker Louis M. Martini had left the Central Valley to hang his shingle up in Napa the same year the Gallo brothers had started their winery. Martini had been at the forefront of the movement from generic jug wine to vintage-dated varietals and was thought to be the first to produce a white Zinfandel wine back in 1941, over forty years before Sutter Home made it one of the most popular wines in the United States. Martini and his son, also named Louis, had built one of the most respected wineries in America. And Ernest had just bought it.

Though Gallo had purchased a number of wineries in Sonoma County, the 2002 Martini purchase was its first major acquisition in Napa. Like so many peers in Ernest's later years, both Martinis, father and son, were deceased. As part of the deal, the Martini family would continue to run the winery their grandfather had founded. Though Ernest's son Joseph had been named CEO of Gallo in 2001, Ernest had insisted on joining him in Napa to meet with the Martinis. He felt he owed it to his old friends.

The tule fog that typically settled over the Central Valley during colder months had lifted and the helicopter pilot noticed his ninety-two-year-old boss stepping off his back porch. He strode over to the shaky old man and extended his hand in an offer of assistance.

"I'm okay." Ernest pulled his elbow away and shouted over the racket created by the spinning rotors. "If you fall, I don't want you taking me down with you!"

He slowly climbed aboard and settled into the cockpit's leather seat. He removed his hearing aids and placed the headset over his ears as the JetRanger lifted over fields he and Julio had cleared over seven decades ago. He wondered who had overcome worse odds: Julio and himself, or the golden vines below. No matter. In both cases, success had only come with perseverance, a fierce will, and blessings from above.

Ernest never ceased to be awed by the wonder of flight or struck by the random memories each trip unearthed. It was as if he were floating above a tapestry that continuously unfurled to tell the story of his life. They rose in a familiar sweep over the bottling plant. His gaze followed the train tracks that had brought him to Chicago and the ones that ended inside a warehouse that was larger than forty football fields and saw over eight million cases of wine come and go every month or so. Sometimes he was struck by the hundreds of sixty-thousand-gallon stainless-steel holding tanks and was reminded of Aunt Tillie's prediction that his wealth would come from oil or wine. From up here, who could tell the difference?

They banked over the home where his father had reached his highest highs and begun his descent to rock bottom—the home where he himself had been loved and humiliated and groomed for the world. As they headed west he looked past the pilot toward Ripon, where he had fallen in love. Oh, how he missed Amelia and ached for the day when they would meet again. The journey toward Napa was like flipping through a photo album. Though the highways were wider and suburban sprawl had claimed its stake, Ernest could still see the smoking vineyards of Antioch, guns drawn on a Livermore cattle ranch, roads that led to a long-gone sanatorium in Napa and a San Francisco asylum, fields of cattle tended by someone he had thought he had known, and mile after mile, acre after acre of vines that had given their fruit to his dreams.

The pilot was well aware of how much the modest man next to him had accomplished with his brother. They had completely transformed and shaped the landscape below. Were it not for Ernest and Julio Gallo he might be flying over nothing but cows and rows of onions and melons rather than vines that grew some of the best grapes in the world that made some of the best wines in the world.

"You know one of the hardest things about getting old?" Ernest asked rhetorically. "Losing all your people. My memory isn't what it used to be. Not so long ago I could've called my brother and said, 'What was the name of that fella who sold us those leaky barrels back when we were still in the warehouse?' But just like that—pfft. No one has the answers. No one I can turn to. Every time you lose a friend, you lose that link to the past."

"I'm sorry, Mr. Gallo. It must be difficult," the pilot sympathized.

"*Ah, così è la vita,* that's life," Ernest shrugged. If only his sorrow were as easily dismissed.

Ernest thought of his parents. And *the troubles*. He was well aware he had been labeled secretive, private, and even reclusive. Critics complained that Gallo didn't offer public tours or tastings. But he knew how people were bewitched by the macabre. One interview would never have satisfied their intrigue. He couldn't prevent the sneak attacks from his own unconscious, but he had been determined to exert control wherever he could. He didn't need people bringing up his demons whenever it suited them. Still, he recognized he had quite a story to share.

Several months before Julio's accident, he and Julio had gotten together to discuss their upcoming joint autobiography, *Ernest and Julio: Our Story*. The project had been borne from a desire to share their story and the history of E. & J. Gallo with those charged with continuing the dream, notably their grandchildren. Julio wanted to address his battles with anxiety and depression in hopes that his candor might somehow help ease the stigma against mental illness. And both reluctantly concurred their story couldn't be told without addressing their parents' deaths.

Since their last conversation about *the troubles,* the country had seen nine presidents, a few of whom the billionaire brothers knew on a first-name basis. Despite their decades-long moratorium, neither was surprised to discover they had come to a similar understanding, acceptance, and forgiveness. With no money in his pockets, Father had left everything he had ever known to come to this country. He had dug ditches and become a land-owner. A businessman. Had he made mistakes? Undoubtedly. Though neither could reconcile why he had taken their mother from them, the Depression had certainly been brutal. Lots of men had lost all hope and taken their lives. But each believed their father had done everything so they could have the opportunities that had never been available to him. And that's why he and Julio had worked as hard as they had. They always wanted to be the best. It wasn't about ego. It was for their father. They had to justify the sacrifices he had made so they could have a better life.

As they outlined their book, Ernest had said, "This is what I want to tell them. What I want our grandchildren and their grandchildren to know. That you can always do better—grow better grapes, make better wine, and sell more. The day you become satisfied is the day you become complacent—fat and lazy—and the company starts to slide downhill. Always strive for perfection. And promise me you'll always keep the company in the family. We never would have gotten this far if we had to answer to others and worry about quarterly reports. And keep an eye on the government. For the life of me I can't understand why they lower import tariffs to help other countries at our expense."

Ernest spent his last years with his remaining family and enjoyed deep-sea fishing as much as his deteriorating body would permit. His estranged brother, Joe, died in February 2007, at eighty-seven years old. And just two weeks later, on March 6, 2007, twelve days shy of his ninety-eighth birthday, Ernest passed away, surrounded by family, in the home he had built in the town he had put on the map. For the last five months of his life he had been awakened by the noise of bulldozers, jackhammers, and cement mixers. The clamor sounded like it was coming from next door…because it was. He and Julio had contributed generously to the construction of the new Saint Stanislaus Church on Maze Road. Plans for the interior of the Romanesque architectural masterpiece were reminiscent of a Cistercian abbey and its concrete copper-covered domes would reach ninety feet high. The hue of its concrete walls would fluctuate with the arc of the sun and the color of the skies. And the church would remain surrounded by grapevines and rosebushes planted by Ernest and Julio Gallo.

Postscript

At the time of this printing, E. & J. Gallo is the largest winery in the world and is worth an estimated $9.7 billion. The family-owned company owns nearly twenty thousand acres of California vineyards and employs more than six thousand people worldwide, including four generations of Ernest and Julio's descendants.

In addition to its eponymous labels—Gallo Estate, Gallo Family Vineyards, and Gallo Signature Series—the E. & J. Gallo Winery's portfolio currently includes:

Alamos, Allegrini, André, Apothic, Ballatore, Barefoot Wine, Bartles & Jaymes, Bella Sera, Boone's Farm, Brancaia, Bridlewood Estate Winery, Canyon Road, Carlo Rossi, Carnivor, Clarendon Hills, Columbia Winery, Copper Ridge Vineyards, Covey Run Winery, Da Vinci, Dancing Bull, Dark Horse, Dolcea, Don Miguel Gascón, Ecco Domani, Edna Valley Vineyard, Frei Brothers Reserve, Ghost Pines Vineyard, J Vineyards & Winery, La Marca, Laguna, Las Rocas, Liberty Creek, Livingston Cellars, Louis M. Martini, MacMurray Estate Vineyards, Madria Sangria, Martín Códax, Maso Canali, Mia Dolcea, Mirassou, The Naked Grape, Orin Swift Cel-

lars, Peter Vella, Pieropan, Polka Dot, Prophecy, Rancho Zabaco, Red Rock Winery, Redwood Creek, Renato Ratti, Souverain, Starborough, Storypoint, Talbott Vineyards, Tisdale Vineyards, Tott's Champagne, Turning Leaf, Vin Vault, Whitehaven, Wild Vines, William Hill Estate, and *William Wycliff Vineyards.*

About the Author

For the past several years Karen Richardson has helped authors of fiction and nonfiction navigate the constantly evolving terrain of independent publishing. She manages production and distribution for The Mentoris Project. Karen is the co-founder of The GoLD Initiative, a nonprofit created to offer afterschool STEAM enrichment programs to teens with learning disabilities. She lives in Southern California with her husband, writer Doug Richardson, their children, and three mutts.

NOW AVAILABLE FROM THE MENTORIS PROJECT

America's Forgotten Founding Father
A Novel Based on the Life of Filippo Mazzei
by Rosanne Welch

A. P. Giannini—The People's Banker
by Francesca Valente

Christopher Columbus: His Life and Discoveries
by Mario Di Giovanni

Fermi's Gifts
A Novel Based on the Life of Enrico Fermi
by Kate Fuglei

God's Messenger
The Astounding Achievements of Mother Cabrini
A Novel Based on the Life of Mother Frances X. Cabrini
by Nicole Gregory

Marconi and His Muses
A Novel Based on the Life of Guglielmo Marconi
by Pamela Winfrey

Saving the Republic
A Novel Based on the Life of Marcus Cicero
by Eric D. Martin

Soldier, Diplomat, Archaeologist
A Novel Based on the Bold Life of Louis Palma di Cesnola
by Peg A. Lamphier

COMING SOON FROM THE MENTORIS PROJECT

A Novel Based on the Life of Alessandro Volta
A Novel Based on the Life of Amerigo Vespucci
A Novel Based on the Life of Andrea Palladio
A Novel Based on the Life of Angelo Dundee
A Novel Based on the Life of Antonin Scalia
A Novel Based on the Life of Antonio Meucci
A Novel Based on the Life of Buzzie Bavasi
A Novel Based on the Life of Cesare Becaria
A Novel Based on the Life of Federico Fellini
A Novel Based on the Life of Filippo Brunelleschi
A Novel Based on the Life of Frank Capra
A Novel Based on the Life of Galileo Galilei
A Novel Based on the Life of Giovanni Andrea Doria
A Novel Based on the Life of Giovanni di Bicci de' Medici
A Novel Based on the Life of Giuseppe Garibaldi
A Novel Based on the Life of Giuseppe Verdi
A Novel Based on the Life of Guido Monaco
A Novel Based on the Life of Harry Warren
A Novel Based on the Life of Henry Mancini
A Novel Based on the Life of John Cabot
A Novel Based on the Life of Judge John Sirica
A Novel Based on the Life of Lenonardo Covello
A Novel Based on the Life of Leonardo de Vinci
A Novel Based on the Life of Luca Pacioli
A Novel Based on the Life of Maria Montessori
A Novel Based on the Life of Mario Andretti
A Novel Based on the Life of Mario Cuomo
A Novel Based on the Life of Niccolo Machiavelli
A Novel Based on the Life of Peter Rodino
A Novel Based on the Life of Pietro Belluschi
A Novel Based on the Life of Publius Cornelius Scipio
A Novel Based on the Life of Robert Barbera
A Novel Based on the Life of Saint Augustine of Hippo
A Novel Based on the Life of Saint Francis of Assisi
A Novel Based on the Life of Saint Thomas Aquinas
A Novel Based on the Life of Vince Lombardi

For more information on these titles and
The Mentoris Project, please visit
www.mentorisproject.org.